DIAGNOSIS DEATH

This Large Print Book carries the
Seal of Approval of N.A.V.H.

PRESCRIPTION FOR TROUBLE SERIES

DIAGNOSIS DEATH

MEDICAL SUSPENSE WITH HEART

RICHARD L. MABRY, M.D.

THORNDIKE PRESS
A part of Gale, Cengage Learning

GALE
CENGAGE Learning

Detroit • New York • San Francisco • New Haven, Conn • Waterville, Maine • London

The verses from Psalm 139 on pages 295 and 296 are from the *New American Standard Bible*®. Copyright © 1960, 1962, 1963, 1968, 1971, 1973, 1975, 1977, 1995 by The Lockman Foundation. Used by permission.

The verses on page 327 are from The Message. Copyright © 1993, 1994, 1995, 1996, 2000, 2001, 2002. Used by permission of NavPress Publishing Group.

Thorndike Press, a part of Gale, Cengage Learning.

Thorndike Press® Large Print Christian Mystery.
The text of this Large Print edition is unabridged.
Other aspects of the book may vary from the original edition.
Set in 16 pt. Plantin.

LIBRARY OF CONGRESS CATALOGING-IN-PUBLICATION DATA

Mabry, Richard L.
  Diagnosis death : medical suspense with heart / By Richard L. Mabry.
    p. cm. — (Prescription for trouble series) (Thorndike Press large print Christian mystery)
  ISBN-13: 978-1-4104-3908-6 (hardcover)
  ISBN-10: 1-4104-3908-9 (hardcover)
    1. Women physicians—Fiction. 2. Large type books. I. Title.
  PS3613.A2D53 2011b
  813'.6—dc22   2011016144

Published in 2011 by arrangement with Abingdon Press.

Printed in Mexico
1 2 3 4 5 6 7 15 14 13 12 11

*To that special group of
health care workers who
perform their healing
labors as a true ministry.
It was an honor to work
alongside you for over four decades.*

ACKNOWLEDGMENTS

This is the third book in the Prescription for Trouble series, all made possible through the efforts of my wonderful agent, Rachelle Gardner; my great editor, Barbara Scott; and the dedicated team at Abingdon Press.

My wife, Kay Mabry, has functioned as my first reader since I began writing eight years ago. She's gentle with her criticism, effusive with her praise, understanding of my times of self-doubt, and supportive throughout the whole process. Besides that, she laughs at my jokes and has taught me to believe in myself.

My children — Allen, Brian, and Ann — have always believed their dad could do anything he set his mind to. I haven't always bought into that premise, but it's constantly motivated me to keep trying. I'm proud of them.

Kay and I have the good fortune to be members of Stonebriar Community Church and to hear our pastor, Chuck Swindoll, preach on a regular basis. I've also been blessed by the Bible teachings of Dr. Steve Farrar and Dr. James Allman (to whom I'm indebted for the inspiring words I've used in the closing scene). Thanks to you all for helping deepen our Christian walk.

I continue to be grateful for the support I've received from the writing community, especially from authors in the genre of Christian fiction and romantic medical suspense. I appreciate everything you've done to help me.

Finally, I'd like to thank my readers. Your purchases of these books, your good reviews, your recommendations to your friends, are so very important to any author. I hope to run into you again somewhere down the road.

PROLOGUE

She stood by his bedside and waited for him to die.

Outside the room, the machines and monitors of the ICU hummed and beeped, doctors and nurses went about their business, and the hospital smell — equal parts antiseptic and despair — hung heavy in the air.

With one decisive move she flipped the switch of the respirator and stilled the machine's rhythmic chuffing. In the silence that followed, she imagined she could hear his heartbeat fade away.

She kissed him and exhaled what passed for a prayer, her lips barely moving as she asked for peace and forgiveness — for him and for her.

She stood for a moment with her head bowed, contemplating the enormity of her action. Then she pocketed the empty syringe from the bedside table and tiptoed out of the room.

1

Dr. Elena Gardner approached her apartment as she had every night for six months — filled with emptiness and dread. The feeling grew with each step, and by the time she put the key in the door, fear enveloped her like a shroud. Some nights it was all she could do to put her foot over the threshold. This was one of those nights.

She turned the key and pushed open the door. The dark shadows reached out at her like a boogeyman from her childhood. The utter stillness magnified every sound in the old apartment, turning creaking boards into the footsteps of an unknown enemy.

She flipped on the light and watched the shadows turn into familiar surroundings. Even though the thermostat was set at a comfortable temperature, she shivered a bit.

Elena dropped her backpack by the door and collapsed into the one comfortable chair in the living room. The TV remote was in its usual place on the table beside her. She punched the set into life, paying no attention to what was on. Didn't matter. Just something to drown out the silence, something to remind her that there was life outside these four walls. That somewhere there were people who could laugh and joke and have fun. Somewhere.

She sighed and picked up the phone. She should call David.

He'd been firm about it. "Call me anytime, but especially when you get home at night. That's the toughest time. It's when the memories butt heads with the 'what-ifs.' "

She dialed the number. Maybe she should put him on her speed dial. But that implied there wouldn't be an end to this soon. And she wasn't ready to think about that.

"Hey, Elena." Although Dr. David Merritt — a resident physician in one of the busiest obstetrics programs in the Southwest — was surely as tired as she was, his voice sounded fresh, almost cheery. "What's up?"

"Oh, you know. Just needed to hear a friendly voice."

"Glad to oblige. How was your day?"

That was one of the things Elena missed most. Now that Mark was gone, there was no one to share her day. "Not too bad until

I was about to check out. The EMTs brought in a thirty-two-year-old woman, comatose from a massive intracranial hemorrhage. The neurosurgeons rushed her to surgery, but —"

She knew David could guess the rest. He cleared his throat. "Did that . . . was it tough to take?"

Elena started to make some remark about it not bothering her. But that wasn't true. And she knew David wanted the truth. "Yeah. Not while it was happening. Then I was pretty much on automatic pilot. But afterward, I almost had a meltdown."

"It'll get better."

"I hope so."

"Any more phone calls?"

Elena felt goose bumps pop up on her arms. "Not yet. But it's Tuesday, so I expect one later tonight."

"Why don't you call the police?"

"What, and tell them that for four weeks I've answered the phone every Tuesday at midnight and heard a woman sobbing, then a hang-up? That's not a police matter."

"And you —"

"I know what they'll ask. Caller ID? 'Anonymous.' Star 69? 'Subscriber has blocked this service.' Then they'll tell me to change my number. Well, this one's unlisted,

13

but that doesn't seem to matter. How much trouble would it be for whoever's calling to get the new one?"

David's exhalation was like a gentle wind. "Well, let me know if there's anything I can do."

"You've done plenty already. You know, after Mark died, I had a lot of people fuss over me for about three days, but you're the only one who's stayed with it. Why?"

His silence made her think she'd asked an embarrassing question. People didn't go out of their way to be nice the way David had with no thought of something in return. Did they?

"Elena, I've been where you are," David said. "Oh, I know. A spouse divorcing you isn't the same as one dying, but a lot of the feelings are the same. I mean, when I saw my wife and little girl pull away from the house for the last time, I wanted to lie down and die."

She knew exactly what he was talking about. "That's me. I wanted to crawl into the coffin with Mark. At that point, my life was over."

"But I got past it," David said. "Oh, I didn't 'heal.' You don't get back to where you were, but you learn to move on. And when Carol sent me the invitation to her wedding, it broke my heart, but it helped me realize that part of my life was over. Anyway, I made up my mind to use what I'd learned to help other people. And that's what I'm doing."

Elena sniffled. "Sorry." She pulled a tissue from her pocket and dabbed at her eyes. "That's another thing. I feel like tears are always right there, ready to come anytime."

"That's normal. Let them out."

They talked for a few minutes more before Elena ended the conversation. She wandered into the kitchen, opened the refrigerator, and looked in without seeing the contents. She wasn't hungry. Since Mark's death she'd lost twelve pounds off a frame that had little to spare. Maybe she should patent the process. "Sure-fire weight loss guaranteed. Withdraw life support and let your husband die. If you don't lose weight, double your money back."

Her lips drew back in what started as a hesitant smile but turned into a grimace of pain. She dissolved into tears.

Elena wasn't sure how long she sat at the kitchen table with her head cradled in her arms before the ring of the phone roused her. She looked at her watch. A little after nine — too early for her midnight caller. Had the routine changed?

She shuffled back to the living room. When she checked the caller ID, she felt some of her tension subside. Dr. Helen Bennett represented the only ray of sunshine in Elena's dark landscape right now.

"Hello?"

"Elena, did I wake you?"

"No, not really. Just starting to unwind. What's up?"

"We need to talk."

That didn't sound promising. "Wow, that sounds like what I used to tell boys in college before breaking up with them. What's going on?"

"I'd rather do this face-to-face. Why don't we have breakfast tomorrow morning? I usually make rounds at six-thirty. Can you meet me in the St. Paul Hospital staff cafeteria at six? We can talk then."

Elena hung up with a growing sense of unease. Mark's death had plunged her into a dark abyss. The only glimmer of hope for a future had been Dr. Helen Bennett's invitation to join her practice. The opportunity to work alongside a woman who was one of the most respected family practitioners in the community, a doctor Elena had admired since her days in medical school, seemed like a gift from above. Was that about to be taken from her?

The evening dragged on as Elena worried about the problem like a kitten with a ball of yarn. Finally, she ate some peanut butter and crackers and forced down a glass of milk. She'd shower in the morning. Right now, she just wanted to crawl into bed.

Sleep was elusive as a glob of mercury. She picked up a book from her bedside table and tried to read, but the words blurred on the page. Finally, she closed the book, turned out the light, and tried to sleep. Instead, she watched the red numerals on her bedside clock change: 10:00, 10:40, 11:15.

She was tossing in a restless slumber when she heard the ring of the phone. The clock showed 12:05 as Elena reached for the receiver. Her left hand clutched the covers tighter around her as her right lifted the phone and brought it to her ear.

At first there was silence. Maybe this was simply a wrong number. Maybe the calls had stopped.

No, there it was. Sobbing. Starting softly, then rising to a crescendo. A woman's voice — a husky alto, like a lounge singer in a smoky, second-rate club.

"Who is this?" Elena said.

No answer. Only sobbing.

"What do you want?" Elena's voice rose

to a shriek.

A click. Then silence.

Elena stabbed blindly at the phone's "end" button, finally hitting it as an electronic voice began, "If you'd like to make a call —"

She turned on the bedside lamp and stared at the cheap lithograph on the opposite wall. In it, a young man and woman were walking through a field of flowers. They looked so happy. Like she and Mark had been.

But he was gone, and she'd never be happy again. Ever.

She reached for the light but withdrew her hand. No, leave it burning. Elena burrowed deeply under the covers, the way she used to do as a child after hearing a ghost story. She closed her eyes and watched the images march across her brain: endless days spent at the bedside of a living corpse, Mark's casket disappearing into the ground, a faceless woman at some shadowy location sobbing into a phone.

As the sound of those sobs echoed through Elena's mind, the image of a face from her past came into focus. Was that who was calling? If so, there was nothing Elena could do. She'd simply suffer . . . because she deserved it.

■ ■ ■ ■

Elena slapped at the snooze button on her alarm clock. Why was it buzzing already? Then she remembered — her breakfast with Dr. Bennett. What had Helen meant by "We need to talk?"

Her stomach did a flip-flop, and she tasted a bitter mix of peanut butter and bile. Maybe some coffee would help.

Elena padded to the kitchen and reached into the cabinet, wishing she'd had the foresight to make coffee before going to bed last night. The weight of the canister told her before she removed the lid — empty. She filled a glass at the sink and drank the contents, hoping to at least wash the bad taste from her mouth.

A quick shower brought her a bit more awake. Now for hair and makeup. Elena had always taken pride in her resemblance to her mother, a beautiful woman with dark, Latina looks. But long days at the hospital followed by sleepless nights had taken their toll.

There were dark circles under her eyes, the brown irises surrounded by a network of red. A few drops of Visine, and she looked less like the survivor of an all-night drinking spree. She'd cover the circles with a little makeup and hope Dr. Bennett wouldn't notice.

Elena ran her hands through her long black hair. She needed a haircut, needed it in the worst way. But there was neither time nor money for that right now. She'd pull it into the always-utilitarian ponytail she'd favored more and more lately.

Dressed, her backpack slung over one shoulder, her purse over the other, she stepped through the door into the early-morning darkness, in no way ready to face the day. It was bad already. She hoped it wouldn't get worse.

The ride in the elevator was three floors up, but Elena's stomach felt as though she was in a free fall. She didn't have to do this today. When Helen Bennett called, she should have put this visit on "hold." But something told her she needed to get it out of the way.

The elevator doors slid open, and the scene before her made memories scroll across her mind like a filmstrip unwinding. The waiting area of the ICU at Zale University Hospital was quiet at 5:30 a.m. The television mounted high on the far wall flickered with silent images as closed cap-tions of the local news crawled across the bottom of the screen. An older man huddled in a chair near the "Staff Only" door, glancing every few seconds toward that portal as though Gabriel himself were about to come through it with news of his loved one.

Elena knew the feeling. For two weeks, she'd spent much of every day in this same waiting room. The rest of the time, the minutes not spent snatching a quick bite in the cafeteria or hurrying home for a shower and change of clothes, were spent at her husband's bedside, holding his hand and listening to the even rhythm of the respirator that kept him alive. Her heart bled for the old man and for every other person who'd ever sat in this room.

Elena was pleased when her final training assignment took her away from Zale, the place where her life fell apart. St. Paul Hospital was less than half a mile away, but she welcomed every foot of that buffer. When she walked out of Zale for the last time, she silently vowed never to return.

Now she was back, and she still wasn't sure of her reason. Was it to add the books from the box balanced on her hip to the dog-eared paperbacks next to the volunteer's desk? Or was it to show she had the courage to revisit the scene of the most terrible two weeks of her life? No matter, she was here. She clenched her jaw and forced her feet to move.

"Dr. Gardner. What are you doing here?"

Elena looked up at the nurse emerging from the elevator. The woman's name tickled at the periphery of Elena's memory like a loose hair. What was it?

"Oh. You startled me."

"Sorry. What brings you back here?"

Elena held up a handful of books and shoved them into the bookcase. "These are some of Mark's —" Her throat closed and words left her. With an effort, she began again. "I was going through some of Mark's things and thought these might help the people in the waiting room pass the time."

The nurse moved closer, and Elena sneaked a look at her nametag. Karri Lawson. Of course. How could she forget Karri? The pretty brunette had been the nurse responsible for Mark's care almost the entire time he was in the ICU. In fact Karri had been Mark's nurse the day —. Elena shook her head. Don't go there. Don't go back.

If Karri noticed Elena's discomfort, she made no mention of it. Instead, she gave Elena a brief hug. "I haven't seen you since . . . since that day. I'm sorry for your loss." She made a gesture toward the closed doors leading to the ICU. "We all are."

Elena had heard "sorry for your loss" so many times, it was almost meaningless. Her response was automatic. "Thank you."

"Would you like to come in and see the other staff?" Karri looked at her watch. "The day shift isn't here yet, but there may be some nurses you remember from when . . . from your time here."

"I don't think so." Elena reached out and touched Karri on the shoulder. "I have a meeting. But tell everyone hello for me. Tell them I said 'thanks.' "

"The coffee here is surprisingly good," Elena said. "Everyone always says that hospital food, especially hospital coffee, is terrible."

"I agree," Helen Bennett said. "I wish my receptionist could make coffee like this. She's a jewel, but in fifteen years with me she's never learned to make coffee that doesn't taste like it's brewed from homogenized tire treads."

"Don't be too hard on her, Helen. I'm looking forward to working with her. And with you, of course."

Helen placed her mug on the table as carefully as an astronaut docking the space shuttle. "Well, that's what we need to talk about." She looked around to make sure there was no one within earshot. Around them, the cafeteria was filled with bleary-eyed residents, medical students, and nurses, but no one seemed interested in the conversation at their table. "I'm afraid you're not going to be working with my receptionist, or my nurse, or me."

"What —"

Helen stemmed Elena's words with an upraised hand. "Let me give you the whole story. Then I can answer questions if you have any — assuming you're still speaking to me by then."

The hollow feeling in Elena's stomach intensified.

"I've been in private practice for fifteen years, going it alone. There aren't many of us left in solo situations, but I've held out. I've managed to get other doctors in various groups to share call with me, but lately that's been somewhere between difficult and impossible."

"I know. That's why you wanted to bring me into the practice," Elena said.

"True, but that's changed. The Lincoln Clinic has approached me to join their family practice section. Actually, they want me to head it. They've made me a great offer.

Not just the money, although that's good. The whole package seems tailor-made for me. I'll be supervising six other doctors, and I'll be exempt from night call. A great retirement plan and benefits." Helen looked down at the tabletop. "I couldn't turn it down."

Elena's mind scrambled for a solution. The ship was sinking, and she grabbed for something to keep her afloat. "So why don't I take over your practice? I can buy you out. I mean, I won't have the money right way, but I can pay you over several years. It'll be sort of like an annuity for you."

Helen was already shaking her head. "No, one part of the deal was that I bring my patients with me. The clinic will hire both my receptionist and nurse, and give them a good package as well. They'll even buy my equipment from me. I've already terminated the office lease. I'm moving out in ninety days."

Elena forced back the tears she felt forming. "Helen, do you realize what this does to me?"

"I know. I just —"

"No." Elena worked to keep her voice level. "You don't know. You don't know how I've struggled to get through my residency after Mark's death. You have no idea what it meant to me to have a practice waiting for me. No need to lease space, to remodel and buy equipment. No waiting to build up a practice. There'd be a guaranteed income and a chance to pay off a mountain of debt."

"Elena —"

Elena shook her head. "I finish my residency in less than a month. Thirty days! Now you've pulled the rug out from under me. I have four weeks to find a way to do the only thing I know how to do — practice medicine." She turned her back to Helen, thinking that Helen had done the same thing to her. "No, I realize this is good for you, but I don't think you really know the effect it has on me."

"Elena, I had to do this. Once you get over the shock, you'll think about it and agree. But listen, I'm not going to leave you hanging."

Elena turned back to face the woman who'd been her mentor, the friend who was now betraying her. "What do you mean?"

"The clinic gave me a very short deadline to accept or reject their offer. I only made my final decision this weekend. But the second call I made, after the one to the clinic administrator, was to your chair, Dr. Amy Gross. She and I are both putting out feelers for a place you can practice." Helen reached across the table and patted Elena's shoulder. "We know how hard this past three months have been on you. We worry about you. And believe me, we won't abandon you now. God has something out there for you. Trust Him."

Elena drained the last of the coffee from her cup. When she set it down, she knocked her fork off the table. The dull clank of silverware on vinyl floor was barely audible over the low hum of voices that filled the cafeteria. "Trust God? I don't think so. I trusted Him when Mark lay there fighting for his life, but it didn't seem to do any good."

"I know. But He's still in control."

Elena shook her head, while one more hobgoblin joined those already dancing in her brain.

2

Elena hesitated in the doorway. She felt her adrenaline titer rise in response to the most ancient of reflexes: *fight or flight.* Unfortunately, neither was an option right now. "You wanted to see me?"

Dr. Amy Gross, chair of the Department of Family Practice at Southwestern Medical Center, sat behind a desk devoid of papers except for a thick file barely contained by a slightly ragged manila cover. To her right, Dr. Bruce Matney, chair of the Department of Neurosurgery, adjusted his white lab coat to better cover his gray-green surgical scrubs.

Dr. Gross waited until Elena settled into the single chair centered in front of the desk. "I appreciate your coming here today."

As though I had a choice. When the chairwoman's secretary calls residents and asks them to be in her office in an hour, it's pretty much a command performance.

"We know that the wound from Mark's death is still tender," Gross continued.

Elena glanced at Dr. Matney and saw the frown that crossed his face. He'd liked Mark, and his inability to save her husband after his intracranial bleeding episode probably still ate at the neurosurgeon.

Gross tapped the file. "But there's something here we need to discuss with you." She flipped to a spot marked by a yellow Post-It note. "Dr. Matney was in Medical Records yesterday to dictate summaries and sign charts. They'd sent Mark's chart back to him for a signature on something he'd missed, and he noticed this. It's an order he didn't write."

No problem there. Lots of doctors wrote orders — residents, staff taking call for a colleague. Stay quiet, Elena.

Gross turned the chart to face Elena. "Tell us what you see here."

Elena leaned forward and read the words she already knew were at the heart of this matter. "DNR."

"And the signature?"

"It's mine."

Gross frowned. "Elena, we all know how difficult it was for you as a physician to let someone else direct your husband's care. And we recognize that the decision not to resuscitate your husband was yours to make. You told Dr. Matney repeatedly that you couldn't bring yourself to withdraw life support. Then, on the same day that a 'do not resuscitate' order appeared on the chart — not written by the attending physician — your husband's respirator was disconnected without the knowledge or participation of any of the staff." She paused like Perry Mason addressing a particularly reluctant witness. "Can you explain that?"

Two pairs of eyes focused like lasers on her. What could she say? Best to keep it simple. "I'd held off as long as I could, but I finally accepted that we couldn't keep Mark on life support any longer. Dr. Matney, you were in surgery, and I was afraid that if I didn't follow through right then I'd change my mind. Writing the order was sort of symbolic for me."

Matney's voice was like polished steel. "And did you turn off Mark's respirator?"

The silence seemed to stretch on endlessly. Elena's shoulders sagged. She looked down at the floor. "I don't know." She swallowed hard. "I honestly can't recall."

No one seemed to know how to respond to that. Finally, Gross said, "I can understand. It was a very traumatic experience, and we often tend to block out those memories." She looked at Matney, then back at Elena. "I believe we can overlook your writing that order, although you recognize it was a serious breach of both protocol and ethics. And, if you did take matters into your own hands to end Mark's suffering, we can understand that as well. But we have to be certain that nothing like this will ever happen again. You can't let this carry over to affect other patients under your care."

Elena looked up at the two doctors with what she hoped was the right expression of contrition. "You have my assurance."

Matney scraped his chair backward and rose. He favored the two women with a single nod and left the room as though marching off to save the world. Gross leaned across the desk and extended her hand. The cold, formal voice she'd used moments before gave way to the kindly tone of an older sister. "Elena, my door is always open. Come and talk with me anytime."

Even as Elena expressed her appreciation, she knew that no help would come from talking with Amy Gross or anyone else. Nothing would help.

"I'm sorry, but I'm paying as much as I can each month. There's nothing more I can do right now." The insistent tones of her pager

31

cut through the conversational buzz and clatter of the hospital staff cafeteria. Elena checked the display. Emergency Room. Stat.

"I have to go." She flipped her cell phone closed and hurried toward the door, shoving her tray onto the conveyer belt without breaking stride.

Elena slammed through the swinging doors of the ER, looked around, and saw a pair of EMTs wheeling a stretcher into treatment room two. She and the head ER nurse arrived at the door right behind them, trailed by a nurse's aide.

"Sixty-eight-year-old male found unresponsive by his wife." The EMT grunted out the words as he and his partner shifted the patient from their stretcher onto a hospital gurney. "Comatose. BP 168 over 90, pulse 56, respirations 12 and irregular. He's on Cardizem, Lipitor . . ."

Elena listened with one ear, her mind already focused on the problem at hand. She ran her hands over the man's scalp, moving aside the silvery gray hair, looking for bruises and lacerations, finding none.

As she bent to check his eyes, she sniffed the man's breath for the smell of alcohol or the fruity odor that signaled diabetic coma. So far, so good.

Elena flexed the man's head forward. No

neck stiffness. She looked for blood in the ear canals. Good, no sign of a basilar skull fracture.

When she thumbed back his eyelids, her pulse quickened. The right pupil was significantly larger than the left. Elena pulled a penlight from the breast pocket of her white coat and shined it into the man's eyes. The right pupil remained unchanged, the left contracted sluggishly.

"Hand me the ophthalmoscope," she said.

Elena used the instrument to look through the pupils to the back of the man's eyeballs. Sure enough, the nerve head of the right optic nerve was already bulging.

"Blown pupil on the right." she said. "Get the neurosurgeon on call down here stat. This patient's had an intracranial hemorrhage." The aide turned and hurried out. "Hang a gram of Mannitol IV. Run the oxygen at high flow. Did you get blood for labs?"

"Did it while you were checking him." The nurse patted her uniform pocket, and Elena heard the muted clink of glass.

"As soon as you get the Mannitol going, send those to the lab for a stat CBC and metabolic profile. When you get a chance, put in a Foley catheter. And he's going to need an MRI, so put radiology on standby."

The aide hurried back in. The nurse paused long enough to hand her the blood samples and whisper instructions. "I'm on it," the aide said, and scurried away.

Elena registered the faint bluish tint to the patient's lips. She checked his fingertips and saw the same coloration creeping into the nail beds. The man's respirations were now weak and shallow. He needed more oxygen.

"Give me the laryngoscope and a tube."

The nurse placed an L-shaped instrument in Elena's left hand, slapped a curved plastic endotracheal tube into her right. Elena pried the man's jaws open with the tip of the laryngoscope and slid the flat end down his tongue. A light at the tip of the instrument showed the opening between the vocal cords, barely visible in a sea of pooled saliva. Elena gritted her teeth and slid the plastic tube downward along the laryngoscope. When the tube disappeared through the cords into the airway, she breathed again. *Made it through another intubation.* Quickly, Elena inflated the soft rubber cuff that provided an airtight seal around the tube. The nurse hooked the patient to the respirator and looked at Elena with raised eyebrows.

"Set it at sixteen," Elena said. Soon the

rhythmic sound of the respirator was accompanied by a regular rise and fall in the patient's chest. She watched for half a dozen cycles before nodding. "There, he's starting to pink up."

Elena ran down a mental checklist. What had she missed? ABC. Airway, Breathing, Circulation: the mantra for handling emergencies, one of the first lessons learned by any doctor. The first two were taken care of. The man's heartbeat was strong, but she'd better check for cardiac damage. "Let's hook him up to the EKG."

A few moments later she scanned the tracing. No abnormalities. Good.

Anything else? As a resident physician at Southwestern Medical Center, Elena was part of a top-notch medical team. Chances were that if she forgot something, someone else would remedy the omission. But when she was out on her own in private practice, it would be totally up to her. That time would be here soon. Better get ready.

Elena looked at the clock on the wall. Sometimes in an emergency, time seemed to slow down. At other times it seemed to be rocket-powered. This was one of those times when the minutes fled by. Where was the neurosurgeon?

At Southwestern there were three separate

hospitals on the campus — four if you counted Children's Medical Center. Chances were that the doctor this patient needed had to travel from Zale Hospital, on the far south end of the campus, to where Elena waited with the patient at St. Paul Hospital, at the far north end of the campus. Whether the neurosurgeon came by car or on the campus shuttle, surely he should have been here by now.

Another glance at the clock. Another five minutes gone. Left unchecked, blood from the intracranial hemorrhage would force the brain down against the bony ring at the base of the skull, compromising the vital centers, shutting down the impulses that kept the heart beating, the lungs inflating. Without surgery to relieve that pressure, the man would die. Where was the neurosurgeon?

"Who's on neuro call?" she asked the nurse.

"Dr. Clark."

"And you paged him stat?"

The aide was back now, hovering behind Elena, awaiting instructions. "I asked the ward clerk to do that." She hesitated. "Do you want me to check?"

"Yes, please." Elena hesitated a beat. "First, get me the tray for an emergency trephine. If he doesn't show soon, I may have to —"

"Okay, I'm here. What's so important?" Dr. James Clark strode into the room and stopped at the foot of the gurney. He stared at Elena, and the look on his face said, "This had better be good."

"Elderly male, hypertensive and probably atherosclerotic, found unresponsive by his wife. Right pupil dilated and fixed, left sluggish to react, definite papilledema. Vitals compatible with Cushing's triad. I've alerted radiology for a stat MRI."

Clark grunted and picked up the ophthalmoscope from the table where Elena had laid it. He checked the patient's eyes, then traded that instrument for a reflex hammer and did a bit of tapping. He ran his thumbnail along the soles of the man's bare feet, frowning when the toes fanned and extended upward.

"Okay, you're probably right." He turned to the ER nurse. "Send him for the MRI. Call the OR and tell them to set up for an emergency craniotomy. I want Dr. Miller for anesthesia. If he's doing another case, have him get someone else to take over. And page the chief neuro resident to help me. Make sure the patient's taken directly from radiology to surgery, along with his films. I'll be up there changing."

He disappeared in a wave of self-importance, without so much as a "good pick-up" or even "please."

"I'll go to radiology with the patient," Elena said. "I'll stay there and take him to the OR myself."

"Dr. Gardner," the nurse said. "You don't have to do that."

Elena didn't answer, just released the brakes on the gurney and started pushing it out the door. Clark might think his MD degree conferred immunity from any of the menial tasks involved in patient care, but Elena had a different point of view. She intended to see to it that this patient got the best possible care. There'd be no delays in his treatment. She knew all too well that delays could be deadly.

After Elena turned the patient over to the anesthesiologist, she lingered in the hallway, praying the surgery would save the life of this man whose name she didn't even know. That he wouldn't be kept alive to simply survive in a coma. Not like Mark.

The patient's name was Chester Pulliam. Elena sat in a corner of the waiting room with his wife, Erma, and explained the situation. "A blood vessel in your husband's brain burst. Usually it's because of a weak place, sort of like a bulging spot on a balloon. This is more likely to happen when there's high blood pressure and hardening of the arteries, and your husband has both these conditions."

The woman looked down at the handkerchief she was twisting. "Can they save him?"

"Dr. Clark is an excellent neurosurgeon. He'll do his very best."

"Oh, I hope so. I couldn't bear to lose Chester. We've been married for forty-eight years. If he died . . . I'd die too."

Elena patted Mrs. Pulliam's hand. "Is there anything I can do for you? Are there any other questions?"

The woman shook her head. "I'm sure there are, but I can't think of them right now." She looked into Elena's eyes. "Thank you for what you've done."

"I'm glad I could be here to help." Elena felt a familiar lump in her throat. She turned and strode away before the woman could see the tears forming in her eyes. Would this happen every time she had a patient with an intracranial hemorrhage? Where was the dispassionate approach she'd been told she had to adopt if she were to survive as a family doctor? Her department chair had put it to her this way, "Elena, Mark's situation wasn't uncommon. You did the best you could. Everyone else did too. The timing was just bad. You can't let that carry over to every patient you see for the next forty years."

In less than a month, she'd complete her training and be out in the world of private practice. She had to get past this. Medicine was all she knew, all she'd ever wanted to do. Surely God wouldn't take that from her after He'd already taken her husband.

Elena's mind was on everything and nothing, churning fruitlessly as she shuffled through the lunch line in the hospital cafeteria. She'd eat, but only because she knew she had to. Her life was coming apart, and she didn't know how to mend it.

"Hey, come join me."

She saw David at a table for two in the far corner of the cafeteria. He stood and waved, as though he was afraid she might miss him. That would be hard to do. He stood a shade over six feet, with a shock of reddish-blond hair above a tan that reminded Elena of a California surfer. He might be quiet, but David was hard to overlook.

She wove her way through the tables and began to unload her tray. She jerked her mind away from the worries that were her constant companion, and struggled for an opening conversational gambit. "Good to see you. I didn't think OB residents ever took time to eat lunch."

"Eat when you can. Isn't that what they teach us as medical students?" David held the chair for her, another of the small things that made her admire him. His bright blue scrub suit and the ring around his forehead from the pressure of his surgical cap told Elena he'd been in the operating room already.

She tried to focus on the man at the table with her, not on the shambles her life had become. "How are things going for you?" she asked.

"Pretty good. I'm on Dr. Cobb's service, and he's letting me do quite a bit. Just finished a case with him." He took a healthy bite of sandwich, chewed, and swallowed. "How about you?"

Elena paused with her fork halfway to her mouth, careful not to drip ranch dressing from the chef's salad she'd chosen. "Right now I mainly divide my time between the FP Clinic and the ER. Sometimes I round with one of the specialists. Good preparation for going out on my own — if I only had a place to practice."

"What's that mean?"

"Are you ready for the next chapter of the

41

Elena Gardner tragedy?" She related the gist of her conversation with Helen Bennett and watched deep concern overshadow David's normally placid countenance.

"I'll add that to my prayers for you," he said. "Be sure to let me know if anything develops."

She nodded before filling her mouth with salad. Doctors learned to eat fast, never knowing when the meal might be interrupted. She noticed David doing the same.

"And did you get a call last night?" David asked.

Elena nodded. "Midnight. A woman sobbing. But I think I recognized the voice."

"You did?"

"I'm pretty sure — but I don't know what to do about it. And until I do, I don't want to say anything — even to you."

"Fair enough. But I'm here for you when you're ready to talk."

Elena dabbed at the corner of her mouth with her napkin. She was opening her mouth to reply when a staccato electronic bleat split the air. Both doctors reached for their belts and extracted their pagers.

"Mine," Elena said. She thumbed the button and read the display. "Dr. Gross's office." She pushed back her chair. "Guess I'd better see what the department chair wants."

■ ■ ■ ■

The chairwoman's secretary was noncommittal in delivering the message. Dr. Gross would like to see Dr. Gardner this afternoon at five. Could she make it?

Elena mentally reviewed her schedule. "No problem. Can you tell me what this is about?"

"Sorry, I'm simply relaying the message."

Elena tried to put the matter out of her mind until time for the meeting, but with little success. It was all she could do to concentrate on her duties for the afternoon. She gave silent thanks that her patients presented straightforward problems: congestive heart failure, early peptic ulcer, migraine headache. She ordered the appropriate diagnostic tests, wrote prescriptions for the proper medications, arranged for referrals to staff specialists when necessary. Somehow she got through the afternoon.

Next she had to finish her clinic charts, go over some X-rays and lab reports, return about a half-dozen phone calls, and change into a fresh white coat before her meeting. She managed to do all this, even run a brush through her hair and redo her ponytail, before she tapped on the open door of

Amy Gross's office at precisely five o'clock.

"You wanted to see me?" Elena waited for Dr. Gross to look up from the papers she was signing.

"Oh, Elena. Come in. Have a seat." The woman motioned toward the couch on the far side of her office. "Let's sit down over there so we can talk without the desk between us."

Elena took this as a good sign. If Dr. Gross planned to deliver bad news, she'd do it from behind her desk, putting a barrier between them.

Elena sat at the end of the couch. Dr. Gross took a seat beside her and half-turned to face her.

"I'm sure you're curious about this 'summons.' " She made quote marks with her fingers to set off the word. "But it's good news, I assure you."

Elena felt the pounding headache she'd experienced all afternoon ease a bit. "Well, I could use some good news."

"I understand you talked with Dr. Bennett this morning."

Elena nodded. She didn't think she could have said a word even if she wanted to. Her throat was in a knot at the reminder of the bombshell Helen dropped on her this morning.

44

Dr. Gross continued. "Helen called me at home Sunday afternoon, right after she decided to take the job offer from Lincoln Clinic."

Elena remained silent.

"You may not believe it, but it caused her a great deal of pain to go back on her offer to you. Both she and I have made lots of calls trying to find something for you. I even looked into the possibility of your working in an emergency room somewhere."

Elena knew that was a possibility, but not one she wanted to consider. In that situation, there'd be no continuity of care. No way to establish a rapport, a long-term relationship with her patients. That wasn't the way she wanted to practice medicine. She hoped that wasn't what this was about.

"But I think I have something better for you," Dr. Gross said. "I got a call shortly before noon from one of the doctors who did her family practice residency here at Southwestern. Do you remember Cathy Sewell? She would have been a couple of years ahead of you in the program."

"I know who she is, but we never had a rotation together and neither of us socialized much, so I don't know a lot about her."

"She went back to her hometown to set up a solo practice. That's in . . ." Dr. Gross

45

pulled a pair of reading glasses from the breast pocket of her white coat and consulted the yellow legal pad she held. "That's in Dainger, Texas. She's pregnant, and she's looking for someone to take over her practice while she's on maternity leave."

"When does she need someone?"

Amy frowned. "She needs someone right now. She's less than two months from her due date. She had a retired doctor lined up to fill in for her, but he was just diagnosed with colon cancer, so he's not coming."

Elena felt hope stir in her chest like the flutter of a bird's wings. Then she saw it — the downside. "Does she want someone temporary? Is this a *locum tenens* situation?"

"Not necessarily. Bringing in the retired doctor was a stop-gap measure, but I think she'd like to find a younger doctor to take into the practice. There certainly seems to be room for expansion. If things work out well with you, she could offer you an association. That's a bridge you'll have to cross when you come to it." Dr. Gross tapped her glasses on the legal pad to emphasize her words. "But I think this is the best you can expect with such short notice. I wouldn't turn it down if I were you."

"Did she give you any more details?"

Dr. Gross shook her head. "She'll do that herself." She tore the top sheet off the pad and handed it to Elena. "Call her. She'd like you to come up this weekend to meet with her. It's only about an hour and a half drive. She'll show you the setup there, talk with you about possible arrangements." She put the pad on the coffee table in front of her and returned the glasses to her pocket. "I've given you a high recommendation. I also told her a bit about your history, about Mark. In fairness, I think you should give her the full story. I believe you'll find her quite understanding."

"Dainger?" Elena said. "I'm not sure that's a very reassuring name."

Dr. Gross chuckled. "I commented on that when we talked. Cathy tells me it was named for some early settler. I don't think you'll find it very dangerous at all."

"Well, I'll certainly be glad to meet with her. Thanks so much for your recommendation."

Dr. Gross rose and extended her hand. "Get someone to look in on your hospitalized patients while you're gone. And I really hope this works out for you."

It was almost seven when Elena pulled out of the medical center parking lot, and traffic had thinned a bit. All the way home, she alternated between elation at the possibility she'd have a position when her residency ended and fear that she was about to jump into a bad situation.

Who had ever heard of Dainger, Texas, anyway? She had a vague notion that it was somewhere northwest of Dallas. Well, driving directions would be the least of her problems, thanks to MapQuest and Google. What worried her more was not knowing what she'd find when she got there. Other than what she'd learned about how the name came about — and that was pretty vague — she had no idea what the town was like. But it didn't matter, did it? It sounded like a chance to get a fresh start. And she certainly needed that.

What about Dr. Cathy Sewell? Right now, that was a familiar name, nothing more. She had a vague recollection of a petite blonde doctor who did her work well and seemed pleasant enough. When Cathy finished her residency, she disappeared off Elena's radar screen. Of course, even if she'd still been around, Elena wouldn't have noticed. She was too busy with Mark, first their courtship, then their marriage, and then . . .

Elena felt her eyes clouding. Her breathing came faster. The shaking of her hands made the car jitter back and forth. She pulled off the busy street and into a mall parking lot, where she put her head on the steering wheel and let the tears flow freely.

"Excuse me?"

She looked up to see an older man, dressed in jeans and a sport shirt, standing beside her car. He tapped on the closed driver's side window. "Ma'am, are you okay?"

She pulled a tissue from the box on the seat beside her and dabbed at her eyes. She felt her nose dripping but wasn't about to blow it in front of this man. She gave it what she hoped was a lady-like wipe and crumpled the tissue in her hand before lowering the window. "I'm . . . I'm fine. I just —" She bit off her response. No need to explain. He didn't need to know.

The man leaned down to her eye level. "Is there anything I can do?"

There was nothing anyone could do. What was done was done. But there was no reason to go into that, either. "Thank you, but no. I need to sit here a moment and collect myself."

It seemed that he might be ready to start a conversation, and she steeled herself to rebuff any efforts to get her to open up about her problem. No one needed to know about it, because no one could help. Instead, he nodded and straightened.

She had the window halfway up when he turned back and said, just loud enough for her to hear. "I'll pray for you." Then he disappeared between the parked cars.

Elena entered her apartment that night to the accompaniment of pounding pulse and jangling nerves. As she crossed the threshold, she asked herself once more, "What's wrong with me?" She was an intelligent woman, a trained physician. There were no demons waiting in the darkness. True, once this apartment had been a home, and now it was only a place to sleep and eat and mourn. But that was no reason to let her grief take over her life.

Then again, it wasn't just the grief. There were the phone calls. If she'd heard heavy breathing or a torrent of obscenities, she'd know what was going on. She could handle that. Any single woman living in the city knew such things occurred. But these calls were more than that. And she thought she finally knew what they represented.

Elena dropped her backpack, slammed the door, and turned on the TV for company. The mail went onto the small table beside her armchair. It could wait. First, a shower and a cup of tea.

Clean, but in no way refreshed, Elena dropped into the easy chair and considered the mail. There was never anything good there anymore. The condolence cards and letters had dried up. She had no family to send her cheery notes. Only her creditors and the people wanting her to spend money she didn't have now accounted for the handful of mail she received.

The envelope was there between her MasterCard bill and an ad for a new textbook. The envelope was a cheap, self-sealing one, addressed by hand in block capitals using blue ballpoint. Two different stamps were affixed to provide the proper postage. The blurred postmark gave no indication of the city of origin.

Elena ran her finger under the flap and pulled out a single sheet of paper from a lined tablet.

The message was printed in the same block capitals. At the end, the writer had pressed down hard enough to penetrate the paper. Elena read the message twice, at first unable to understand and then unwilling to believe it.

**I KNOW WHAT YOU DID AND
YOU'LL PAY.**

She dropped the paper onto the table and pressed both hands to her temples.

3

"Mrs. Gardner, you really need to make arrangements to clear this entire balance." The woman's voice was level and calm. No threats. No pressure. But, nevertheless, the words made Elena's stomach roil.

As it had so many evenings for several months, Elena's phone rang at about 8:00 p.m. When she checked the Caller ID, she knew what the call was about. This was the collection agency for the ambulance that took Mark to the hospital. Other nights the call would be about the balance due for Mark's hospital care or his funeral. There'd been so much expense, and his insurance coverage wasn't the best. The doctors caring for him discounted their fees, often writing off the balance. But there were other expenses — so many other expenses.

Elena took a deep breath and made a conscious effort to loosen her death grip on the phone. "Not that it makes any difference to you, but it's Dr. Gardner. I'm well aware of the situation, and I have no intention of letting this debt slide. But right now I'm in residency training, working eighty hours a week. The pay's not much, certainly not what you'd expect a doctor to make. Then there are deductions for taxes and Social Security. Some of what's left goes for utilities, groceries, rent, car payment. You know, living expenses, although I don't know if you could call what I'm doing living. I've tried to pay something on my debts every month since Mark . . ." The words trailed off. What was the use? Elena leaned forward onto her desk and watched her tears drip onto the blotter.

"Mrs. Gardner?" The woman might have been a robot for all her response to the emotion in Elena's voice. Maybe she was. Maybe they used robots for this. Certainly, it seemed to Elena that the people she'd talked with so far had no living, beating hearts.

"I'll keep paying you as much as I can," Elena said. "My employment situation is sort of up in the air right now, but you can rest assured that this debt and my medical school loans will be the first things I repay." Elena took a deep breath. "Now please stop calling me. I know how much I owe. I know where to send the payments. I know all of it. Actually, I can't seem to get it out of my head."

The emotionless voice was saying something when Elena hung up. It was just too much. She put her head on the desk and let the tears flow unchecked.

"Good dinner."

"Will, the worst meal you ever ate was wonderful." Dr. Cathy Sewell grinned. The way to her husband's heart might not be through his stomach, but it certainly represented an easy shortcut. "Coffee?"

She poured coffee for Will, herbal tea for herself, and followed him into the living room. "Good news," Cathy said. "I got a call from Amy Gross today."

Will put down the paper. "Did she find someone?"

"Dr. Elena Gardner, one of the residents who's finishing in less than a month, had her practice offer fall through. Amy thinks she might be a good fit here. She'll drive up this weekend to talk with me."

"Do you know her?"

Cathy sipped her tea. "Vaguely, although I didn't recognize her name at first. Apparently she took her husband's name when they married." Cathy smiled. "Personally,

I'm glad you were okay with my continuing to practice as Cathy Sewell. Can you imagine the hassle of changing the name on all those documents?"

Will grinned. "Yeah, and I'm glad you didn't make me take yours. 'Law offices of Will Kennedy-Sewell, how may I help you?' "

"Amy said Dr. Gardner has had some problems recently."

"Professional problems?"

"No, Amy says she's the sharpest resident they've had since I graduated. I waved that off as flattery, but if she practices the way I do that'll be good."

Will got up from his chair and moved toward the small kitchen adjacent to the living room. "I want a couple of cookies to go with my coffee. Want anything?"

"No, I'm good," Cathy called. She waited for him to return and settle into his chair. "You mentioned professional ability, and I guess it does affect that, although indirectly. Her husband had a ruptured berry aneurysm —" She caught herself and corrected her doctor-speak explanation.

"A little over six months ago, a blood vessel in her husband's brain burst, and by the time they got him into surgery, the damage was too great for him to recover. He was left in the deepest level of coma. He could be kept alive, but he was never going to recover. Elena struggled with the decision to take him off life support. Apparently she finally agreed, but I get the impression there was some irregularity about the way it was done. Amy says Elena has had problems since then."

"Such as . . . ?"

"I tried to get details from her, but she said I'd have to ask Elena about them."

Will took a sip of coffee, winced, and blew across the surface of the cup. "I'll be glad to sit in on the interview if you'd like my opinion, but I'm pretty sure you can trust your own judgment."

Cathy began to run through the things she wanted to discuss with this new doctor. She took a deep breath and blew it out slowly through pursed lips. She smiled. Could it be that she was unconsciously practicing cleansing breaths to help her through labor?

"Earth to Cathy? Where'd you go?"

"Sorry. I was wondering how my patients might relate to Dr. Gardner. It won't be a problem for me, but I'm afraid it might be for a few of them."

"Sorry," Will said. "I'm not following."

Cathy pushed aside her cup and saucer. "I didn't recognize her from her married name, but when I heard her maiden name I remembered her."

"Okay, I'll bite. What was Elena's maiden name?"

"Perez."

"And you think this might present a problem?"

"As I said, not for me, but the potential is there. Since Doc Gladstone retired, I trade call with Dr. Brown. You and I know that Emmett Brown is a competent doctor, but there are still a few of my patients who refuse to see him because they're uncomfortable being treated by an African American."

Will pushed his cup and saucer aside. "And you think they might feel the same way about this Dr. Gardner?"

"I don't recall a lot about Elena, but I do remember what she looks like. And I remember you could take one look at her and know she was Latina — a very beautiful one, by the way. Whether she uses the name Gardner or Perez, people are going to know her heritage."

Will watched as Cathy clenched her jaw. He knew that look and felt sorry for anyone who stood in her way when she displayed it. "But it's not going to sway your decision, is it?"

"Not in the least."

"Come in." The response to Elena's light tap hardly carried through the closed door of the ICU room.

Elena had dreaded this visit all morning. After talking with the neurosurgeon, she was more certain than ever what was ahead for the patient and his wife. Now she owed it to Erma Pulliam to share her knowledge. Elena steeled herself and pushed through the door.

"Mrs. Pulliam, I'm Doctor Gardner. I took care of your husband in the emergency room."

The lines in the woman's face were etched more deeply than Elena remembered. Her eyes carried a sadness that seemed beyond utterance. She sat at her husband's bedside, one hand covering his. "I remember you." Mrs. Pulliam's voice cracked. She cleared her throat. "You came out to the waiting room and told me what was happening. I appreciate that so much. I guess . . . I guess Dr. Clark's a busy man, but I keep missing him. I spend most of my time here. Just go home to change clothes and catch a nap. The nurses have trays sent to me, so I don't have to leave the room to eat. But still, I've only seen Dr. Clark once in the past two days. And when I ask him how Chester's doing, he just says, 'All we can do is wait.' "

Chester Pulliam lay pale and still. A large bandage covered his head. A ventilator puffed oxygenated air into his lungs via a tube into his windpipe. The monitor at the head of Chester's bed displayed blood pressure and pulse readings in the high normal range. IV fluids dripped slowly through a tube into a needle in the back of the man's right hand. The plastic bag hanging off the bed rail told Elena a urinary catheter was in place.

Elena lifted Chester's eyelids. His eyes were fixed straight ahead, the pupils midsize. She grabbed his Achilles tendon and squeezed. No reaction. She ran her thumbnail along the sole of his foot. The toes splayed and flexed upward. She frowned.

"Mrs. Pulliam, your husband had a very serious episode of bleeding inside his skull. That put a lot of pressure on his brain. Dr. Clark relieved that pressure and sealed off the blood vessel that burst, but the damage that was done has left Chester in a very deep coma."

"Will he be all right, Doctor?"

In Elena's mind a scene played out, one she knew as certainly as if she'd written the script. Chester would never recover from his coma. He'd go to a rehab facility. Despite decent care, he'd get contractures and bedsores. Eventually he'd get pneumonia or an overwhelming urinary tract infection with sepsis, and that would be his terminal event.

Tell her what's coming, Elena. She took a deep breath. "Every day he remains in a coma makes it less likely that he'll regain consciousness. And if he does begin to react, we can't know how much permanent damage there is, how much function he'll have." Elena surprised herself with her next words. "But there's still hope."

Mrs. Pulliam dabbed at her eyes. "Thank you, Dr. Gardner. That's all I want — to know that there's hope." She eased out of the chair with obvious effort. With one hand still grasping that of her husband, she reached with the other and took Elena's arm. "Thank you for giving me that."

Why did you lie? You know what's ahead. Elena swallowed hard. "There's always hope."

David wasn't sure why he felt the need to call Elena. Call it a premonition. Call it a divine prompting. Call it a surfacing of his suppressed desire to spend more time with Elena. For whatever reason, as soon as he reached his car to start the drive home, he pulled out his cell phone and punched her speed-dial number.

"Dr. Gardner." The tone of those two words painted a clear picture, and David was glad he'd called. Elena was really down. Time to step in.

"Elena, it's David. Can you talk right now?"

"Oh, right. Yeah, I guess so. I'm on my way to pick up my dry cleaning and buy a few groceries."

Run with the hunch. "Why don't you meet me at the El Fenix on Lemmon Avenue? I'll buy you some good Tex-Mex and we can talk."

"Oh, I couldn't — I mean, that's not . . ." He could hear a car honking in the background. Elena was probably working her way through the same type of traffic he was. "David, do you really want to do this?"

"Why not? We both need to eat. I'll bet you're too tired to cook, and I'm really not in the mood for a bologna sandwich tonight." He grinned, thinking there was no need to let Elena know about the pot roast simmering in the Crock-Pot at home. No need to puncture that "men can't cook" myth. "So, what do you say?"

"Why not? I'm probably about half an

hour away. Will that work?"

"Whoever gets there first gets a table," David said.

Twenty-five minutes later, he was munching on tortilla chips when Elena walked in. He rose and gave her a brotherly hug. "Bad day?" he asked.

"Not great, but not as bad as it could be. At least it's not Tuesday."

The waiter approached, but before he could speak Elena said, "Diet Coke with lime. Chicken taco salad."

David added his own order. When they were alone, he said, "So you expect another phone call next week?"

"I'm not sure. It's possible that she's escalated the action."

He listened as she related her story of the note and its cryptic message. "And you think it's from the same person?"

"It all fits together. Mark's birthday was four weeks ago — on a Tuesday. That's when the calls began. The message reached me Wednesday, but it was mailed on Tuesday."

David dipped a chip in salsa and crunched it, then took a sip of iced tea. "I'm hearing you say this is all related to Mark's death — the calls, the note, everything. Is that right?"

"I think so. Mark's mother . . ." She shook

63

her head.

"You don't have to talk about it if you don't want to."

"No, I need to. You see, Mark's mother didn't like me from the get-go."

"What about Mark's father?"

"He died when Mark was in his teens. Left the family comfortably fixed, and Lillian never let anyone forget that. She's spent most of her life parading her social status."

David nodded. "So Mark's mother opposed the marriage."

"Actually, 'marrying beneath him' was the way she put it, because, to her at least, I was a Mexican, born in Monterrey. Never mind that Mama was a U.S. citizen, the daughter of an American diplomat, that she was cultured and sophisticated, spoke flawless English, came from an upper-class background. Forget the fact that she married a wealthy Monterrey businessman."

A waiter deposited more salsa and a fresh basket of chips on the table. Elena murmured, *"Gracias,"* and he padded away. She pushed the chips toward David. If she was hungry for anything, it was conversation, not food.

"If you were born in Mexico — ?" He left the question hanging.

Elena took a deep breath. She was tired of

explaining this, but she'd brought it up and David deserved to know all the details. "My parents wanted their only daughter to be raised in the U.S., so they moved to Texas when I was an infant. I don't know how it happened — some law or other — but anyway, I was a U.S. citizen because of my mother. My father got his citizenship later." She lowered her head. "After my parents were killed in an auto accident when I was eight, my mother's sister and her husband raised me. There was no Spanish spoken in that home. I grew up like an Anglo. But none of that mattered to Lillian. All she cared about was my name, the color of my skin, the appearance of my features."

David paused with a chip halfway to the salsa. "So there was an uncomfortable relationship there."

"There was no relationship. We saw Mark's mother when we had to, but it was obvious she disapproved of our marriage."

"And this continued?"

Elena shook her head. "It got worse. You see, when Mark had his cerebral aneurysm, Lillian figured the dumb Mexican should have been smarter. I was a doctor. I should have seen it coming. I should have gotten him to the hospital more quickly. I should have pulled strings to get him a better surgeon." She bit her lip. "I should have saved his life — instead of ending it the way I did."

"What do you mean?"

Elena shoved her plate away. Score another one for the widow's diet. "To Lillian, so long as Mark's heart was beating and that monitor hadn't flat-lined, even though it took a respirator and a bunch of IV medications to keep him going, he was alive."

"And when you stopped all that?"

"Lillian is of the opinion that when I discontinued life support, I murdered her son."

Dr. Milton Gaines laid his half-specs on the desk and looked across at his colleague and patient. "You're doing fine, Cathy. In another few weeks you'll give birth to a healthy baby. Sure you and Will don't want to know whether it's a girl or boy?"

"No. We've decided to wait and be surprised." Cathy shifted in her chair, seeking a more comfortable position and finding none. "I appreciate your seeing me this late in the day, Milton. It's tough for me to get out of the office."

"Glad to do it. And I know how it feels to be swamped with patients."

66

Cathy felt a foot bury itself in her side. "Are you about ready to take on an associate?"

"I hadn't planned to quite yet, but some things have changed. This is going to come out at the hospital staff meeting next week, and I suppose you can keep it to yourself until then. Arthur Harshman's retiring. He and his wife are moving to Florida."

That surprised Cathy. Somehow, she'd pictured Arthur Harshman as sort of an ageless icon in the medical community, always here, always the same, holding sway in hospital staff meetings because most doctors didn't dare disagree with him. He had the bedside manner of Attila the Hun, but there was no question about his competence in obstetrics and gynecology. She was surprised to realize she'd miss him. "So, what about —"

"About someone to fill in when I can't be here? For now, Tom Denson in Bridgeport has agreed to drive over to cover if I have to be away, which won't be often. And I have an associate who'll be starting soon. He's finishing his residency June 30."

"Good for you, Milton. I know that practicing OB can wear you down. I'm glad you've found someone to help with the load."

Gaines frowned. "What about you? I hope you're not expecting to work right up to the day you deliver. What are you going to do for coverage? Can Emmett take up the slack?"

"Emmett has offered to help, but . . . well, some of my patients have balked at seeing him. Then I lined up a retired doctor from the temp agency, but he's developed health issues so that's off."

"What will you do?"

"I have a young woman coming in for an interview this weekend. I hope she'll be a good fit for the practice."

"Will this be to fill in temporarily?"

"Originally, I wanted a *locum tenens,* but if things work out between us I might want to take her on as an associate. You know, the town is growing."

Gaines chuckled. "So are you, Cathy. So are you."

Her footsteps echoed in her ears and her pulse raced as Elena negotiated the dark sidewalk leading to her apartment door. She fumbled in the depths of her purse to retrieve her keys. *Get a grip.*

With the lights on and the TV pumping out *Wheel of Fortune,* she felt the knots in her neck unwind a bit. Elena collapsed in her usual chair and thumbed through the mail. She caught her breath when she spotted the square envelope, but it was only an invitation to a bridal shower. She tossed it back onto the table and made a mental note to send a gift. She had no money for bridal gifts, but she'd squeeze out enough to do something. She wouldn't be at the shower, though, even if her schedule allowed it.

Now her social activities consisted of an occasional meal with David. She'd miss him when they left for their respective practice locations. That thought brought to mind her trip to Dainger in a few days. She'd promised to call Dr. Sewell and confirm her visit. Elena looked at her watch — half past nine. Too late to call? Not for a doctor.

She located the number, punched it in, and listened through four rings. She expected to hear a voice mail message. Instead, a soft voice answered. "Dr. Sewell."

"Dr. Sewell, this is Elena Gardner. Dr. Gross told me you're looking for someone to help out in your practice."

"Elena, thank you for calling. And please, call me Cathy. I was so sorry to hear about your husband."

Elena had learned the best response, and she gave it. "Thank you, Cathy." She paused a beat, inserting a verbal paragraph mark.

"Dr. Gross says you'd like me to come to Dainger this weekend to talk with you."

"Yes, I'd like to show you around, talk with you, see if we can work out an arrangement."

They talked for about ten minutes, and Elena was glad to find that Cathy was as detail-oriented as she was. Most of the questions she had would be answered during the interview, but Elena had a good feeling about the situation as Cathy described it. She hung up with a smile on her face.

Had Helen Bennett been right? Was God behind this opportunity? Or was it a random set of circumstances? She'd withhold judgment for now.

Elena fired up her computer, deleted a mountain of e-mail spam, read the two or three messages that were actually significant, and finally opened Google maps.

She plugged in the address Cathy gave her and, after a few minutes, found that the drive to Dainger, Texas, would take her about ninety minutes, maybe less if traffic was light. She printed out the directions and put them in a manila folder labeled "Dr. Sewell." Elena left the folder on the desk in plain sight, where its presence could remind her that there was hope for her future.

For about the millionth time after his

death, Elena wished Mark were here so she could talk with him about the practice opportunity. That led to another crying spell. Should she call David? No, she'd seen him only a few hours before this. She had to learn to get through these times on her own.

She read for a while, or at least she turned the pages of a book. When she put it down, she had no idea what she'd read.

Elena channel-surfed long enough to decide that the guy — she couldn't recall who — was right. Television was indeed a barren wasteland. She left the set on for noise.

She wandered into the kitchen, opened the refrigerator, stared into it as though waiting for some secret to be revealed, then closed it again.

Elena showered, laid out her clothes for tomorrow, and crawled into bed, where she lay and stared at the ceiling for what seemed like an eternity. She must have fallen asleep, although she didn't know how or when. She was struggling through a nightmare where she defended herself in court on some unspecified but terribly serious charge when the phone woke her. She squinted at the bedside clock and was immediately wide awake, one nightmare replaced by another. Midnight.

What day was it? Was it Tuesday? She snatched up the phone and whispered, "Hello?"

"Are you all still open? I want to order a pizza."

Elena sighed. "No, I'm sorry. You have the wrong number."

She returned the phone to its cradle and sat up on the side of the bed. Might as well have a glass of milk and read. Sleep was probably going to be a long time coming. A long time.

4

Elena turned off the alarm well before it was time for it to sound, swung her feet over the side of the bed, and wondered how she could face the day. Her head pounded. Her mouth was dry. Sweat plastered her pajamas to her. She had never been drunk, but this had to be what the mother of all benders produced.

Had she slept at all? She wasn't sure. Last night's wrong number had been innocent enough, but the dreams that followed it were nonstop torture. Elena wondered if they represented the guilt that filled her subconscious, boiling to the surface like the bubbles in a witches' cauldron. They'd all been there — her late husband, her mother-in-law, her colleagues — all asking the same question. "Why did you do it?"

She stumbled through some semblance of morning ablutions, threw on the clothing she'd laid out the night before, and headed for the kitchen to make coffee. Thank goodness she'd bought more. It was bad enough to face another day. Doing it without coffee was unthinkable.

Elena spooned coffee into the pot, daydreaming about her future, when the open can slipped from her grasp and bounced three times on the tile, rolling to a stop against the refrigerator. The entire contents, almost a full can of coffee, formed a dark brown trail across the floor. Elena wanted to scream. She wanted to cry. But instead, she laughed. One more thing had gone wrong, so how many more could there be? Maybe she could use up all her bad luck before she left the house today. Meanwhile, she'd stop at the convenience store on her way to the hospital. Maybe some caffeine would help. Then again, maybe nothing could help.

Whether it was the tall cup of coffee she drank or the fresh air blowing into her face through the wide-open car window as she drove, by the time Elena wheeled into the doctor's parking lot at St. Paul Hospital, she felt almost human.

Elena made her way through the hospital, following signs to the Family and Community Medicine Clinic. Funny, the medical center had changed the name to keep up with the times, but everyone still called the department Family Practice. Well, that was what she wanted to do in her own practice — help families. If she just had the chance.

She took particular comfort that today was Friday. Not because it marked the start of the weekend, though. Illness and accidents don't observe a calendar, and physicians are as likely to be called upon for their services on a Saturday as on a Tuesday. But this weekend was different. Tomorrow she would meet with Dr. Sewell.

By now Elena wasn't feeling particularly nervous about the meeting. Maybe she'd felt disappointment so many times the possibility of one more held no terror for her. Then again —

"Dr. Gardner, are you ready to see patients?"

Elena turned. Mary, the pert, dark-haired clinic nurse, held out a chart.

"Thanks, Mary. Yes, I'll start."

For Elena, the patients in the family practice clinic presented the same challenge as a Sudoku puzzle — except the stakes were much higher. She opened the chart and scanned the notes Mary had made. "42 y/o WF. 3 mo. Hx vague aches, lack of energy. BP 110/60, P 68."

"History of vague aches and lack of energy." *Could be something, could be nothing.* Elena tapped on the door and entered. "Hi, I'm Dr. Gardner." She extended her hand.

"Emily Gunderson." The woman's handshake was lukewarm, matching her expression.

"How can I help you?"

The woman perched on the edge of the exam table appeared to be closer to 55 than 42. Her eyes were dull. Her voice was husky and soft. She picked at a broken nail as she spoke. "I'm tired all the time. I feel like I've got a lump in my throat. I ache all over. I . . . I feel terrible."

A century ago, doctors would have attributed these symptoms to emotional problems and called the condition "neurasthenia." Elena gave thanks for the strides medicine had made since then. "When did this start?"

"Maybe three or four months ago."

Elena moved behind the woman and placed her fingers lightly on her neck. "Swallow for me, would you?" She increased her pressure slightly. "Again."

Elena continued to ask questions as she examined the woman's chest, heart, abdomen. Finally, she took a rubber-headed reflex hammer from the table and tapped gently at the bend of the woman's elbows and below her kneecaps. Reflexes diminished, no doubt about it.

"Mrs. —" She checked the chart. "Mrs. Gunderson, I'm going to order a couple of blood tests. If they confirm what I'm thinking, we should be able to get you back to your old self pretty quickly."

For the first time since the exam began, there seemed to be a spark in the woman's eyes. She leaned forward, apparently eager to catch Elena's words. "Did you say what I think you did? You can do something about this?"

"I think you've had an episode of what we call thyroiditis — an inflammation of the thyroid gland. It left part of the gland unable to make thyroid hormone, which is why the rest of your thyroid enlarged to compensate." Elena ran her fingers over the area to demonstrate. "But it still isn't making enough thyroid hormone. That makes you tired. It causes you to ache all over. Does cold bother you? Do you have trouble in an air-conditioned building?"

The woman looked at Elena like she'd pulled a rabbit out of a hat. "How did you know?"

"It's my job to know that, Mrs. Gunderson. No trick to it." Elena ticked a few boxes on the lab request sheet clipped to the front of the chart. "The nurse will draw some blood for tests. I want to see you back in a week. If I'm right, we'll start you on a medication called levothyroxine. It may take a bit of dosage adjustment, but I think you'll soon feel like your old self."

"No surgery?"

"No, did someone suggest that?"

Mrs. Gunderson ducked her head. "Well, I saw another doctor last month about this. He said I probably needed surgery. I guess now he meant surgery on my thyroid. But when he found out I didn't have insurance, he sent me here to the charity clinic."

Elena fought to keep her voice level. The surgeon might have made a diagnostic mistake. Then again, he could have decided that, in the absence of insurance, a referral would be a good idea. "If you'll tell me the name of that doctor, I'll call him. I'm sure he'll be pleased that no surgery is necessary." *And if he punted this poor woman because there was no fee in sight for him, he's going to get an earful.*

Elena struggled upward from sleep like a diver returning from the depths. She opened one eye and frowned at the strident tones that assaulted her eardrums. Phone? She lifted the receiver and was rewarded with a dial tone. Pager? Her frontal cortex slowly ground into gear and returned the message: nope, different sound, not the same cadence as her pager. She reached across her body, pushed down the pillow in which her head was nestled, and saw the flashing red numerals on the bedside clock: 6:01.

She slammed her palm down on the bar to silence the alarm and tried to recall why she had to get up. Did she have early morning rounds at the hospital? Was there a conference at the medical school? No and no. What is today? It had to be . . . Saturday. Then it all came tumbling back.

Today she was driving to Dainger to meet Cathy Sewell. Driving to Dainger? No, if anything, she hoped she was driving away from danger. Away from the midnight phone calls, leaving behind the notes with the threatening messages, trying to flee the guilt that enveloped her every time she came near the ICU at Zale Hospital. Surely no danger awaited her in Dainger — only the hope of a better tomorrow.

Elena rolled out of bed, scuffed her feet into slippers, and hurried to the kitchen. She needed coffee, lots of it. She flicked the switch to set the already-prepared pot brewing and padded off to the bathroom, thankful she'd stopped at the store and bought yet more coffee last night.

Back in her bedroom, she chose and rejected three outfits before settling on a blouse and slacks that seemed casual yet professional. Wasn't that coffee ready yet? Elena walked through the kitchen door in time to hear the coffeemaker give one last gurgle and fall silent. She poured a cup and burned her tongue with the first sip.

She stumbled to the bathroom and risked a glance at herself in the mirror. She recoiled when she saw her eyes — a network of red lines turned the whites into a roadmap. She recalled a movie based on the life of dancer Bob Fosse, a man who burned the candle at both ends on a regular basis. Scene after scene portrayed him gazing at his dissolute face in the morning mirror and murmuring, "It's showtime." Eye drops and a stimulant pill and he was off for another day.

Well, there'd be no Dexedrine, but some eyedrops and a bit of wizardry with makeup wouldn't hurt. It was indeed showtime.

"If you don't like that rug, tell me," Will said.

Cathy turned to where he sat in the living room, newspaper in hand, coffee at his elbow. "Excuse me?"

Will lowered the paper and gave her a smile. "If you don't like that rug, tell me. Don't keep pacing, trying to wear it out." He looked at his watch. "It's ten-twenty. Dr. Gardner said she'd be here about ten-thirty. She's not late. Does everybody have to be early, simply because you always are?"

Cathy shrugged. "I guess I'm nervous about this interview. I want it to work out — I mean, I need someone to cover my patients while I'm out with the baby — but I don't want to take her into the practice and then regret my decision." She resumed pacing, caught herself, and stopped to rearrange the magazines on the coffee table.

Will gestured toward the easy chair that sat at right angles to the one he currently occupied. "Get a cup of coffee. Sit down and relax."

"You know I can't have coffee," Cathy snapped.

"Sorry. I forgot. Maybe some herbal tea. But —"

The sound of the doorbell put an end to the conversation. Will's eyes followed his wife as she made her way to the door. Cathy stopped, took a deep breath, and admitted the visitor.

Will didn't listen to the conversation. He

already knew what it would be like. "Dr. Sewell?" "Call me Cathy." "And I'm Elena." "Now I remember you." "You haven't changed a bit." Instead, he focused on Dr. Elena Perez Gardner.

Will was happily married, rarely looked at another woman, but Elena's appearance was more than enough to get his attention. Mid-length, black hair was pulled back into a ponytail to frame a beautiful oval face with high-set cheekbones and flawless skin the color of honey. Will decided her body would be the envy of most women and definitely merit a second and third look from almost any man.

Then Will looked into Elena's eyes. If, as some poet said, the eyes are the windows of the soul, this woman's deep brown eyes clearly showed that her soul was troubled. Maybe it was the aftermath of her husband's death, maybe something else. Will hoped they'd know the answer to that question before the day was out.

Will realized Cathy was saying something to him. "Excuse me?"

"I said, 'Elena, this is my husband, Will Kennedy.' You know, I hope you pay better attention when you're in the courtroom."

"Sorry. My mind was a million miles away." He extended his hand. "Elena, it's a pleasure to meet you."

"Likewise." Elena's grip was firm, but he noticed that when he withdrew his own hand it was moist. Well, he couldn't blame her for being nervous. If she only knew how nervous Cathy was as well.

Cathy reached for her purse and keys. "I'm going to show Elena my office and the hospital. We'll probably break for lunch about twelve. Want to join us at RJ's?"

Will turned to Elena. "Okay with you? You won't think we're ganging up on you?"

"Not at all," Elena said. "Cathy, I'd like to freshen up before we leave, if you don't mind."

"Of course. Just down that hall."

As soon as the door closed, Cathy turned to Will and raised her eyebrows. "Well?"

As he advised his witnesses to do, Will hesitated before he answered. "She's nervous, but that could be the pressure of a job interview on top of what she's already been through. Let's see what we find out after we get to know her better."

Since she started medical school, Elena always had a stack of blank three-by-five cards with her. She might use them in class to jot down particularly salient points, later tucking each in her textbook at the ap-

83

propriate page, handy for last-minute exam cramming. On clinical rounds, she'd pull out one of the cards and make notes about each patient, often flipping through them later in the day to be sure she hadn't missed something. The cards proved invaluable when she presented cases to an attending physician. Notes on three-by-five cards became so ingrained in her life that her pocket or purse generally held cards with grocery lists or reminders to pick up cleaning or have her car serviced.

Today she had to stop herself several times from reaching into her purse for a blank card. Somehow, it seemed almost disrespectful to make notes during her meeting with Cathy. If Elena's observations jibed with Cathy's assessment that the facilities at the hospital were excellent, she accepted that fact and moved on, knowing she could always ask specific questions later. If Cathy told her that night call in her practice wasn't as bad as being on call at Parkland, Elena heaved a sigh of relief, realizing that only time would prove or disprove that assessment. And when Cathy mentioned a salary arrangement that included a generous base salary and benefits, Elena gratefully filed the number away in her head, not on a card.

As they spent time together, Elena

warmed to her host. Some of the glow Cathy exuded might be attributable to her pregnancy, but she also had about her a sense of security that Elena envied. Maybe this would be a good match. If only Cathy felt the same.

They wound up their tour in the front foyer of Summers County General Hospital. Cathy extended a hand and turned a half-circle like Vanna White showing a prize. "Well, that's our hospital. What do you think?"

"Frankly, it's more than I expected," Elena said. "You have a very nice facility."

"Here's someone you need to meet." Cathy pointed to a man walking down the hall toward them. A blue dress shirt with a blue and gold tie peeked out from under a spotless white lab coat with creases so sharp they could cut cheese. He was about four inches shorter than Elena's five feet ten inches, but carried himself with the bearing of someone used to being in charge.

The man halted two steps from them, and Elena half-expected him to click his heels as he drew himself up to his full height and nodded once. "Dr. Sewell, good to see you."

"Nathan, this is Dr. Elena Gardner. Elena, Nathan Godwin, our administrator."

Godwin favored Elena with a curt nod.

"Doctor, pleasure to meet you. Are you interested in our hospital?"

Before Elena could speak, Cathy said, "That's what we're about to discuss, Nathan. I'm sure you have things to do, so we won't keep you from your rounds."

"Nice meeting you," Elena mumbled.

When Godwin was around the corner, Cathy said, "Self-important little man, but he keeps the place running well."

"He scares me a little."

"Never mind. You won't have a lot to do with him. Now how about some lunch? Since I'm eating for two, it's all I can do to keep my hands off every bit of food I see."

"Cathy, to be in your third trimester, you don't look like you've been overeating."

"That's all right. I don't want the town gossips saying, 'Isn't it too bad she never lost all that pregnancy weight?' Our city is big enough to offer everything you might want, but at heart it's still a small town, and news travels fast around here."

Elena suppressed a shudder. She'd hoped to leave her past behind with the move, to start fresh. But if anyone in Dainger started asking questions about Mark's death . . . No, she wouldn't let that happen.

When they arrived, Will was already inside the restaurant, seated at a table in the back corner. Cathy dropped her purse into the chair opposite him and said, "I'm going to freshen up."

Elena took an empty chair between Cathy's spot and Will. He smiled and said, "So did Cathy convince you that our fair city isn't exactly a medical backwater?"

"Frankly, when she first mentioned Summers County General Hospital, I had a mental picture of a little facility with no specialty care, antiquated equipment, and a scraper outside the front door to clean the barnyard residue off the boots of the patients and doctors alike."

"I'm sure Cathy showed you otherwise."

After the waiter took their drink orders, Will chatted amiably and Elena began to relax. Maybe she wasn't going to get the third degree from Cathy's lawyer husband.

Cathy returned, and Will rose to pull out her chair. Elena recalled when Mark used to do that for her, and as she often did when something brought to mind her loss, she felt herself die a little. She turned away and dabbed at the corner of her eyes with her napkin.

"Did I miss anything?" Cathy eased into her chair and set her purse near her feet.

Will shook his head. "I was giving Elena the third degree, but you got here before I could get out the rubber hose."

Cathy picked up a menu. "Well, there'll be none of that now. Let's have a relaxing lunch."

During the meal, the two women shared anecdotes and discovered mutual acquaintances. Will chimed in from time to time with comments and stories of his own. Both women declined dessert. Will asked for coffee, and Elena decided to join him.

The waitress left the bill, and Cathy slipped a credit card into the folder. She waved off Elena's attempt to cover her own lunch. "This is definitely a professional expense. I hope we can come to an arrangement. If we can, the cost of a chef's salad and iced tea is a pretty small price to pay for finding someone to watch over my practice while I'm on maternity leave."

Elena felt her lunch creeping back up into her throat. She'd hoped for something permanent, a move to somewhere she could put down roots. Now she wasn't sure. "So you're looking for someone on a temporary basis? A *locum tenens* arrangement?"

"Not necessarily." Cathy looked around. "Wouldn't you be more comfortable talking about this in my office?"

Elena wasn't sure she could wait one more minute to hear Cathy's offer — if there was to be one. "I'm fine doing it right here if that's okay."

"Sure." Cathy looked around the nearly empty room. "RJ's a friend of ours, and we eat here a lot, so they shouldn't mind if we keep this table a bit longer." She beckoned to the waitress. "Peggy, we're going to discuss a little business. Would you top off everyone's beverages, and then ask Darlene not to seat anyone near us?"

Even though there was no one within earshot, Cathy leaned a bit closer to Elena. "This is a two-part deal. What I need now is a *locum tenens* to cover my practice while I'm on maternity leave. I've told you about the salary and benefits. Do you have any questions there?"

Elena shook her head.

"But I'd like the contract to include an option for a permanent association." Cathy said.

Elena was afraid her dry throat could only emit a croak. She sipped from her cup. "The option would rest with you?"

"No, with both of us."

"Is the practice big enough to support two doctors?"

"I think there's room for another primary care doctor here in town, but I'll have a better idea about that later. First I have to fill the *locum tenens* position."

Elena had to concentrate hard on the words as they came through the high-pitched hum in her ears. It was happening. She had a place to practice.

"So far as your capabilities, there's no question there," Cathy said. "And I think you and I would be a good fit. There's only one thing."

Elena felt the muscles in her shoulders tighten like a violin string. *She thought it was all behind her, but here it came again.* "What's that?"

"Amy hinted that your husband's death is still affecting your professional behavior. Let's clear the air about that."

The sound of breaking glassware from the kitchen split the air. The noise might as well have been the sound of Elena's composure shattering. She squeezed her eyes closed in an unsuccessful attempt to stop the tears she already felt forming there.

5

Cathy was sorry to trigger the emotional display, but Amy had made it clear that Elena still carried some baggage after the death of her husband. Cathy had to know the extent of that baggage.

Will, bless him, was unflustered. Most men didn't know how to react to a woman's tears, but his reaction was immediate and unembarrassed. "Elena, let's go over to my office for this conversation. We can all ride together, and I'll bring you and Cathy back here to pick up her car afterward."

He didn't wait for a response. He shepherded the two women out of the restaurant and helped them into his pickup truck. Once inside the building, Cathy showed Elena to the restroom and suggested she splash some water on her face and repair her makeup. "We'll be here in Will's office."

As Elena disappeared down the hall, Cathy said, "So there's something there."

"I sort of figured there was. Why don't you let me see if I can get it out of her? In this situation, I think it would be better if you just provided a comforting female presence."

Cathy recalled a time when she'd sat in this office and poured out some significant secrets to Will. She hadn't intended to, but at the time it had seemed so easy, so natural to confide in him. She wasn't sure whether the knack came from his training as a lawyer or his growing up with a pastor for a father. In any event, she decided to go along with him.

"I'm so sorry I broke down like that." Elena eased through the door and took a seat on the sofa that occupied one wall of Will's office. She appeared to be holding herself together by a supreme effort.

"No problem," Will said. "Would you like some water, a Coke?"

Elena shook her head. "No. Really, I'm okay." She rummaged in her purse, pulled out a tissue, and dabbed at her eyes.

Will rested one hip on the edge of his desk and said, "We know you've had problems since Mark's death, and we need to understand what they are."

"It's sort of complicated," Elena said.

"It usually is," Will said. "Start at the

beginning."

Cathy took a seat on the sofa beside Elena and turned halfway so she was facing the woman. She tried to make her expression and her body language nonjudgmental and encouraging.

Elena took a deep breath. "Mark and I met right after I graduated from med school. One of my classmates was dating his roommate, and she fixed me up on a blind date with Mark. I know it sounds hokey, but it really was love at first sight. We were married six months later, halfway through my first year of residency."

"What did Mark do for a living?" Will asked.

"He started out as a computer programmer. Then, after we were married, his company made him sort of a troubleshooter. You know, if a company was having IT problems their in-house staff couldn't solve, Mark was the guy they called."

"Did he travel a lot?"

"Not really. I was the one who was always gone." She looked at Cathy. "Not travel, of course, but you know how it is. Nights on call at the hospital. And when I was home, I barely had time to keep things going. Mark did his share — more than his share, I guess — of the housework. We . . . we had a great marriage."

Cathy noted the hesitation and filed it away. Most marriages weren't great a hundred percent of the time, and she was willing to bet Elena's hadn't been, either. But she guessed it was normal to remember things as perfect once they were out of reach.

Will's voice was so soft Elena had to lean forward to hear him. "Then what happened?"

"It was almost seven months ago. He woke me sometime after midnight. He had a terrible headache. His speech was sort of fuzzy. I turned on the light and saw his eye was drooping." She swallowed hard. "I called 911. He was unconscious by the time the paramedics got there. I rode with him to the hospital. He stopped breathing halfway there, so I intubated him and kept him going with an Ambu bag. At the hospital, I pulled every string I could think of to get a neurosurgeon there stat."

Cathy felt herself drawn into the story, first as the clinical picture unfolded, then as Elena told about her relationship with her mother-in-law. Her heart was touched by the enormous responsibility thrust on Elena when Mark's prognosis became obvious.

"And how did Mark's mother react to all

this?" Will asked.

"She thought I should have noticed symptoms earlier and gotten Mark to the doctor."

Cathy couldn't help herself. "But he had a berry aneurysm." She looked at Will. "A weak spot in the wall of an artery in the brain. Most often there aren't any symptoms. The first you know of it is when it ruptures, like this one did."

Elena nodded. "Makes no difference. She was convinced I'd missed the diagnosis, that I should have somehow gotten him better treatment. But the thing that put the final barrier between us was that she kept holding on to the idea that, if Mark were kept on life support long enough, he'd eventually recover. I think she had visions of his being moved into her home where she could nurse him back to health — and get him away from me."

Cathy spoke softly, but still her voice seemed too loud for the circumstances. "How did it finally play out?"

"The neurologic damage Mark sustained was extensive. There might have been a chance — a very slim chance — that he could be weaned off the respirator, but he'd remain in a coma. He'd never function as a sentient human again."

"So it was up to you to withdraw life support," Will said.

"That's right. But Lillian kept arguing." Elena paused and chose her words carefully. "After two weeks, Mark came off life support and —" The words seemed to hang in her throat.

"I understand how you must feel." Will's voice was calm. "I know a little about survivor guilt, not from firsthand experience, thank goodness, but from counseling with lots of widows and widowers when we prepare to probate wills."

"Oh, there's that," Elena said. "I live with survivor guilt every day. But I know that I'll get over it eventually. What I can't get away from are the phone calls that come at midnight every Tuesday."

Elena told them about the phone calls and the card, and explained why she thought Mark's mother was behind them. She told them about the financial morass in which she was trapped because of Mark's final expenses. More and more came rushing out. She appeared not so much to finish as to simply run out of steam.

Cathy exchanged glances with Will. He gave a faint nod. Elena appeared to be telling the truth. *Now for the big question.*

"Elena," Cathy said, "I realize how this

must have weighed on you. I need to know how this affects your ability to function as a physician."

"Of course, it's made it more difficult for me to see stroke patients. I guess I tend to identify more with their families, but that's probably not all bad. It makes me work harder to make sure the patients get the best possible care."

"And you have no problem functioning in an ICU environment?"

"I'll admit, there were some flashbacks early on, but it's never interfered with my clinical performance, never affected my judgment that I can tell. Actually, I have a patient in the ICU at St. Paul Hospital right now who's postsurgical after an intracranial bleed. I don't think he's going to make it, and I believe my experience has made me more empathetic, better able to counsel his wife."

"Two more questions and we'll let this go," Cathy said. "First, can we help you stop those harassing phone calls? Will is an attorney. Maybe he can get some kind of injunction or something."

Elena was shaking her head before Cathy finished. "I hope a move will be all it takes. I plan to have my Dallas number disconnected, no notification of the new number.

I want it to be a dead end."

"How about your cell number?"

"To my knowledge, Lillian doesn't have it. I called her from my cell a couple of times when Mark was in the ICU, but I doubt she'd be savvy enough to check her call logs that far back."

Will said, "If you change your mind, let us know. I think the other thing Cathy intended to ask was whether you'd like some counseling to help you get past this more quickly."

"As usual, my husband has read my mind," Cathy said. "There's an excellent therapist in Fort Worth. Maybe a half-hour, forty-minute drive from here. Close enough to be relatively convenient, but far enough away that no one here in town will know about any visits you make."

"I guess I'd have to think about that."

"Well, I can highly recommend him. I saw him myself when I first moved here and was working through some issues."

Elena forced a smile. "Thanks. I'll give it some serious consideration."

Cathy had the sense that Elena wasn't about to consider seeing a therapist. But things could change. She'd be certain the option remained open.

Will drew a line through the last string of

words on his legal pad. "I think we've covered everything. That's the gist of the contract. I'll print it out and send it to you, and I'd suggest you have your own attorney read it over before you sign."

"Do you have any questions?" Cathy asked.

Will let the exchange that followed wash over him, taking one final stab at sizing up Elena Perez Gardner. Her brown eyes still bore the evidence of deep inner turmoil. The furrowing of her brow might be explained by concentration, but he was willing to bet there were some deeply troubling thoughts running through Elena's brain.

He tuned back in to the conversation in time to hear Cathy say, "Call me next week. Meanwhile, I guess that's it."

"One second," Will said. "Elena, we might be able to save you a trip back to Dainger. It occurs to me you'll need someplace to live. Do you want to drive around and look for a place to rent?"

It was obvious Elena hadn't thought this far ahead. Will opened his mouth to make some suggestions, but Cathy beat him to it.

"Why don't I make a phone call? I know a wonderful couple who have a spare room they'd probably be glad to make available until you've been here long enough to know what you want."

Without waiting for an answer, Cathy picked up the phone and punched in a set of numbers she obviously knew well. The conversation lasted only a couple of minutes, and when she hung up she was beaming. "Let's go meet these people. This is a very special couple, and I think you'll really enjoy living with them."

"Well . . ." Elena stammered. "I don't . . . I mean, I suppose . . ."

"Don't worry. I stayed with them myself a few years back before Will and I were married. You'll love them, and they'll love you."

Will frowned. At this point, he was pretty sure Cathy still had designs on getting Elena to open up. That's why she was setting her up to stay with his parents, Matthew and Dora Kennedy, in the parsonage of the First Community Church.

"Matthew, Dora," Cathy said, "This is Dr. Elena Gardner."

Elena studied the couple who stood in the doorway. Matthew Kennedy was whip-thin and sinewy. When she took the hand he extended, she found it slightly callused but the grip gentle. His white hair was thinning a bit. Blue eyes sparkled behind rimless glasses. Elena had the feeling she was look-

100

ing at a preview of Will Kennedy thirty years hence.

Dora Kennedy wiped her hands on a plain blue apron and stepped past Elena's outstretched hand to enfold her in a hug. Dora was a bit plump, a head shorter than her husband, but her twinkling eyes and white hair matched his. "Oh, Dr. Gardner. We're so thrilled that you're going to help Cathy. And when she called to ask if we'd put you up in the spare room, why that was the frosting on the cake." She stepped back and gestured the group inside. "And speaking of cake, I just took a peach pound cake out of the oven, and I have some fresh peaches to go on top of it. Let's go into the kitchen."

"I don't really —" Cathy's faint headshake made Elena stop in mid-sentence.

"Thanks, Dora. We'd love to," Cathy said. "I suspect a few days of your cooking will do wonders for Elena. I don't think she's felt much like eating the past few weeks."

As the group trailed Dora and Will through the living room into a cozy kitchen, redolent with the enticing smell of fresh cake, Will whispered in Elena's ear, "My mother is the best cook in seventeen counties. I know we've just eaten, but I've learned it's better to take whatever she offers than argue with her. Besides," he added,

"I'll bet you finish a piece and ask for seconds."

Elena noticed that even Cathy, who'd said not an hour ago that she was trying to watch her weight, took the proffered cake.

"Coffee?" Dora asked.

Elena and Will accepted; Cathy said water would be fine.

"Oh, yes," Dora said. "What am I thinking, offering you caffeine? I'm going to have to get used to your being pregnant. I need to get my grandmother hat on."

Matthew gave a "What are you going to do?" glance, and Cathy combined a nod with a brief, wry smile.

Elena picked up her fork but stopped when Matthew Kennedy said, "Will, this is the first time you and Cathy have broken bread with us in a while. And we're so glad to have Elena in our home. I'd like to express our gratitude for all that. Why don't I pray over the food before we eat?"

Elena eased her fork back onto the table and bowed her head, wondering what she'd gotten herself into.

"Dr. Gardner, we know what you did. We know what you did, and you have to pay."

Elena squirmed in the hard chair. She was so far back from the tribunal that she had to squint to see the three doctors. One man had a gray tonsure ringing an otherwise barren dome, giving him the appearance of a very unhappy and unforgiving monk. The second peered out through Coke-bottle glasses that made him look bug-eyed. The third was surprisingly young for a doctor charged with such a solemn responsibility. His dark good looks reminded Elena of some TV star. The name tickled at the edge of her consciousness, but stayed hidden.

She raised her hand like a third-grader. "But I'm a good doctor. Doctor Sewell said so yesterday. She's going to take me into her practice."

"But not as a partner," said the monk clone, his voice thundering as though coming from the cloisters his appearance suggested. "She didn't offer you a partnership. You're on probation."

"That's right," said the TV star. "And when we tell her what you did, you'll have to pay."

"You'll have to pay," joined in the doctor with the thick glasses, his eyes growing more prominent with every word. "We're calling her now to tell her."

The near-bald doctor picked up the phone sitting at his elbow and punched in ten digits.

"Please don't call her. I'll do anything. Anything."

"Too late. It's ringing."

Elena heard the synthetic tone that sufficed for a ring in most phones. But why could she hear it? Maybe if she could answer before Cathy did, she could talk her way out of this mess. Her fingers scrabbled around on the table beside her until they felt the hard, cold plastic of a phone receiver. She fumbled it to her face and fairly screamed, "I can explain. I can explain."

"Explain what?" a familiar voice asked. It wasn't that of the doctor/judge. It was someone she trusted — someone who could help her.

"David!"

"Hey, did I wake you? I'm so sorry. It's almost 9:00 a.m. I figured you'd be awake by now."

Elena swung her feet out of bed and squinted at the clock. "No, no, I should be up. You woke me from a nightmare. I should be thanking you."

"Are you okay to talk?"

"Give me time to splash some water on my face and get coffee going. I'll call you back in five minutes."

She took ten. Elena could smell the coffee brewing as she dialed David's number. "I'm so sorry. I must have sounded like an absolute nut."

"Not a problem. I've had nightmares that were so real it took me most of the day to shake them. Want to talk about it?"

"Not really." She didn't want to think about what it meant. She already knew.

"I don't suppose you'd like to go to church with me this morning?" David asked, hope mixing with resignation in both his tone and words.

Church? Oh, it was Sunday. But all Elena wanted to do was start planning for her move. "David, I appreciate the offer, but I'll have to pass."

"Well, would you like to meet afterwards for lunch? You can tell me about your interview."

She had to give him full marks for persistence. And he was a friend — perhaps the only one she had. "Sure. Call me when you're ready."

The coffee was brewed by the time Elena hung up. With cup in hand, she sank into a kitchen chair, leaned her elbows on the table, and wondered if her nightmare had been an attempt by her subconscious to cleanse her soul of the guilt it felt. Or was it a portent of trials yet to come?

6

The ICU was a terrible place to start the week, but Elena was drawn to it this morning like iron to a magnet. She had to talk to Erma Pulliam again. If the woman was to do the right thing for her husband and herself, she had to do it soon.

Elena pushed through the double doors into the unit. Off to her right, a nurse glanced at her and ducked into a patient room. Did the nurses resent her visits now? Chester Pulliam was no longer her patient. There was never any change to report, but conveying that information to her took precious minutes out of their already overcrowded day. Should she stop bothering everybody? But just as it was impossible not to explore a sensitive tooth with your tongue, Elena couldn't stay away.

As she paused outside Pulliam's door, Elena heard the rhythmic *chuff, chuff, chuff* of the respirator. Apparently the patient still had no spontaneous drive to breathe. The machine was keeping him alive.

Elena tapped lightly on the door and entered the room.

"Dr. Gardner." Erma Pulliam tried to smile, but Elena saw there wasn't much behind it. "Nice of you to come by."

The first thing Elena noticed was a plastic tube taped to Chester Pulliam's right nostril, the end plugged to keep a milky fluid from dripping out. There were a couple of vials of pills at the bedside, along with an old-fashioned pharmacist's mortar and pestle. The nurses would use those to grind medicines before inserting them into the feeding tube. No more need for IVs.

The feeding tube represented an intermediate stage. Surgical procedures came next: a gastrostomy to provide a permanent means of feeding and a tracheotomy to allow unrestricted airway access. These operations were an accepted part of the road to what physicians called a vegetative existence. Nice words, but they failed to describe what would happen to the patient — and to his family.

Mrs. Pulliam didn't know what lay ahead of her, but Elena did. Once more, she led the woman into the hall for their conversation.

"Has your family been here yet?" Elena asked.

Mrs. Pulliam shook her head. "We have two sons, both married and living on the other side of the country. They couldn't get away to come here, but they both said it didn't matter." She nodded toward the room they'd just left. " 'That's not my dad in there,' they said. They want to remember him the way he was."

"And what did they say about taking him off life support?"

Mrs. Pulliam wiped her eyes with a tissue, then began shredding it. "They think I should do it. But I . . . I can't. It seems so wrong."

"Do you have religious scruples about it? I can ask the hospital chaplain to talk with you."

"No, I recognize the difference between taking someone's life and not prolonging the existence of a body with no brain function. It's just that I don't know if I have the courage to do it."

Elena patted the woman's shoulder. "I know how you feel. I've been where you are."

Surprise showed on the woman's face. "And what did you do?"

Elena swallowed hard. When could she

stop reliving that awful experience?

"That's all right. I can see it's hard for you to talk about. I shouldn't have asked."

Elena shook her head. "No, you need to know that you're not the first person to agonize over this decision. I finally came to the conclusion that it was best for Mark — and for me — to take him off life support and let him die with dignity."

"I just don't know if I can do that."

"It's hard," Elena said. "But not doing it can lead to things that are much harder."

Mrs. Pulliam put her hand on Elena's arm. "Would you mind staying here with Chester for a few minutes? I want to walk down to the coffee shop. I need to get away for a bit. And somehow, I can't leave him alone."

"Of course. I'll be here when you get back."

The woman kissed her husband's forehead. She'd taken two steps toward the door when she turned back and kissed his cheek once more. "I love you, Chester."

Alone in the room with Chester Pulliam, Elena pulled a chair to his bedside. She drew back the sheet a bit to expose his hand. Gently, she covered it with her own.

A tap on the door jarred her away from her thoughts. Elena turned to see a nurse peek into the room, wheeling a medication cart in front of her. "Oh, Dr. Gardner."

"I can step out if you like."

"No, I was just checking on him. Do you think there's any change?" This wasn't the nurse who'd avoided her earlier. This one seemed to care.

Elena glanced at the woman's nametag. "Not for the better, Ann. And I don't think there'll be any. Do you?"

"No, I don't." The nurse nodded toward the figure on the bed. "It's pitiful, isn't it? You're so good to stand by Mrs. Pulliam through this. I know it can't be easy. I hope you help her do the right thing."

A beeping noise issued from Ann's pocket. She consulted her pager. "Oh, they need me stat. I guess the cart will be safe here with you." She looked up and it seemed that her gaze went to the center of Elena's soul. "I'll pray for you." With that, Ann hurried away.

Elena tried to recall all the people who'd told her they'd be praying for her. Most of her recent thoughts had been questions, not supplications, but surely God would count them as prayers. Other than that, she hadn't prayed since Mark's death.

She closed the door and began to look around the room. Everything she saw reminded her of a way to end Pulliam's marginal existence.

The most obvious action would be to disconnect the respirator from his endotracheal tube. Two or three minutes, and it would be over.

She scanned the medication cart. Pills? It would be difficult to get them down the feeding tube. Something injected? The IV had been removed, but there were needles and syringes on Ann's cart along with vials of various medications. One intramuscular injection would release Chester Pulliam from his prison.

She looked down at the frail figure on the bed and located the pulsations of his carotid artery. Enough pressure on one spot — a spot she could easily find — and his heart would slow and stop.

Elena knew how to spare Chester from a living death. If she did that, Erma Pulliam would be spared too — spared the guilt that comes from making the decision that ends the life of a loved one. Sure, she'd grieve for a while, but eventually she'd move on. She wouldn't be tied for who knows how long to a husband whose brain no longer functioned, whose body shriveled with contractures and wept with bedsores.

Mrs. Pulliam was waffling. Elena recognized all the signs. And delaying the decision would just bring about a host of problems. Chester would have recurring kidney infections because of his catheter. Despite frequent suctioning through his tracheotomy, pneumonia would finally come. The staff would turn him frequently, but eventually he'd develop decubitus ulcers — ugly sores that smelled foul and ran pus, poisoning his system. He'd shrink to a husk of the man Erma Pulliam had known. And thanks to the miracles of modern medicine, his life — if you could call it life — would go on.

Elena could prevent all that. And that knowledge was what made her heart sink, as she stood alone at the bedside, pondering what to do.

Twenty minutes later, Elena tapped the keys of a computer in the hospital library to call up the last of the articles and research papers she needed. She snatched the papers from the printer as quickly as it spit them out, turned, and moved toward the elevator. Had she done the right thing? Well, what was done was done. From here on, it was out of her hands.

Her pager went off as she stepped off the elevator. Elena pushed through the doors of the ICU and stopped. Something was going on in Chester Pulliam's room. A resident,

112

one whose name she couldn't recall, bent over the bed. He listened for a few moments, then straightened and looped his stethoscope around his neck. The nurse, Ann, stood next to him. He murmured something to her. She nodded assent and pulled the sheet over Pulliam's face.

As the doctor edged through the door, he saw Elena. "I didn't expect you to be around for this."

She plucked at his sleeve, but he kept walking. She hurried after him, matching his long strides. "What do you mean? I got a page and came in here to use the phone."

He ducked into the head nurse's office and closed the door behind them. "We told Mrs. Pulliam it was time to take him off life support, but she couldn't bring herself to do it. The nurses saw you talking with her this morning. They figured you told her about Mark."

"I did, but the decision still had to be hers."

He grunted. "Pulliam's nurse had to help when one of the other patients in the unit went sour. Half an hour later, when Ann went in to check him, Pulliam's respirator was turned off. His wife was at his bedside, holding his hand."

Elena couldn't believe what she was hearing. "Maybe Mrs. Pulliam decided to do it herself. Say good-bye, flip the switch, sit there with him while he died."

"No, she said it was off when she returned to the room. The nurse figured you did it to save Mrs. Pulliam from having to make the decision. That's the way I see it too." He frowned as his pager beeped. "I'm going to sign it out as death due to his stroke." He thumbed the pager button, looked at the display, grimaced. "For the record, I think it was probably all for the best. I saw the DNR order you wrote on his chart today. I hope Dr. Clark is okay with it."

The resident rose from his chair. "Gotta answer this page. See you around."

"Wait!" she called. But the young doctor was already out the door, on his way to handle the next emergency.

Elena slumped into a chair and buried her head in her hands. What next?

Elena stumbled through her clinic duties that afternoon. Time after time she had to ask patients to repeat themselves, their answers drowned out by the words that still rang in her ears: "I saw the DNR order you wrote on his chart today."

"Mrs. Murchison," Elena said, "Your blood pressure is creeping up a bit, but so is

114

your weight. Are you following that diet I prescribed?"

"Well, doctor . . ."

Elena knew what the answer was before the woman was halfway through her detailed justification for ignoring her diet. High blood pressure was truly the silent killer. Until the symptoms were severe enough — headaches, dizziness, shortness of breath — people tended to ignore the warnings of their doctors. Mrs. Murchison was no exception.

"I'm going to ask the nutritionist to talk with you again. Meanwhile, let's add this to the blood pressure medication you're already on." Elena filled in the prescription as she talked. "Let's see you back in two weeks. I want you to be two pounds lighter by then. Will you try?"

Mrs. Murchison left, trailing promises and good intentions behind her. Elena wrote a note and tossed the chart into the basket beside her desk. She wondered if she'd be here in the clinic in two weeks when Mrs. Murchison returned.

The clinic nurse stuck her head through the door. "That's your last patient."

"Thanks, Mary." Elena sat for a moment, torn between going home to lick her wounds and picking up the phone to make a call that would either resolve her problem or make it much worse. The strident bleat of her pager put an end to her indecision.

The number included the medical school prefix. She felt that she should recognize it, but the identity danced in her head just out of reach. She dialed it, and the voice that answered reminded her why it seemed familiar. It was one she'd heard on a daily basis while Mark was in the ICU.

"Dr. Matney."

"This is Elena Gardner. You paged me?"

The chairman of neurosurgery cleared his throat. "Elena, I believe we need to talk. How soon can you come to my office?"

"I'm at St. Paul, but I can be there in fifteen minutes. Is that okay?"

"Come as soon as you can. We'll be waiting."

Dr. Matney's call set alarm bells ringing in Elena's head. His use of the word "we" increased the cacophony a dozen-fold. What "we"? Who else would be waiting for her? She thought she knew, and the prospect was far from pleasing.

No condemned man ever walked his last mile any more slowly and unwillingly than Elena trudged down the hallway to enter Dr. Bruce Matney's outer office. His secretary gave two sharp raps on the closed door of the chairman's inner sanctum, opened it, and motioned Elena in. The closing of the door behind her made Elena want to bolt, but there would be no escape from this meeting.

It was his office, his meeting, and Matney held center stage. He sat behind his desk, flanked by Dr. Amy Gross on his right and Dr. James Clark on his left. Matney motioned Elena to the straight chair across from him.

"Elena, thank you for coming."

She wanted to say, "I had no choice," but decided that silence had served her well before so it was worth a try here as well. She simply nodded.

Matney picked up a thick manila folder. "This is Chester Pulliam's chart."

Elena felt her heart creep into her throat. Droplets of sweat trailed down her backbone. She hunched her shoulders, but the muscles remained tense as bowstrings.

Clark took the chart from Matney's hand and flipped it open. This time the page was marked with a paper clip, but otherwise the feeling of *déjà vu* was complete. "I believe I intimated that Chester Pulliam had virtually no hope of recovery. I know you communicated this to his wife, and frankly, I appreciate that. It's difficult to break this

117

kind of news. But there are some questions about the way he met his end, and we think you can answer those questions." He tapped the page with a manicured fingernail. "Here is a DNR order you wrote — an order about which I knew nothing. And Pulliam was found dead, disconnected from his respirator, immediately after you were alone in his room. The inference is obvious."

Elena licked her lips but remained silent.

Matney frowned. "If it were not for the similarities between this case and that of your late husband, this might have gone unnoticed, or at least been ignored. As it was, because of your involvement in the case, Dr. Clark brought this to my attention. We thought it best to deal with the matter in this setting, rather than mounting any kind of official inquiry."

Amy leaned forward. "Elena, you're about to finish your residency. I don't want you to go out under a cloud of suspicion. It's possible that what you say in this room can stay in this room, but the three of us need assurance this sort of action won't be repeated."

Elena cleared her throat. "Could . . . could I have some water, please?"

Matney swiveled in his chair and plucked a bottle of water from a mini-fridge behind him. Elena took it and drank deeply. "Thank you."

Matney came right back on point. "Can you give us the assurances your chairman has asked for?"

"I can give you assurances, but not the ones you want," Elena said. "I can assure you that I neither wrote that DNR order nor disconnected Chester Pulliam's respirator."

7

Elena's words hung in the silent room like the last notes of a grand symphony dying away in a concert hall.

Clark pinched his lip and furrowed his brow. Matney leaned forward and opened his mouth, but Amy Gross spoke first. "Elena, I recognize how difficult it must have been for you to be involved with a patient whose situation so closely mirrored Mark's. Are you sure you're not simply denying — even repressing — an action you regret?"

Elena scanned the tribunal before her. She realized that's exactly what they represented: a tribunal. As surely as Caesar and his buddies decided the fate of a gladiator, these people held her professional life in their hands. Thumbs up or thumbs down. Well, she wouldn't go without a fight.

"I've admitted that I wrote the 'do not resuscitate' order on Mark's chart. After I made up my mind, I decided to write the order before I backed out." She fixed her gaze on Dr. Matney. "I didn't think it would matter whether I told you or the resident about it or wrote it myself. Obviously, that was a bad decision, a breach of protocol, but I wasn't exactly at my best after practically living in the ICU for two weeks waiting for Mark to show some sign of recovery."

Matney raised a hand like a sixth-grader trying to get the teacher's attention, but Elena plunged ahead. "I don't think I was the one who disconnected Mark's respirator. I have no memory of doing so, but it's possible that I did and repressed it. I've told you — at least, two of you — all that before." She picked up the water bottle and finished it in two greedy gulps.

"But —" Amy said.

"But in this circumstance, I'm absolutely clear about my actions."

"You don't deny you were alone in Pulliam's room," Matney said.

"Why deny it? It's true. There was even a witness. A nurse — Ann was her name — came in after Mrs. Pulliam left. We talked briefly before she left the room to help with another patient."

Matney bored in for the kill. "Turning off the ventilator would only take a few seconds.

How long were you alone in the room?"

"I don't know. Maybe five minutes." She read the doubt in their eyes. "Yes, long enough to do any number of things to end Pulliam's life. And I thought about every one of them. But I didn't."

Amy pushed Pulliam's chart across the desk and pointed to a line on the order sheet. "This is the order not to resuscitate Pulliam. There's your signature. Do you deny writing it?"

Elena didn't even look at the chart. Instead, she pulled a blank sheet from the notepad on Matney's desk and scribbled on it. "*This* is my signature. Does it match?"

Amy took the sheet of paper and the chart. Her gaze ran back and forth a couple of times before she passed them to Matney. He scrutinized them and handed them to Clark, who spent almost no time comparing the signatures before he dropped the chart on the desk, saying, "They're not the same."

Elena scanned the group. "Get a handwriting expert to compare them if you want to."

"That won't be necessary," Amy said. "It's pretty obvious that someone else wrote this."

Matney tapped his fingers absently on the chart cover. "If you didn't write that order, who did?"

"I think there's a more important question," Elena said.

Amy was the first to voice it. "Who took Chester Pulliam off his respirator? And why did they want the blame to fall on you?"

David waved to Elena and motioned her to the corner of the hospital cafeteria where he sat with the remains of his breakfast. She shuffled over and slumped into the chair opposite him.

"Bad night?" he asked.

"Bad week. Bad month. Bad year." She drank deeply from the coffee cup she held. "Bad life, I guess."

"Do you want something to eat? I'll get it for you?"

Elena shook her head and emptied her cup. "Just coffee for me this morning. If I ate anything, I'm afraid it would come right back up."

David rose and took her empty cup, returning in a moment with two full ones. "Here. If you're going to be caffeinated, you might as well go all the way."

That brought the faintest trace of a smile to her lips. She nodded her thanks.

"What's the problem? Want to tell me about it?"

She launched into a retelling of the circumstances of Chester Pulliam's death and her meeting with the neurosurgeons and Dr. Gross. Elena's voice was flat, her face showed no emotion, but it was obvious to David that her composure hung by the merest thread.

He waited until he was sure she was finished. "So how did they leave things?"

"Matney is going to talk with the ICU nurses. Maybe one of them knows who had the opportunity to write that note and discontinue Pulliam's life support. Personally, I don't hold out much hope there. And I sure don't see someone coming forward to say, 'Oh, I did it.' In the meantime, I'm to finish my residency and keep my nose clean."

"So you're not in trouble over this."

"I don't know why I should be! I did nothing wrong." She lifted her cup, but put it down without drinking. "I want to leave here with a clear record instead of going out with a cloud hanging over me, labeled as a doctor who practiced euthanasia."

David had never felt so helpless. "If there's anything I can do —"

She shook her head. "Thanks. I'll let you know if you can help. Right now, I don't know what anyone can do to make this better." She brushed away a tear.

"Hey, you'll get through this. You've handled worse."

"That's not it. With everything else that's happened, I forgot — this is Tuesday. Tonight is my night to get another call."

"Do you think this business with Pulliam is connected to your mystery caller?"

"I don't see how it could be," Elena said. "I still think the calls are coming from Mark's mother. And there's no way she could get anything done inside the hospital."

"I guess that's good."

"No, it's terrible. It means that there are at least two people out to get me. And I have no idea how to fight back."

Elena brushed a strand of hair from her eyes. "Mary, please tell me I'm about finished."

The clinic nurse held up a chart. "One more patient. After that, I promise you can go home and forget about this place."

If only I could. "Thanks. Put him in room two. I'll be right there."

Elena walked to the workroom and took a Diet Coke from the refrigerator. She held the cool can to her forehead until she heard, "Ready, Dr. Gardner." She popped the top and took several long swallows before heading for the exam room.

"Mr. . . ." She looked down at the chart. "Mr. Emerson, how can I help you?"

"My wife's been after me to get a physical. I keep telling her it's old age, but she insisted."

How many times had she heard that excuse? She hoped the man was right, but her intuition told her different.

"Let me get a bit of history. Then I'll have a look at you." She eased onto the rolling stool and propped the chart on her knee. "What's the main thing that's bothering you?"

"It's really nothing. I just get out of breath real easy."

"How far can you walk without getting tired?" Elena asked.

"Maybe from here to the front of the waiting room out there."

The distance he indicated was less than a hundred feet. "Do you ever wake up short of breath?"

"Sometimes. But it helps if I prop up on two or three pillows."

Thirty minutes later, Elena sat in the exam room with the patient and his wife. "Mr. Emerson, you have what we call congestive heart failure." She saw the look of shock that the words "heart failure" always produced, so she hurried on.

"There's no need to panic. This is fairly common, and we can treat it. I need to start you on a medicine to improve the efficiency of your heart. It's called digitalis, and doctors have been using it in one form or another for over two hundred years, so you know it must work."

"I've heard of digitalis," Mrs. Emerson said. "Is that all that's needed?"

"No. In this condition, the body accumulates fluid." Elena looked at Mr. Emerson. "This is why your feet and ankles are swollen. We treat that with medicines called diuretics. You've probably heard them called 'water pills.'"

"Anything else?" To Mrs. Emerson's credit, she hadn't berated her husband for putting off this visit so long. But Elena got the distinct impression that Emerson's wife would definitely make sure he followed orders from now on.

"There's salt restriction," Elena said. "That means you cook without added salt. And hide the salt shaker so your husband doesn't use it."

While Mary phoned to set up an appointment with a cardiologist, Elena answered a few more questions. She rose and handed Emerson the appointment slip. "If you have

127

problems before then, call us. We're here to help."

On his way out the door, Emerson offered Elena his hand. "Thanks, doctor. I'm glad she bullied me into coming." The loving look he gave his wife took any sting out of the words.

Elena decided that Emerson was lucky on two counts. He'd sought medical help before his disease became irreversible. And he had a partner, someone who'd help him through the days ahead. She wished she could say the same for herself.

Elena must have eaten something that evening, but she couldn't remember what it was. Anyway, she wasn't hungry. She'd flipped on the TV when she got home, just as she did every night, but there was no comfort in the noise, and the flickering images made no sense.

She slumped in a chair in her living room and tried to sort out the tangled mess that was her life. Mark was gone. She'd almost come to grips with that, although there were still times when she couldn't quite believe she'd never see him again. The thought brought a few tears to her eyes, but she counted that an improvement over the floods that came without warning right after his death.

The harassment from her mother-in-law apparently wasn't going to stop, but maybe she could outrun it when she moved. In the meantime, she still had those Tuesday night calls and threatening letters to contend with.

Her finances were in ruins. Mark's insurance — he'd been so stubborn about having his own coverage through work instead of being included with hers — had only paid a part of the expenses of his illness. There were still unpaid obligations for ambulance services, lab and X-rays, even the cost of his funeral. She'd been able to stave off her creditors, but eventually she had to pay those debts. And that meant hanging on to the position Cathy Sewell offered.

Which brought her to her next quandary. The tribunal — she'd come to think of Matney, Gross, and Clark in that fashion — had promised they'd conduct their investigation discreetly, but would Amy Gross think it best to warn Cathy of this latest hiccup in Elena's professional career? Had they talked already? Would the practice offer, the lifeline to which she clung so desperately, be yanked out of her reach?

No, it was better to face it head-on. She'd call Cathy and tell her the truth. At least, as much of the truth as Elena was prepared to offer. Maybe that would be enough.

The first time Elena dialed Cathy's home number, the line was busy. Was Amy talking with Cathy even now? Elena cradled the phone, looked at her watch, and decided to give it fifteen minutes before she called again. She made a cup of tea. It sat untouched on the table beside her chair when she roused herself from thoughts that went round and round like horses on a carousel, ending where they started with no progress.

She dialed again. One ring. Two. Three. *Oh, please answer.*

"Dr. Sewell."

"Cathy, this is Elena. Do you have a minute to talk?"

"Sure. What's up?"

How do I say this? "Listen, there's a problem here. I hope it won't affect your decision to offer me the contract, but you need to know about it."

Elena told the story as unemotionally as possible. She started with Pulliam's presentation in the emergency room. She freely admitted that, because of the similarity to Mark's situation, she'd been drawn to Erma Pulliam and felt a need to counsel her. Elena told how she stood alone in Chester Pulliam's room and wrestled with the concept of putting an end to an existence

130

that was hardly a life. "But I didn't do it."

"Elena, that's all understandable," Cathy said. "I'm glad you felt free to unburden yourself to me, but this isn't going to affect our relationship. Matter of fact, this was probably a breakthrough for you. Maybe it will help you get past Mark's death."

"Unfortunately, the story doesn't stop there. Yesterday afternoon, I met at their request with Pulliam's neurosurgeon, the chair of the neurosurgery department, and Amy Gross."

As she spilled out the rest of the story, Elena envisioned Cathy's face darkening, her thoughts already centered on how she could break the employment contract they'd signed. "So that's where I stand," Elena concluded. "They say I'm okay so long as I stay out of trouble, but it seems to me that trouble is actively seeking me out. If you don't want an associate who's tainted with a reputation for mercy killing, I'd under-stand. But I swear to you that I didn't discontinue Chester Pulliam's respirator."

The silence on the other end of the line spoke volumes to Elena. Cathy was about to cut her loose. And then what would she do?

"Elena, I accept what you tell me as truth. But let's look at it this way. Was there any

131

hope for Chester Pulliam to live?"

"Maybe one chance in a thousand he could come off the vent, but even then he'd never be a sentient human being again."

"And his wife was leaning toward pulling the — Sorry. I've got to stop using that expression. She was about ready to discontinue life support?"

"Yes."

"So this isn't a case of murder, or manslaughter, or any other crime. What it represents is someone who wanted to get you in trouble professionally, for going outside protocol, for ignoring policy. Right?"

Elena found herself nodding. "Yes, I guess so."

"So the question we have to answer —"

"Right, it's the same one Amy asked. Why did someone want to blame me?" Elena reached for the cold cup of tea and drained it, but her throat was still dry. "Does this mean you still want me there?"

"More than ever. I think the sooner you leave Dallas and the medical school complex behind, the safer you'll be."

Hours later, as Elena lay in her bed, Cathy's words made her shiver. Was this more than harassment? Was she actually in danger? And wasn't it ironic that her escape from danger hinged on a move to Dainger?

She determined to keep a low profile for the next couple of weeks. If a patient with an intracranial hemorrhage presented to the emergency room, she'd get them into the hands of a neurosurgeon as quickly as possible, but there was no way she'd participate in their care. And afterward, she'd avoid their room like the plague. Matter of fact, she wouldn't even visit the ICU unless she was called there to help with a procedure. For the next two weeks and two days, she'd walk the straight and narrow.

She'd start packing tomorrow night. In a couple of weeks, she'd jam cardboard boxes with the remnants of her life into every available space in her little Ford and set out for a new life, a new chance.

Elena's positive thoughts crashed about her when the phone rang. She looked at the bedside clock. Midnight.

She brought the phone to her ear and held her breath. She expected to hear sobbing, but this time there was none. Only silence.

Finally, when she could stand it no longer, she said, "Hello?" Her voice shook, and she hated herself for it.

No answer.

"Hello?"

The reply came in the same rough whiskey

alto as the other calls, but the words were different this time. "I know what you did, and you have to pay. This makes twice."

8

The night brought no rest. Elena tumbled and tossed, wracked by dreams of faceless women who chased her through dark winding corridors. Before she left her bedroom, she stripped the sweat-soaked linens from the bed and deposited them along with her still-damp pajamas in the laundry hamper.

Elena made coffee and decided to skip breakfast in favor of a donut on the way to the hospital. She was halfway to the front door when the envelope caught her eye. It peeked from the pile of bills and ads she'd chosen to ignore yesterday when she came in. Elena started to pick it up between her thumb and forefinger before she caught herself. *Don't be silly. No one is going to fingerprint this. Just open it.*

It was like the other envelope — plain, self-sealing, available at a hundred stores — addressed in block capitals. This one bore only a single stamp. She squinted to read the smudged postmark — mailed from the central post office on Monday evening.

Elena ripped the flap and pulled out a single sheet of plain paper. The same block capitals, written in blue ballpoint, spelled out a new message:

THAT'S TWO STRIKES. WILL THERE BE THREE?

Elena made it through the morning on autopilot. Clinic was mercifully light. At noon she took her bowl of soup to a quiet corner of the cafeteria. The bowl was empty when she returned her tray to the moving belt, but she had no recollection of what she'd eaten. All she could think about was "two strikes."

This changed everything. The person who made the phone calls was connected with the circumstances of Chester Pulliam's death. Maybe they were the same person, maybe not, but they were certainly connected. Did Lillian's reach extend to the hospital? Could she know the effect of the cloud cast over Elena's professional reputation by recent events in the ICU? And if Lillian was behind this, how had she managed it?

Elena consulted the large clock that hung

over the door of the cafeteria. She had half an hour before she was due in the neuro-surgery department's monthly M&M con-ference. She'd been in medicine so long she no longer thought of candy when she heard those initials. No, this was the Morbidity and Mortality Conference, the meeting where the menu centered on complications and death, neither a sweet subject.

One of the "mortality" cases was that of Chester Pulliam. Matney promised that her possible role in the termination of his life support wouldn't come up, but although her attendance was *pro forma,* it was neces-sary. Now she had twenty-five minutes to make it across campus for the conference. Ten minutes to the shuttle bus stop, ten or more for the ride to the building that housed neurosurgery, another five to make it to the conference room. No, there was no time for what she wanted to do.

Elena started for the door. First the conference, then the phone call. She prom-ised herself she wouldn't forget it. She dreaded making it, but she had to know. This had to come to an end.

Twenty-seven minutes later Elena opened the door of the neurosurgery conference room a cautious six inches and peered inside. A huge conference table occupied at least two-thirds of the room. A mixture of faculty and residents filled the chairs around it, with Matney at the head. Dr. Clark sat immediately to his right with the department vice chairman, Dr. Bruce Mickey, on Matney's left. The chairman whispered something, and the three men laughed. Elena took the opportunity to ease into the room and slide into a vacant chair along the back of the room.

Two junior faculty members were seated to Elena's right. She wasn't particularly trying to eavesdrop, but their whispers came through as though channeled through a megaphone.

"Did you hear about Dr. Matney?"

"Yeah. Dunston's leaving, and Matney's the prime candidate to succeed him as dean. The Search Committee's giving him the once-over right now."

The first doctor looked around. Elena casually directed her gaze to the bound journals lining the walls. Satisfied, he continued. "Matney's already given the word to the faculty. He wants this department squeaky clean. Anything that might look bad, sweep it under the rug or deep-six it some way. If it could bring attention, don't do it."

"I know. He caught me in the surgeon's

lounge and told me to stop giving a particular IV med to patients with cerebral edema because that was off-label usage."

"Man, I'll be glad —"

"Let's get started." Matney's eyes swept the room. All conversation stopped as though someone had hit a "mute" button. The chairman leaned back in his chair, apparently relaxed and comfortable.

"Gershon?" This was a first-year resident, who presented the case of a patient who'd developed an infection at the operative site after an otherwise uneventful craniotomy. Elena knew that the most serious neurosurgical complications were vascular — either hemorrhage or obstruction to circulation. This one was unexpected but not what she'd consider major. Indeed, the patient responded well to antibiotics and had no further problems. Nevertheless, Matney spent fifteen minutes questioning the resident and his staff surgeon about how they might have prevented this postoperative infection.

Elena felt her stomach doing flip-flops. If Matney handled the morbidity portion of the conference this way, what would he do when the mortality discussions started? She tried to dry her palms on her white coat, but it didn't seem to help. Her throat was parched, her heart was in her throat. She hardly heard Matney's next words.

"Dr. Neely, tell us about Mr. Pulliam."

This was the resident whose name Elena hadn't been able to recall, the one who had pronounced Chester Pulliam dead. He presented the facts in a monotone more appropriate for delivering an annual report to stockholders than a description of the death of a human being. Elena wondered if this was a coping mechanism adopted early in their training by neurosurgeons because they dealt every day with matters of life and death. She hoped she'd never become that callous about the loss of a human life. Then the irony of that thought brought her up short.

Neely ground to a halt with, "The patient was maintained on life support, but showed no effective respiratory efforts and required IV dopamine to maintain his blood pressure. He had a diffuse dysrhythmia on EEG, showed a positive Babinski reflex, and we observed early decorticate rigidity developing. We discussed withdrawal of life support with his wife. Subsequently that was done and he expired quietly."

That was it. No mention of an unidentified person disconnecting the respirator, or of the questionable DNR order. No finger-pointing by Clark or Matney. Instead, Clark encouraged the residents to maintain a high index of suspicion for arteriovenous malformations, the snake-like tangle of blood vessels around the brain that had ruptured and sent Chester Pulliam to his death. For the first time he looked at Elena and said, "Dr. Gardner, who's joined us today, did all the right things in getting immediate treatment for Mr. Pulliam. Unfortunately, his intracranial bleed wasn't a survivable one. That's why it's imperative to find these before they rupture."

Matney and Clark engaged in a low-key debate about the best surgical approach to AVMs, as they called them, and one of the residents had a follow-up question. Then Matney called on the next presenter, and the discussion moved on.

Elena let out a breath she didn't know she'd been holding. That was it. Could she slip out now? The clock was on the wall behind her. If she looked at her watch, Matney might see it. She decided to sit quietly until the conference ended. She might even learn something.

After another half-hour the last presentation wound down. Matney made a few perfunctory announcements, and the conference was over. Faculty members and residents moved toward the door, most with pagers and cell phones at the ready. Elena insinuated herself into the crowd and inched out of the room, her shoulders hunched as though she could make herself smaller and avoid further contact with Matney or Clark.

Once she was safely in the hall, she took a deep breath and strode rapidly toward the elevators. Three paces from safety, an all-too-familiar voice brought her up short. "Dr. Gardner. May I see you for a moment?"

Elena followed Dr. Matney into his office.

"Please have a seat." He hung his white coat carefully on a hook behind the door and took a seat behind his desk. "Thanks for coming to the conference. Your input wasn't necessary, but I wanted you to see for yourself that we are making an effort to put behind us the controversy about how Chester Pulliam's life ended. In the final analysis, whether you or someone else disconnected the respirator, the result was expected. Mrs. Pulliam remains convinced you were responsible, and tells Dr. Clark she hopes to see you again to thank you."

Elena inclined her head, although she wasn't sure why she would be thanking Matney. After all, he hadn't yet said anything that indicated a belief in her innocence.

"I spoke with two of the ICU nurses this morning," he continued. "One is new at St. Paul, a transfer from the Zale Hospital ICU. I didn't catch her name. She saw you go into Pulliam's room. She has no recollection of when you came out, or of anyone else going in until he was found dead."

"So that doesn't help," Elena said. "What about Ann?"

"I talked with her. She recalls speaking with you in Pulliam's room. She left you alone there when she was needed elsewhere in the unit. She doesn't know when you left. The emergency kept her tied up until the time Pulliam was found dead."

"So no one saw anyone enter or leave Pulliam's room after I was there?"

Matney's expression was that of a teacher sorely disappointed in a star pupil. "Although neither of these two nurses saw anything, there remain fully half a dozen people who might be interviewed." He held up a warning finger. "But I've chosen not to go further. As I told you, it's immaterial whether you or someone else wrote that DNR order and disconnected Pulliam's respirator. It's not homicide or manslaughter. It's not even malpractice. The acts merely brought to an inevitable end an unfortunate chain of events. Therefore, we plan to let the matter drop."

Anything that might look bad, sweep it under the rug or deep-six it some way. Elena couldn't believe this. "What about the person behind this, the one who wants to cast suspicion on me? Aren't you going to look for them?"

"We have no desire to keep this going and risk any hint of scandal for our department or the medical center. And, as for your reputation — because I know that's foremost in your mind — Dr. Gross and I talked earlier today about the best way to handle the problem. I was adamant in my insistence that the incidents be allowed to fade away without further mention." Matney looked down at the immaculate surface of his desk. "To this end, Dr. Gross will give you a terminal leave for the last two weeks of your training. Your certificate will show a graduation date of June 30, but as of now you're relieved of all clinical duties."

"I don't —"

The chairman steamrolled on, apparently anxious to get this done. "Since the doctor whose practice you're entering is pregnant, it's likely she'll be grateful for your early arrival. Perhaps a change of scene will be beneficial to you. It would, after all, take you away from a setting that was the scene of a very traumatic event in your life — an event that could possibly have influenced the way you react to subsequent patients in that same situation."

Elena tried unsuccessfully to wrap her mind around this change. "You're treating me like I'm the guilty party in all this. You're sending me into exile just to get me out of the way."

Matney cleared his throat and put on his best hyperadministrator manner. "I am neither affirming nor denying any culpability you have in the matter. What I am doing is protecting the reputation of the department and this institution by avoiding an investigation into a matter that, although the outcome was in no way unexpected or even improper, is best left alone."

"So I'm out of here," Elena said.

"Actually, when I first approached her, Dr. Gross was inclined to let you continue your residency to its conclusion. However, I felt it best that you leave the campus and managed to convince her to go along with my recommendation. You may consider yourself on probation under the supervision of Dr. Sewell for the next three months. If, at the end of that time, we find no further incidents of this nature, I will accept that you were blameless in the ones about which we've already talked. On the other hand, if a pattern emerges of — shall we say — early termination of life, I will turn the matter over to the authorities for investigation."

And, of course, by the time any of that happens, you'll be safely in the Dean's office and it will be someone else's problem. Elena sat, stunned. Even though she was certain that given enough time she could prove she had nothing to do with Pulliam's death, she was being sent away under a cloud. Even worse, the person or persons willing to go to these lengths to discredit her remained unidentified and unpunished. They were still out there somewhere, perhaps poised to strike again. And she wasn't sure that leaving Dallas would make a difference.

Elena's first instinct was to make a beeline to Amy Gross and confront her face-to-face, but she never made it to the shuttle bus stop. Halfway across the plaza, she collapsed onto a bench like a marionette abandoned by its handler. Spots danced in front of her eyes. A high-pitched ringing overrode the noise from the people who flowed around her in a steady stream, a part of the endless activity of a medical center.

"Are you all right?" The question came from an older woman in a business suit. Elena guessed she was probably from the administrative offices in the tall building to her right, the so-called Tower. "Can I get you anything?"

"No, thank you. I've . . . I've had some bad news."

"Dear, I've lived long enough to know that there's very little bad news we can't survive. What's your name?"

The sudden change in subject caught Elena off guard. "Elena Gardner."

"And are you a resident? Research fellow? Maybe an instructor?"

What was she, exactly? She guessed that, officially at least, she was still a resident. "I'm completing my FP residency."

"Well, Dr. Gardner, why don't you sit here and fill your tank? It seems to be pretty empty right now." She laid her hand on Elena's shoulder, squeezed, then turned and walked away.

In a few moments, Elena felt a bit better. She pulled out her cell phone and dialed the Department of Family Practice office. Yes, Dr. Gross was in, but she was on another call. Would Elena like to hold? She did.

She was serenaded by the strains of a classical piece while her mind worked a mile a minute. The knowledge that her tormentor would get off scot-free offended her innate sense of right and wrong. And the manner of her leaving was certain to cause some talk among her fellow residents. "Did you hear about Elena?" "One of her patients died under suspicious circumstances." "They terminated her." "I hear she negotiated an early release." The truth might be in there somewhere, but it wouldn't be easy to find.

Amy's voice broke into Elena's thoughts. "Dr. Gross."

"This is Elena. Dr. Matney told me you're terminating my residency." Not exactly accurate, but maybe it would force her chair to explain her actions.

"I know you're upset, but look at it this way. Cathy Sewell needs help, the sooner the better. You're under a great deal of stress here. If someone tried to make it look like you took things into your own hands with Chester Pulliam, it makes sense to me that you'll be safer in a different location — preferably one that makes you hard to find."

"What about — ?"

"I know. Your sense of justice rebels at this, but I'm not so interested in justice as I am your safety and well-being." Elena heard pages turning. "I'm looking up Cathy's number right now. When we hang up, I'll call her and tell her that we're able to let you go a couple of weeks early if she could use the help. If she says 'no,' I'll buy you a steak dinner."

"I guess you're right."

"I know I am. Now go home and start packing. Come by my office at eight in the morning and we'll talk. After that, it will take you a couple of hours to clear the campus. I'm going to tell Cathy to expect you this weekend."

At home, Elena dropped her backpack by the door, grabbed a soft drink from the refrigerator, and pawed through a desk drawer until she located her address book.

It wasn't difficult to find the number. The page was unwrinkled, the writing crisp and clean. She'd called it perhaps half a dozen times in her life. This was the hardest.

She settled into the armchair by the phone but made no move to pick up the receiver. What would it matter if she confirmed the identity of her Tuesday caller? Would the woman be likely to tell how — or even if — she'd managed to cast a pall over Elena's professional life? No, the call made no sense. But Elena decided to make it anyway.

She had to confront Lillian, and it was probably for the best that it wouldn't be face-to-face.

She punched in the numbers and waited through half a dozen rings before a wavering tone assaulted her ears. Then an electronic voice told her that number was no longer in service.

She redialed, thinking she must have made a mistake. Same results. Elena called directory assistance and received the news that there was no listing for a Lillian Gardner at that address, nor in that city. *How could that be?* Lillian would be as likely to cut off an arm as to move. The house sat in a ritzy neighborhood. It was perfectly set up for entertaining, something Lillian loved to do. "See me. I'm important. People scramble for invitations to my parties. And I hire Mexicans to serve my guests — I certainly don't expect my son to marry one."

Elena decided maybe she wasn't fated to talk with her ex-mother-in-law today. It was probably a good thing, the way she felt. But tomorrow she'd get on the Internet — amazing what one could find out using that tool — and track down Lillian Gardner.

The ring of her phone startled her. The Caller ID showed "Private Number." Cathy's first reaction was to let it ring. Then

150

again, it might be important. She answered the call just before it rolled over to voice mail.

"Hello?"

"What time do you close tonight?"

"I beg your pardon?"

The caller repeated the question.

"What number were you calling?"

"Sorry." And there was a click.

Cathy breathed a sigh. Was she going to dread every phone call in the future? Not if she could help it. Tomorrow, she'd have her landline disconnected. Anyone who really needed to contact her could do so via her cell phone, and only a limited number of people had that number.

That reminded her of a call she wanted to make. She dialed the number, one she knew by heart. David answered his cell phone on the third ring.

"Can you talk right now?" she asked.

"Sure. I'm in the surgeon's lounge waiting for my case to start. What's up?"

For the next ten minutes, Elena poured out her heart. David listened without comment or question. "So I guess I'll start packing tomorrow. I don't think I could stand to start tonight."

"No, that's probably not a good idea," he said. "Tell you what. Join me for one last dinner in Dallas. You pick the place. I'm buying."

They settled on Del Frisco's Steak House after David assured her that price was no object. "After all, I have a job too. Starting in two weeks, I'll be the junior partner of an established obstetrician. Salary, benefits, the works."

"Oh, David. I'm sorry. I've been so upset the past few weeks, I never asked you about your practice plans. Where are you going?"

David chuckled. "I've been dying to tell you this, but somehow the time never seemed right. I'm joining the practice of Dr. Milton Gaines, in a beautiful town with the unlikely name of Dainger, Texas."

David walked her to the door. "I enjoyed dinner."

"So did I," Elena said. "Thanks."

She unlocked the door and replayed the evening in her mind. She'd been grateful for David's support after Mark died. It was wonderful to have someone to talk to, someone who understood what it was like to lose a loved one. But tonight, he'd acted like more than a friend. Was David developing feelings for her? And after just six months was she ready to open up to that possibility? No. Definitely not. It was too soon, and her life was too hectic.

Elena turned in the doorway. "I'd invite you in for coffee, but to tell the truth, I'm exhausted. Think we might hook up for lunch tomorrow after I clear the campus?"

David shook his head. "I'm in surgery, with back-to-back cases from dawn to dusk."

"That's okay. Now that I know you're going to be in the same city with me, I don't feel so bad about making the move."

Once inside, Elena dropped her purse on the desk beside a pile of mail. Idly, she thumbed through it. Bills went into one pile. She'd write checks tomorrow and notify her creditors of her new address. She tossed the ads and junk mail. Maybe they wouldn't follow her without a forwarding address. That left one first-class envelope.

This wasn't the envelope she'd come to dread, the cheap one addressed in block capitals. This was heavy stock, computer addressed, and it bore a Houston return address: the offices of Gilmore, Chrisman and Rutledge, whoever they were.

She ripped open the envelope and withdrew a letter on stationery that matched the envelope. Along the left side was a list of attorneys. At the bottom of the letter was the signature of the senior managing partner, one Jerry C. Gilmore. Interesting, but what could they want from her?

Elena's dealings with legal matters had been limited, but the phrases that jumped out at her were easy enough to decipher. "We regret to inform you of the death of your former mother-in-law, Lillian Gardner — Her will provided a specific bequest to you of one dollar, with the balance going to a number of charities, including the Daughters Of The American Revolution — In accordance with her wishes, she was cremated and interred beside her husband without a public ceremony."

Lillian was dead. But when did she die? The last midnight call came less than twenty-four hours ago. How did she manage that? Did this mean that there would be no more calls, no more letters? And, if Lillian had managed to arrange for someone at the hospital to disconnect Chester Pulliam's life support, would there be further efforts against Elena?

Elena dug inside the envelope and withdrew three pieces of paper. The first was a check from the law firm in the amount of one dollar. She tore it to shreds and dropped it into the wastebasket. Elena ground her teeth as she considered Lillian's last dig at her former daughter-in-law. *See, I could have left you an inheritance, but I didn't.*

The second piece of paper was an obituary, detailing the death of Houston socialite Lillian Gardner. "Predeceased by husband . . . son Mark. Survived by daughter, Natalie, of Santa Fe, New Mexico . . . No services. Memorial gifts to . . ." Brief, sterile, to the point.

Who was Natalie? Mark had never talked about a sister. She hadn't been at the wedding. Lillian had certainly never mentioned her. What had Natalie done to merit being effectively erased from her family's life? Well, at least Elena had company in that regard.

The third piece of paper was an article neatly clipped from the *Houston Chronicle.* This went into a great deal more detail about Lillian's life, but there was nothing about the mysterious Natalie. Apparently she'd been reduced to a vital statistic, included in the obituary but not meriting further mention in a story that seemed no more than a puff piece praising Lillian, the Houston socialite.

Elena read the first paragraph again. "Despondent after her son's death, prominent Houston socialite Lillian Gardner took her life with an overdose of sleeping pills." And the date of her death was five days after

Mark's funeral.

The voice on the phone yesterday hadn't been Lillian's, was never Lillian's. The letters hadn't come from her. She hadn't manipulated Pulliam's death to cast suspicion on Elena.

But, if not Lillian . . . who? And why?

9

Elena's exit interview with Amy went as expected. They both said all the right things, while they carefully ignored the elephant in the room: the person who tried to throw the blame for Chester Pulliam's death onto Elena.

The mechanics of "clearing the campus" mainly involved shuttling between buildings and offices. Elena collected signatures on a form, gave a forwarding address only when it was absolutely necessary, said a few heartfelt "good-byes" and a lot of "see ya"s. Then it was over. She'd severed her connection with the medical center that had been her home for the past six years with less ceremony than the lowering of the flag at day's end. In her head, she began humming "Taps." Well, tomorrow was a new day, and she'd better get ready for "Reveille."

She wasn't really hungry, but she knew if she didn't eat something her blood sugar would dive, and she'd be even more depressed than she was now — if that was possible. Automatically, Elena reached for her cell phone. She stopped with it halfway out of her purse. David was in surgery all day. Was there anyone else whose company she'd enjoy? Not really.

So she'd have lunch on her own. Where? She could go back to one of the cafeterias on campus. Bad idea. She'd see people who'd want to know how she was doing. They'd offer sympathetic words as sweet as cotton candy, but with no more substance. *Poor Elena. Her husband died — she may have killed him, you know — and now she's been asked to leave the campus before her residency is up. Wonder what's behind that?*

Elena climbed into her car and said a silent "See ya" of her own to the campus. She navigated down Harry Hines Boulevard and turned onto Maple Avenue, sad that this might be her last trip along this street that boasted so many excellent Tex-Mex restaurants. She hoped Dainger offered a few of its own.

David wadded his surgical mask and paper head-cover into a ball. Without breaking stride, he dropped them in the trash-can outside the operating room.

"You handled that case very well. Removing a tubal pregnancy via laparoscope requires good hand-eye coordination and a smooth touch, and you have them both." Dr. Steve Cobb accompanied his words with a manly slap on the back.

David appreciated the praise of the staff surgeon, although he could have done without the slap. Although Cobb was now a part of the medical school faculty, only a decade ago he'd been an All-American linebacker at SMU, and while many college football players tended to get soft after their playing days were over, Cobb not only stayed in shape, he bragged that he could bench-press more now than in his football heyday. Based on what he'd just felt, David had to agree. He shrugged his shoulder and rubbed his left arm.

"You want to write the orders and op note?" Cobb asked.

"Sure. Seems fair, since you let me do the whole case."

"Got to get you ready for private practice. Tell me again where you're going."

David fished his wallet from the hip pocket of his scrubs and extracted a card. "I'm going into practice with Milton Gaines."

Cobb glanced at the card and nodded.

"Good man. He trained here, you know. Finished a year ahead of me. Tell him 'Hi,' will you?"

David hung back at the swinging doors to the recovery room, mainly because there wasn't room for anyone to walk through them side-by-side with Dr. Cobb. He cleared the doorway in time to hear, "This woman's going into shock."

The anesthesiologist, Ron Ward, was at the patient's bedside. "I extubated her in the OR. Her vital signs were stable when we started the transfer to the recovery room. But as soon as we got in here, her pressure had dropped twenty points systolic. Pulse rapid and thready."

Cobb was the first to respond. "Run that Ringer's full speed. Start another IV in the other arm." He turned and called to the ward clerk. "She's got three units of blood holding in the blood bank — send for them and start one as soon as it gets here."

The nurse adjusted the IV while Dr. Ward hurried around the bed to insert a second intravenous line. David didn't wait to be told. He started toward the door. "I'll scrub up."

Minutes later, the patient was back on the operating table, her abdomen reduced to a rectangle of skin colored a muted orange by the antibacterial prep solution, outlined by green drape sheets, and illuminated by strong overhead lights.

"She's under, but very lightly. Let me know if she moves." Ward's voice was steady. "Fluids running full. First unit of blood going up in a minute."

Cobb motioned David to stand on the patient's right, the spot reserved for the surgeon. "Your case, doctor, start to finish. I'm here to help."

David breathed a silent prayer and held out his hand for a scalpel. His brain riffled through hundreds of mental index cards, each the product of countless hours of study. Anatomy, physiology, surgery, everything had to be collated and applied.

Here goes. David cut through the skin of the patient's abdomen in a ruler-straight vertical incision. He dropped the scalpel onto the instrument tray and held out his open hand. "Deep knife. Get the Bovie up to co-ag the bleeders."

Cobb was the perfect assistant. He was a big man, but his hands were those of a concert pianist — fast and accurate. The dissection went smoothly: skin, fat, muscle. Suddenly, dark blood mixed with clots welled out of the incision.

David's words were crisp and confident.

161

"Suction."

Cobb held out his hand for the suction tube and inserted it into the wound.

"Lap pads."

David took moistened gauze packs from the scrub nurse and shoved them into the depths to absorb blood.

"Self-retaining retractor."

David spread the incision widely, and almost immediately saw a tiny scarlet fountain spurt with every beat of the patient's heart.

"Aberrant branch of the ovarian artery." There was no condemnation in Cobb's voice. Just a simple statement of fact.

"I don't recall coming close to it," David said, as much to himself as to his mentor.

"Well, it didn't cut itself, but we can talk about that later. Tie it off, then put a stick tie on for good measure."

After both he and his staff man were satisfied the problem was corrected, David closed the wound. But while his fingers were busy with catgut and nylon, his mind churned over other matters. Again and again, he went through the sequence of the laparoscopic operation. Had he seen that artery? Was there a possibility he'd nicked it? An injury to an artery could cause the tiny ring of muscles in the wall of the blood vessel to go into spasm. Sometimes this was sufficient to staunch any bleeding. Later, as the vessel wall relaxed, hemorrhage could occur. That must have been the sequence here.

"I know what you're thinking." Cobb's offhand comment made David look up from tying a suture.

"What?"

"You're going over and over the laparoscopy. You want to know what you might have done to cause this. More important, you want to be sure it doesn't happen again."

David focused on finishing the knot. "How do you know that?"

Cobb snipped the suture to the proper length. "Because that's what I'd do. It's what any surgeon worth his salt would do."

"So, what's the answer?" David dropped the needle holder on the instrument tray. "Staples, please."

Cobb blotted the incision line, although there was only a bit of blood there. "There's no magic formula. Personally, before every operation I review a mental checklist of the things that could go wrong. Then I try not to let them happen."

"And if they do?"

Cobb used a pair of fine-toothed forceps

to pinch the skin of the incision closed while David applied staples. "Good surgeons know they're human, and they operate in a less-than-perfect world. Mistakes happen. When they do, good surgeons admit it and address them."

"And bad surgeons?"

"A bad surgeon is the one who says he never makes mistakes. That's a doctor I don't want holding the knife if I'm on this table."

"Drat!" Elena dropped the cardboard box and picked her way among its mates, through the maze from her bedroom to the living room, toward the ringing phone.

She stretched out her arm and snatched the receiver off the cradle. "Hello."

She heard only silence. *Oh, don't hang up just when I get here.*

"Hello," she repeated.

"Elena?"

"David?"

"I meant to call earlier, but I had a complication in the OR this afternoon, and after that everything ran late. How about dinner?"

She looked at her watch. Six o'clock. "I don't know. I still have quite a bit of packing to do. And I'd have to clean up, change clothes."

"Why don't I pick up some Chinese and bring it over? I won't stay long. I might even be able to help you pack."

"Sure, why not?"

Elena figured she had maybe an hour before David arrived. That should give her time to clean out Mark's clothes. After his death, she couldn't bring herself to give them away. It seemed too final. Now, the move made the decision for her. Any clothes David couldn't wear were headed to the Goodwill drop-off box in the morning.

She decided to start with things she was sure David wouldn't want. Underwear and socks went into the box first. Then pajamas. Handkerchiefs.

How about shirts? Mark had some nice ones. She'd put them aside and let David decide.

The shirts were folded because, in the days when he traveled, Mark found it easier to pack them. The habit carried forward, and now she stared at a large drawer filled with folded dress shirts. She carefully transferred the three stacks to the bed.

She opened the closet. Suits, pants, sports coats — each of them bore the scent of Mark's cologne. Elena's eyes filled and overflowed. She couldn't do this. Not even this long after Mark's death. She'd ask David to go through them. He could choose what he wanted and put the rest in boxes for her.

Her stomach knotted as she considered the finality of her actions. Mark wasn't coming home. Ever. That had been true before she started to clean out his things. It would still be true when she was in the car with her suitcases and boxes, on the way to a new life. But right now it was too much to contemplate.

Enough! She had to put an end to the pity party and get back to packing. While she was staying with Will's parents — and she still wondered about that — she'd determined to get by with a few boxes and a couple of suitcases of clothes. A mover was coming to pack and move the rest.

She pulled a large suitcase out of the closet and opened it on the bed. When she shoved the shirts aside, one stack toppled, uncovering an envelope. Elena pulled it out and studied it. No address. The flap had come unsealed. Was this some sort of message from the grave? Or just a letter Mark had picked up that was trapped between clean shirts when he put them away?

She pulled a single sheet of paper from the envelope. As she did, she noticed that her hands trembled a bit. Who could blame her? This might be a love letter Mark had meant for her.

Elena opened the sheet. It was computer-generated, covering about half a page. She scanned it, then dropped to the edge of the bed and read it again. A third reading didn't change the words that by now were burned into her retina and her heart.

I've struggled with this for days and weeks. In the end, maybe I'll deliver this news in person. But in case I'm weak and take the coward's way out, I'll say it here.

It's over between us. I can't continue living a lie. There once was passion in our relationship, maybe even love. But there's someone else whom I love even more. And if I'm to be true to her, our relationship has to end.

That was it. No salutation. No signature. Just simple words that spelled the end of a love she thought would last a lifetime.

Elena wondered how long Mark had put off delivering this news to her. If he'd lived, how would their marriage have changed? Would he have destroyed the letter and devoted himself to her once more? Or could he have summoned up the courage to deliver this deathblow to her in person?

The doorbell rang. That would be David. Could she share this latest development with him? Could she admit that her husband had gone outside their marriage because he found her so lacking? No. Not to David. Not to anyone.

That's when it hit her. She was alone — totally alone. Even the memory of her dead husband was no longer there to sustain her.

Elena locked the door of her apartment. The click was like an audible punctuation mark that ended this part of her life. The last two days had gone by in a blur, but she had no wish to recapture them. All she wanted to do was move on.

When David walked through the door on Thursday night, Elena's determination not to share her news about Mark's infidelity disappeared like a wisp of smoke before the north wind. After her first few blubbering sentences, David dropped the bags of food in the living room and extended his arms to her. She wasn't sure how long he held her, but she recognized that there was more there than just a good friend offering support in a time of crisis. And, God help her, she found herself wishing she could stay in those arms.

Eventually she'd disengaged from his arms, dried her eyes, and tried to gather herself. They'd talked for over an hour after that, carefully avoiding any mention of their embrace. When David left, they'd divided the Chinese food, joking that doctors could eat anything, including reheated Lo Mein, for breakfast.

Elena had managed to fill yesterday with enough to keep her mind occupied. There'd been packing, phone calls, two trips to the dumpster, one to the local Goodwill center to dispose of all of Mark's clothing after David declined it. Elena didn't blame him.

She shoved the apartment key into the pocket of her jeans and climbed into her car. The little Ford fairly bulged with luggage and boxes. Despite Elena's intentions to take only essentials on this trip — she'd be coming back soon to meet the movers — now she wanted as much familiar stuff with her as possible. She needed security.

She punched a button on the dash, and the sweet strains of piano music filled the car. The song was "It Is Well With My Soul," and Elena thought nothing could be further from the truth right now. The CD had been a gift from a friend after Mark's death. Elena hadn't listened to it since, but now she hoped the music could help her purge the bitterness that clutched her heart.

As she passed the Dallas city limit sign, she felt she should say something to mark the occasion. Something like, "Goodbye, Dallas; hello, Dainger." No, she didn't much like the ring of that. Finally, she settled on a brief wave into the rearview mirror.

Elena drove for about an hour, navigating pretty much on automatic pilot, when she noticed the car in front of her weaving from side to side. She eased off the accelerator and dropped back a bit. If the driver was on the verge of an accident, she didn't plan to be involved in it. The car was a dark blue Buick, at least ten years old but polished and shiny as a new dime. One head showed through the rear window, silver hair that bobbed forward, then backward, like a cork on a windswept lake. Was the driver drunk? Or asleep?

She honked her horn, but there was no reaction from the driver. Then the head slumped forward onto the steering wheel and stayed there. Elena scanned her surroundings. She'd gone from the urban sprawl of Dallas to the farmland right outside Dainger. She couldn't recall seeing more than three cars in the past ten minutes. An occasional gravel road led off to the side of the highway, but there wasn't a house in sight. Wire strung between stout posts created fences that framed green fields and pastures where horses and cows grazed.

Elena retrieved her cell phone and punched in "911." Her finger was poised over the "send" button when the Buick started a steady drift to the right. Elena leaned on her horn, without any evident effect on the driver. The car slowed as it moved inexorably off the road, onto the shoulder, across a wide patch of grass, rolling to a stop against a fencepost.

Elena closed the distance to the car, pulled onto the shoulder, and hit the button to activate her emergency flashers. When she reached the Buick, the motor was idling but the car was held fast by the stout post in front of it. The driver, an older man, was neatly dressed and clean-shaven. There was no odor of alcohol in the car, although Elena did note a scent that reminded her of Juicy Fruit gum. The man's head rested against the steering wheel that his hands still clutched at the ten and two positions. She felt in his neck for his pulse — strong and steady. He was breathing rapidly but seemed to have no problem with air exchange.

She did a quick once-over of the car's

contents. An overnight bag rested on the passenger-side seat. A larger suitcase and a suit hanger bag lay across the back seat. She sniffed at the travel cup that rested in the console on the driver's side — coffee.

Elena reached across the unconscious man, jammed the transmission into park, and turned off the ignition key. She backed away from the car and punched the "send" button on her phone.

"Summers County 911. What is your emergency?" Elena had a brief moment of panic. She seemed to recall that cell phone calls to 911 were routed to the nearest city, but was that foolproof? Was this Summers County? She had no idea.

"I just came up on a man who lost consciousness and ran his car off the road. I need EMTs and the police or sheriff or whoever is responsible for this area."

"Is the victim breathing? Does he appear to be injured? Is he bleeding?"

"He's breathing and has a strong pulse. There's no evidence of an injury. But we need medical attention here."

"What's your location?"

"I'm not sure. I'm new here. I . . . I know I'm about an hour or so out of Dallas, going north toward Dainger." Elena looked around her. What was the number of this highway? "I'm pretty sure I'm on highway 287."

"Are there any billboards there? Mile markers?"

Elena turned a full circle. "None that I see."

There was a brief pause. "That's all right. The units are rolling now, going south on 287. Turn on your flashers. They'll find you."

"Please, can you get some help here as quickly as possible?"

Elena heard radio chatter in the background. "They're on their way. Stay with the victim. Cover him to keep him warm. Don't move him."

"I know what to do. I'm a doctor. Get those EMTs here ASAP."

"Don't —"

Elena ended the call and turned back to the man, who didn't appear to have moved since she discovered him. The fruity scent was stronger now, and his breathing was faster than before. Diagnoses ran through her head at lightning speed until one clicked: diabetic ketoacidosis. Blood sugar through the roof, no insulin to help burn it, so he was metabolizing his own body fat and the by-products were poisoning him.

She grabbed the man's overnight bag and

opened it on the car's left front fender. Clothes, a shaving kit, but no medications. If this man was a diabetic, where was his insulin?

As Elena replaced the overnight bag, she saw something she'd missed earlier: a cord ran from the console's cigarette lighter into the back seat to a travel mini-fridge on the floor behind the driver. Of course. A diabetic would travel with insulin, but insulin required refrigeration.

She opened the refrigerator. Bingo! Insulin syringes and needles, packets of cotton wipes, and two bottles labeled "Insulin, NPH." Good for him, bad for her. The man was on a regimen that only required insulin once or twice a day, so he carried a long-acting preparation. What he needed right now was insulin that would be effective in minutes, not hours. And every minute of delay meant the death of more brain cells. She could give him some of the long-acting preparation, but that, plus the proper treatment later, would probably send him into hypoglycemic shock, also carrying the potential for brain damage.

The sound of a siren in the distance saved Elena from a difficult decision. The MICU — the mobile intensive care unit that had replaced the "ambulance" of prior years —

would have a glucometer to give a rough reading of blood sugar, and a supply of rapid-acting insulin.

The first vehicle on the scene was a white SUV with black trim. Its light bar spit out rays of red and blue, and its siren was loud enough to make Elena cover her ears. The SUV made a U-turn across the road's grassy median and came to a stop behind Elena's Ford. Two men in tan uniforms emerged. The younger of the two opened the vehicle's trunk, pulled out some flares, and hustled down the road. An older man climbed out of the driver's side. The sun glinted on the badge pinned to his shirt. He adjusted his sunglasses, hitched up his gun belt, and made his way quickly toward Elena.

The lawman touched the brim of his straw Stetson. "Ma'am, I'm Sheriff J. C. Dunaway. The medics are about a minute behind me. What do we have here?"

"I was following this car when it started weaving. Then the driver collapsed onto the wheel, and the car veered off the road. I believe the man is a diabetic who didn't take his insulin this morning, and now he's in a coma from high blood sugar."

Dunaway bent through the open door of the Buick and scanned the interior. He touched the driver's neck lightly with two fingers. Without moving the man's head, he lifted the eyelids and checked the pupils, then ran his hand lightly over the driver's scalp.

The sheriff straightened up and turned back to Elena. "We'll let the medics sort it out." He cupped a hand to his ear. "I think I hear them coming right now. I'll need a statement from you for my report. I can get it here, but it would be a lot easier if you came to my office and dictated it. Were you headed into Dainger?"

"Yes." She extended her hand. "Dr. Elena Gardner. I'm going into practice with Cathy Sewell."

Dunaway removed his hat and shook her hand. "Doctor, I'm pleased to meet you. Cathy — I mean, Dr. Sewell — told me you were coming. I guess I shouldn't have been trying to play doctor when a real one was already here."

"That's —"

Elena realized Sheriff Dunaway wasn't going to hear her next words over the commotion from the whoopers of the arriving vehicles. First came a fire engine. It followed the tracks Dunaway had made across the median, coming to rest behind the accident scene to form a much more effective road-

176

block than the flares the deputy had placed. It was followed by a bright red MICU that skidded to a stop beside the stalled Buick. Two men in tan coveralls spilled out. The man on the passenger side opened the double back doors of the vehicle and brought out an emergency kit. Elena recognized it as the twin of the ones she'd seen in Dallas MICUs.

The driver hurried up to Dunaway. "What's up, Sheriff?"

"I'll let the doctor here tell you. Dr. Elena Gardner, this is Eric Burson, one of our EMTs."

Eric nodded, obviously impatient to get to work. "What do we have here?"

Elena summarized her findings and suspicions in a few terse sentences.

Eric called out to the other EMT, "Perry, he may be a diabetic. You get his vitals. I'll check his blood sugar. Let's get an IV going."

"What can I do to help?" Elena asked.

"Just let us do our job," Eric threw over his shoulder. "I'll call you if I need you."

Hmmm. Not a very auspicious welcome to the medical community. Oh, well, at least I won't be blamed if something bad happens to this patient.

10

"Doctor, I think that ought to do it." Sheriff Dunaway rose from his desk and offered his hand. "I'll give you a call if we need anything more. And thanks for stopping to help that man. I know a lot of people would just pass on by. Like in the story of the good Samaritan."

Elena decided to ignore the Bible reference. Those days were behind her. She paused at the door to the sheriff's office. "I think I'd like to go by the hospital and see how that patient's doing. I'm afraid I've only been there once. Can you give me directions?"

"I can do better than that," Dunaway said. He called to the deputy who sat at the front desk. "Frank?"

The deputy turned. "Yes, sir?"

"Would you get in one of the cruisers and lead Dr. Gardner over to the hospital? She's new in town, and I don't want her to get lost on her first day."

Frank rose from his desk, and when he turned toward them Elena felt her knees buckle. At first glance, he was the spitting image of her late husband. Frank's smile displayed gleaming teeth in a face that belonged on a movie star. He was about her age, trim and fit, with dark hair and sparkling gray eyes.

He stuck out his hand. "Frank Perrin, doctor. Pleasure to meet you."

"Well, I'll leave you in Frank's hands." Dunaway turned back to his office.

Frank gestured toward the door. "The hospital's only a few blocks from here. I can lead you there, if you'd like." He took a couple of steps, then turned back. "Better still, why don't I take you there? I can wait for you and bring you back here for your car when you're through." He glanced at the sheriff's open door and lowered his voice. "I could even buy you a cup of coffee if you'll let me."

Elena's thoughts churned like water in a fishpond at feeding time. She wanted to see "her" patient at the hospital. She should move her things into the Kennedys' house. She ought to call Cathy and check in with her. But it would be so very nice to put herself in the hands of this man for a little while. Even though she knew he wasn't Mark, being near someone who was so like her late husband, even for a bit, was appealing. "I . . . I think that would be nice."

She'd never ridden in a police car before. Elena took note of the radio, the scanner, the radar unit. She flinched when she saw the shotgun mounted behind her, in front of a mesh screen that separated the driver's compartment from the back seat. She fastened her seatbelt, almost afraid to touch anything in the process.

Frank laughed. "Pretty impressive, isn't it? I guess that's one reason little boys want to grow up to be policemen — so they can play with all these toys." He clipped his seatbelt. "Want me to turn on the lights and siren for the ride to the hospital?"

Elena had her mouth open to reply when she realized he was kidding. "I appreciate your doing this."

Frank waved it off. "No problem. Things are pretty quiet, and this gets me away from that desk for a while. Besides —" He nodded toward the microphone clipped to the shoulder loop of his immaculate tan uniform. "If they need me, they'll call."

At the hospital, Frank wheeled into the Emergency Room parking area and left the unit in a slot marked "Police." He stopped at the ER admissions desk and was told that the emergency patient, whose name was John Daniels, was in room three with Dr. Baker.

"I'll only be a minute," Elena said. "I want to see if the patient's going to be okay, and introduce myself to the doctor taking care of him."

Frank pointed to a door. "I'll hang out in the break room there. See you soon."

Elena tapped on the half-open door of room three and eased inside. Mr. Daniels lay on a gurney with a woman in hospital scrubs at his side, adjusting the flow of an IV. A middle-aged man in a white coat worn over slacks and a sport shirt stood to the side, scanning what Elena took to be an ER chart.

She cleared her throat. "Dr. Baker?"

The man looked up but said nothing.

"I'm Dr. Elena Gardner. I'll be going into practice with Dr. Sewell. I'm the one who found Mr. Daniels right after he lost consciousness. I wanted to introduce myself and see how he's doing."

Baker's smile was minimal but real. He offered his hand. "Evan Baker. Nice to meet you. The EMTs checked Mr. Daniels's blood sugar with a glucometer and started insulin. Even at that, his sugar was through the roof and his electrolytes were totally out of whack when he arrived in the ER. Typical diabetic ketoacidosis. We're bringing him under control, and I think he'll come out of it fine."

"Good."

"I understand you made the diagnosis on the spot, just from Kussmaul respiration and the smell of ketones on his breath."

"I . . . Yes, that was my first impression."

"Well, nice pick-up. I look forward to working with you."

Elena left the treatment room feeling somewhat better. At least one doctor in town seemed to be on her side. Better than the reception she had received from Eric, the EMT. And, speak of the devil . . .

"Doctor, come to make sure we didn't foul up with your patient?"

"Eric, I don't know what I did to get off on the wrong foot with you, but whatever it was, I'm sorry. And, to answer your question, I dropped by to make sure I didn't miss something at the accident scene. As it turned out, my evaluation was correct, and your treatment was good. Mr. Daniels is going to be fine."

Eric's reply was a sniff. He turned on his heel and headed out the door, where his MICU idled in the intake bay.

Okay, I'm one for two. I'm not sure what Eric's problem is, but obviously he's got something against doctors. Or maybe it's just me.

She found Frank in the break room, deep in conversation with one of the male nurses about the relative merits of the Dallas Cowboys and the Houston Texans. "Ready to go?" he said.

"Yes, thanks."

Elena climbed into the sheriff's SUV with a bit less apprehension this time. Actually, it felt kind of cool riding up here. And she had to admit she enjoyed having a handsome man beside her. It gave her a thrill — a guilty thrill, but nevertheless it was a sensation she hadn't felt in a long time. Part of her wondered what she was doing. Part of her said, "Relax. Enjoy."

"Are you going to have enough room here?" Dora Kennedy reminded Elena of a bellman in a nice hotel, anxious that the guest would find the accommodations comfortable.

Elena stood in the doorway and surveyed the room that would be her home for a while. It wasn't large, but the overall effect was cozy. A double bed was butted head-first against the near wall to her right, with a double dresser and bookcase taking most of the wall opposite. The room's only window was at the far end of the left wall, with an easy chair, reading lamp, and end table nearer the hall on that side. The right-hand wall contained two doors, with a picture hanging between them. The door closest to the hallway was closed. The open door, nearest the outside wall, afforded a glimpse of a cozy bathroom.

Elena wrestled a large suitcase onto the double bed. "I'm sure it'll be fine. Thanks so much for opening your home to me."

"Not at all." Dora pointed to the open door. "You have your own private bath. Linens are in the cabinet."

"Very nice."

"This was Will's room. Since he left, we've used it for guests." She opened the closed door and shoved aside several hangers draped with coats. "Here's your closet. It doesn't get much use, so I'm afraid it's accumulated some things we don't want to throw away but don't use much, either."

Elena took a handful of empty hangers and filled them with blouses, slacks, and dresses. "I'm sure there's still plenty of room. Besides, I hope to find a place of my own soon."

She reached into the closet to deposit her

clothes and bumped a long, khaki-colored canvas case on the top shelf. Elena started to move it, then jumped back as though she'd felt a snake. "Oh!"

"What's the matter, dear?"

"There's a gun up here. That's not exactly the kind of thing I expected to find in a preacher's home."

"That's Will's shotgun," Dora said. "He and his friends used to go dove hunting in the fall. When he got married, Cathy told him he couldn't keep the gun in their house. Matthew's checked it, and I can assure you it's not loaded. Matter of fact, there aren't even any shells in the house. So it's perfectly safe." She reached out her hand toward the shelf. "Would you like me to move it?"

"No, no. It'll be fine there."

As Elena unpacked, Dora kept up a running commentary on the town. There was not a shred of what might be termed "gossip" in the whole conversation, but Elena got the impression Dora and Matthew Kennedy were tuned in on most of the comings and goings in the community.

Elena moved to the bathroom and started to stow her makeup. "I had quite an introduction to Dainger," she called over her shoulder. "Even got to meet a sheriff." She sketched out the highway incident for Dora.

"The lead EMT wasn't too pleasant, though."

"That would be Eric. Poor man. Lost his wife, and he's blamed doctors for it ever since. But Cathy tells us he's good at what he does, so she ignores his jabs."

"Well, there are always a few people like that around." Elena closed the last suitcase and shoved it into the back of the closet. "The good news is that I sort of made friends with the sheriff and one of his deputies."

"Oh, J. C. Dunaway's a fine Christian man. Our police force is good, mind you, but if I had a real problem, I'd trust it to J. C. in a heartbeat."

"He was very nice. Even had one of his deputies drive me to the hospital so I wouldn't get lost. We had lunch afterward."

"Which deputy?" Dora asked.

"Frank Perrin. Do you know him?"

In the short time she'd been around her, Elena had never heard Dora Kennedy say anything bad about anyone. The preacher's wife kept that record intact by saying, "Yes, I know Frank." But the expression on her face was what Elena imagined Dora would display if she found two-day-old roadkill in her driveway.

■ ■ ■ ■

Cathy laid down her book and reached for the phone. Who could be calling her at home on Saturday afternoon? She hoped it wasn't the hospital. Wasn't Dr. Brown on call? Then she saw the caller ID.

"Elena. What's up?"

"I just got into town and wanted to check in with you."

"Glad you made it. Where are you?"

"I'm at the Kennedys' now, but I started out at the sheriff's office."

A myriad of thoughts, all of them bad, flashed through Cathy's head. "Is there a problem? Do you need a lawyer? Will and I can be there in ten minutes. Let me call Sheriff Dunaway. He knows me. We —"

"Take it easy. I saw the driver in front of me slump over the wheel of his car, and I called it in. The sheriff asked me to stop by his office for a formal statement. Then he had one of his deputies drive me to the hospital so I could check on the patient."

"Whew. I had visions of something bad happening," Cathy said. "So you've been at the hospital all this time?"

"Not really. After I finished looking in on the patient — he's a diabetic who went into a coma, and Dr. Baker's taking care of him — anyway, the deputy asked if he could buy me a hamburger. We sat at the Dairy Queen for half an hour. Then he took me back to get my car and led me to the Kennedy house."

"I know most of the deputies here in town," Cathy said. "Which one were you with?"

"Frank Perrin. Know him?"

Cathy took her time answering. "Yes, I know him." She'd been wrong. Something bad had happened to Elena. Her new associate just didn't know it yet.

Talk about embarrassing! It was Monday, Elena's first day in her new job, and she had to ask her landlady for directions to her office.

Mrs. Kennedy waved it off. "No need to be embarrassed. You haven't had time to learn your way around." She topped off Elena's cup and refilled her own before sitting down at the breakfast table. "Tell you what. My husband has to go visit a couple of folks in the hospital. You can follow him, and he'll lead you right to Cathy's office building."

Fortified with more breakfast than she'd eaten in years, Elena followed Pastor Matthew Kennedy's black Olds sedan as it wove its way through the streets of town. In about five minutes, he pulled over and pointed to his right. Sure enough, there was Cathy's office building. A bit further down the road, Elena saw the hospital.

Elena waved her thanks and wheeled into the parking lot. Even though it was early, there were about a dozen cars scattered throughout the lot. Probably staff. Most of them were parked at the far end, but she recognized Cathy's auto in a space near the door. A stand-up sign showed the slot was reserved for "Dr. Sewell." Nothing was designated for "Dr. Gardner." Elena was halfway to the end of the lot when it dawned on her: she was a staff doctor now. No more thinking like a resident. She deserved to park next to Cathy. She did a quick K-turn and slid her little Ford in next to Cathy's Chevrolet Impala.

Elena promised herself she'd have a new car someday. And not just a new car — she wanted a home of her own and freedom from the debt that hung heavy over her head. But if she intended to get any of those, it was time to go to work.

She lifted her purse from the passenger seat. She'd brought a white coat with her, one with "Dr. Elena Gardner, Family Practice" embroidered over the breast pocket. She pulled it from the back seat, beeped the car locked, and started toward the office.

When she was with Cathy, Elena had gone in and out through a back door, but for the life of her she couldn't remember how she got there. She took her cue from the glass-enclosed signboard in the lobby and made her way down the hall to the front door of Cathy's office. She took a deep breath, turned the knob, and walked into the waiting room.

"May I help — Oh, it's you, Dr. Gardner." Cathy's nurse rose from behind the desk and hurried to the door to meet Elena. "I'm Jane. Jane Wilson. I know it's going to be hard to keep everyone's name straight for a while, but believe me, it won't be long before you know most of the folks in town."

Cathy came out of her office to add her own greetings, and the next few minutes were controlled chaos. One woman, then the other, bombarded the newcomer with things they thought she should know. Finally Elena raised her hands in mock surrender. "I give up. How about I walk around and familiarize myself with the layout." She turned to Cathy. "Then, if it's okay, I'll watch as you see a few patients. If I have questions, I'll ask them later."

"Of course," Cathy said. "We haven't made any appointments for you yet. I want to let you get your feet on the ground. However —"

Elena didn't like the sound of that "however." But this was her boss, and she'd better get used to it. So much for being out on her own and independent. "Yes?"

"I'm on emergency room call for the hospital this week. I thought it might be a good idea for you to take those patients. That should help you build a patient base."

That didn't sound so bad. Elena had been to the hospital only two days ago, not to mention the brief tour with Cathy on her first visit. And she'd seen it from a distance just this morning. She was fairly certain she could find it again without getting lost — or calling Frank Perrin for help. At the thought of the deputy, she found herself wishing she could see him again.

Elena tried to put her finger on why she felt attracted to Frank. Maybe it was his resemblance to Mark. After the not-so-subtle distaste her landlady showed, maybe Elena's feelings were the same ones that drive people to test a wet paint sign or to see if an iron's still hot. Anyway, it was nice to have a friend here, one who wasn't also a colleague. Maybe she'd call Frank and offer to buy lunch. Sort of return the favor from the other day.

The morning passed uneventfully, and Elena picked up Cathy's routine quickly. The office was well organized. The diseases and problems presented by the patients were diverse but not particularly challenging. Cathy took the time to introduce each patient to Elena, following the same pattern each time. "This is Dr. Gardner. She'll be joining my practice. She's very well-trained, and I think you'll like her."

While the two women waited in Cathy's office for Jane to prepare a female patient for an examination, Elena said, "Why did that last patient frown when you introduced me?"

Cathy gnawed for a moment on her lower lip. "You won't see a lot of this, but there's a bit in every community. I introduce you as Dr. Gardner. They expect to see someone who looks like them. Instead, they see a woman with darker skin, long black hair, high cheekbones — a classic Latin appearance. Most patients are fine with this. But a few are thinking, *This woman is a Mexican. Did she train in Guadalajara? Does she even speak English?*"

Elena's stomach knotted like the fists her hands were forming. "Did you expect this when you took me into the practice?"

"Of course I did. And maybe I should have mentioned it to you ahead of time. But, frankly, the color of your skin doesn't matter to me. As I've said, you won't find a lot of this here, and once these folks get to know you, it won't make any difference to them, either. You speak clear, unaccented English. You trained at Southwestern, which in my opinion is second to none. You're an excellent doctor, whether your name is Gardner or Perez or whatever."

Elena saw Cathy's dilemma. She couldn't very well introduce her new colleague by saying, "This is Dr. Elena Perez Gardner. She's a U.S. citizen. She was raised as an Anglo. She trained at UT Southwestern Medical Center. Don't let the color of her skin bother you."

"Okay, I see where you're coming from," Elena said. "I guess it's up to me to overcome any prejudices these folks might have." She frowned. "What do you think is the best way to do that?"

Cathy smiled and patted Elena's shoulder. "Be yourself. Let the real Elena come through. After that, things will take care of themselves."

"That's the last patient," Jane said, and disappeared down the hall.

Elena had been surprised at how busy the morning was. No wonder Cathy wanted help — pregnancy or no pregnancy. But it was a good experience for Elena. Now she had a decent working knowledge of the way the office ran. All but a couple of the patients warmed to her. And, as the morning wore on, she began to relax.

Cathy stopped Elena in the hall. "How about letting me buy your lunch? We can go to RJ's. As I recall, our last meal there started out okay but ended up sort of intense. Maybe this one will be better."

"I guess that —"

Jane's voice carried clearly from the front desk. "Dr. Gardner, there's a call for you on line one. Do you want to take it? It's Deputy Perrin."

Elena could hardly miss the way Cathy's lips pinched at the mention of the name. She'd have to pursue that later. Right now, though, it seemed as though Frank had read her mind. Lunch with him was certainly appealing. She'd been with Cathy all morning, and the furthest thing from Elena's mind was a lunch where the sole topic of conversation was the practice of medicine in Dainger. She needed a break, and Frank Perrin promised to provide a lovely one.

"Yes, I'll take it." Elena held her hands out palms up in a "what are you going to do?" gesture. "He probably wants to ask me more about the accident report I filed yesterday. Why don't you go ahead? I'll pick up a sandwich somewhere around here."

"We start again at one," Cathy said, lowering the temperature in the office at least ten degrees with her attitude shift. She shucked out of her white coat, grabbed her purse from a desk drawer, and disappeared out the back door.

Elena closed the door to the office before she picked up the phone and punched the blinking button. "Frank, this is a surprise."

"Just keeping my promise to show you the town. Why don't I pick you up in about five minutes? We can grab a quick bite and still have time to drive around before you have to be back."

"That sounds great. But I have two requests."

"Name them."

"Pick me up outside the back door of the office."

"Secretive, but I'm game. What's the other?"

"Let's go somewhere other than RJ's."

Elena dawdled in Cathy's office for five minutes, then stuck her head out the door like a teenager trying to sneak off to a concert. No movement. No sound. She tiptoed down the hall and saw that the front desk was empty. Apparently Jane was at lunch. Good.

She grabbed her purse and hurried out the back door. As he'd promised, Frank sat in his sheriff's department SUV outside the rear entrance.

Elena climbed in and waved her hand toward the dash. "Don't you get tired of riding around in the midst of all this equipment? I'd be afraid I'd touch something and bring a SWAT team running."

Frank laughed, a throaty, full laugh that made Elena smile. "You get used to it. And it's nice to know that if I needed backup, I could get a SWAT team here in a flash." He reached out his hand. "All I'd have to do is —"

"Never mind! I'll take your word. Now how about that lunch?"

The place Frank chose was a tiny building, apparently a converted home, where, according to the menu, the "best Tex-Mex in Summers County" was served. Everyone there seemed to know Frank, and he seemed proud to introduce Elena as "my friend, the new doctor in town."

They ordered and Elena sampled the

chips and salsa. If the rest of the food was this good, she could see herself coming here regularly. But something bothered her. "Frank, why did you bring me here? Was it because I'm Hispanic? Do you think that's all I eat?"

Frank spread his hands wide. "Hey, I didn't mean to offend you. If you ask any of the staff, they'll tell you that I eat here about three times a week. Sure, I noticed your looks don't exactly scream 'Caucasian,' but I don't pay any attention to that sort of thing."

The food arrived, and Elena decided to let the matter drop. Maybe she was sensitized by her conversation with Cathy this morning. She took a bite of her tamale. It tasted wonderful. She definitely wouldn't have to drive back to Dallas for a Tex-Mex food fix.

Frank dug into his meal as though he hadn't eaten in a week. How could he eat that much and maintain his physique? He had a classic swimmer's build: broad chest, narrow waist, hips that were — *Stop it, Elena. You've only been a widow for a few months, and you're already checking out men. Besides, there's David.* Wow! Despite her best intentions, she was already comparing the relative merits of two eligible men. She wondered if it might be a reaction to her late husband's letter. *Careful. Right now you're the poster girl for rebound.*

Frank's voice made her look up from her plate. "I was wondering if you'd like to —"

Elena's hand went to her purse to silence her cell phone. Then she recalled she was on emergency room call. "Sorry, I've got to take this." She punched the button to answer. "Dr. Gardner."

"Dr. Gardner, this is Glenna Dunn. I'm the head nurse in the ER at Summers County General. I understand you're covering for Dr. Sewell. One of her patients just came in by ambulance with a possible MI. Do you want to see him, or shall I contact the internist on call?"

"No, I'll be right there. Thank you for calling." Elena could imagine the reaction of an internist who was called out to see a "heart attack," only to find that the patient had acid reflux, or some similar uncomfortable but by no means life-threatening problem. Of course, if it was a myocardial infarction, there was a limited window of time for administration of proper treatment. In either case, she needed to be on her way. Elena dropped her fork on her plate, crumpled her napkin beside it, and rose. "Frank, I'm sorry to interrupt our lunch, but I've got to get to the ER. Let's put those lights and siren to use."

11

Elena knew the moment she walked into the treatment room that this was no case of simple acid reflux. According to his paperwork, the man on the gurney was in his mid-50s, but he looked ten years older than that. His complexion was ashen and dotted with beads of perspiration. The collar of his dress shirt was loose, his tie at half-mast.

One glance at the monitors above the patient's head confirmed her suspicion. Definite T-wave inversion, ST elevation — myocardial ischemia for certain. No Q waves yet, so it was early. Blood pressure down a bit, although she had no idea what his normal level was. Pulse a little rapid.

Elena ran her eyes down the chart. Oxygen by mask, an aspirin chewed and swallowed, IV started but no drugs given yet, lab work drawn and sent stat. "Nice job, Glenna. But will you raise the oxygen flow to eight liters per minute?"

The ER nurse adjusted a dial. "Our standard protocol is six. Will eight be your usual?"

"Yes, please." *Nice. No argument.* Elena addressed the patient for the first time. "Mr. Nix, I'm Doctor Gardner, Doctor Sewell's new associate. Tell me what happened."

A middle-aged woman stood beside the patient. Her hands fluttered about like frightened birds. She responded before Nix had a chance to speak. "I'm his wife. He came home for lunch, and right after his first bite of chicken fried steak he clutched his chest and slumped over. That's when I called 911."

Mrs. Nix looked younger than her husband. Elena figured there might have been some nips and tucks along the way to help that image. A few dark roots showed that the woman's blonde hair owed more to Clairol than to Nordic genes. Mrs. Nix would call herself "pleasingly plump." Elena's assessment was "running to middle-age spread."

Elena turned back to Nix. "Are you having any pain?"

He pointed to the midpoint of his chest.

"Anywhere else?"

"My neck and jaw." He indicated his left side.

"Are you on any medications?"

Mrs. Nix dug into her purse and pulled out two bottles. "I thought you'd want to see these."

"Let's have a look." Elena studied the labels. Generic versions of Digoxin and Toprol. "So Dr. Sewell has been treating you for heart failure and high blood pressure."

Nix forced out the words through clenched teeth. "Dr. Sewell, and Doc Gladstone before that."

"Excuse me, Doctor." The ward clerk hurried in and handed Elena a slip of paper with several values written on it. "The lab just phoned with the results of Mr. Nix's chemistries."

"Thank you." Elena studied the figures for a moment. The enzyme levels were rising but were not too high yet. "Mr. Nix, right now you're in the early stages of a heart attack. So far there's been very little heart damage. We need to keep it that way."

"How?" Nix grunted.

"A heart attack occurs when the blood flow to the heart is interrupted. The blockage can be due to a blood clot or an obstruction by what we call plaque — hardening of the arteries. What we need to do is unblock the vessels and get circulation restored." Elena turned to Glenna. "Get some tPA ready, please."

"May I speak with you, Doctor?" Without waiting for a reply, Glenna stepped into the hall.

Elena excused herself and joined her. "What's the matter?"

"You probably don't know this yet, but we have an interventional radiologist on staff. Dr. Rosenberg does all our cardiac angiography. I thought I'd better tell you before you ordered tPA."

Elena felt like kicking herself. She needed to get out of the mindset that when she left Southwestern Medical Center to practice in a smaller community hospital she'd be without all the modern technology on which she'd depended. She silently blessed Glenna for discreetly pointing out the availability of cardiac angiography. If she'd given Nix the "clot buster," the risk of hemorrhage with any subsequent procedure would be multiplied. The angiogram should come first, if one was available.

"Thank you, Glenna. That's my mistake for not asking. Would you please page Dr. Rosenberg for me? And I might as well ask: Do the internists here normally follow these patients, or do FP privileges extend to post-MI care?"

Glenna grinned. "Dr. Sewell fought this

battle when she came here. Those patients can be cared for by either family practitioners or internists."

"Good. Since Mr. Nix is already Dr. Sewell's patient, we'll keep his care in the practice. In the meantime, let's get Dr. Rosenberg down here. We have ninety minutes from symptom onset to get an angioplasty done, and the clock's running."

A gentle tapping noise diverted Cathy's attention from the lab reports spread out on her desk. "Yes?"

Jane stood in the open doorway. "Doctor Sewell, there's a call on line one. It's Dr. Gardner."

"Thanks. Would you close the door on your way out?" Cathy punched the flashing button on the phone. "Elena, what happened? Where are you? We tried to call, but you didn't answer your cell phone."

"I'm at Summers County General. Apparently cell phone reception inside the hospital isn't very good. I've had to step outside to get a signal."

"Okay, that explains where you are. Now, why are you there?" Cathy heard the exasperation creeping into her voice. "I'm sorry. I didn't mean to come off sounding like your mother."

"My mother's been dead for so many years, I have no recollection of how she sounded."

Score one for Elena. "I apologize. Poor choice of words. What happened?"

She listened to Elena's story of Milton Nix's myocardial infarction. "Dr. Rosenberg did a cardiac cath. There was a forty percent blockage of the anterior descending coronary artery. Rosenberg was able to open it with a balloon angioplasty. He didn't think a stent was necessary."

"How did Mr. Nix come through it?"

"So far, so good. He's in the cardiac care unit. They tell me that FPs can take care of their own post-MI patients here. I'd imagine you'd want that, but if you'd feel better passing Nix off to an internist, I'll contact one. Your call."

"No, tell him and his wife that I'll be by this evening after I finish in the office."

"Do you want to do that? I can make sure he's okay before I leave, and you can see him on rounds in the morning."

"Fine. Be sure to call me if you have any questions. And thanks for taking care of this."

Cathy was about to hang up when she heard Elena's voice. "What was that?"

"I said I'm going to need a ride to pick up

my car when I leave the hospital."

"Why is that?"

Elena cleared her throat. "Well, I was at lunch with Frank Perrin when I got the call. He took me to the hospital, but my car's still back at the office."

Cathy had her choice of sharp retorts, but she bit back all those words. She fought to keep her voice level. "Do you think you'll be finished in another hour?"

"Should be."

"Be at the ER door at that time. I'll ask Will to come by and pick you up."

"Thanks."

Cathy hung up the phone and leaned back. She'd hoped Elena's relationship with Frank Perrin would be limited to the time they'd already spent together. It was nice of J. C. Dunaway to have someone guide the new doctor until she got her bearings. But why did he pick Frank Perrin? Surely J. C. was aware of the rumors.

Of course, Cathy knew they were more than rumors. She had some facts. But how much could she tell Elena?

She picked up the phone again and punched in Will's number. Bless his heart, he was always there to help out — with a ride for a stranded colleague or with advice for his wife who found herself facing an

206

ethical dilemma.

Will pulled his pickup into one of the parking spots designated "Medical Staff." He'd decided long ago that when he was acting as Cathy's agent he was sort of a medical staff member by proxy. *Thinking like a lawyer, again.* He was out of the vehicle and halfway to the emergency room door when it opened and Elena hurried out.

She climbed in and had buckled her seat belt by the time he resumed his spot behind the wheel. "Thanks for coming by," she said. "I guess I could have walked, but it's a bit too far. Besides that, there's a pretty good chance I'd get lost."

Will stifled a smile. He couldn't imagine anyone getting lost in this town. Then again, he'd lived here pretty much all his life. "It's not that bad. We'll drive you around and help you get your bearings. Pretty soon you'll know our fair city like the back of your hand." Will pulled out of the parking lot, turned left, and pointed. "The office building is up there, less than a mile away."

Elena ignored Will's pointing finger. "Cathy seemed angry that I had lunch with Frank Perrin. Was it because I didn't accept her invitation to lunch? Did I violate some sort of unwritten rule?"

"I don't recall putting anything into your employment contract about mandatory lunches with your associate. No, I think she was concerned that the person you ate with was Frank Perrin."

Will sensed more than saw Elena grow tense beside him. "Wow. I've made one friend since I arrived in town, and Cathy doesn't like him. Why?"

"Elena, none of us likes to spread rumors, and that's all I have."

"I understand, and I can make up my own mind when I have more facts, but what's the basis for those rumors? Does he kick dogs, take candy away from little children, give tickets for three miles an hour over the speed limit? What?"

Will wondered if this was a mistake, but Elena deserved to at least have more than a nonspecific warning. "All I can say is the consensus around town is that nice women don't go out with Frank Perrin."

Elena kept silent through the remainder of the trip. When Will pulled into the professional building's parking lot, she had the door open almost before the vehicle had rocked to a halt. "Thanks for coming by for me."

Will watched Elena beep her car unlocked, climb in, and drive away. Maybe he'd said too much. On the other hand, maybe he hadn't said enough.

"Good morning." Elena felt her words drop like icicles from a roof, cold and sharp. So be it. That was how she felt.

"Morning," Cathy replied, her voice about thirty degrees warmer than Elena's. "Why don't you get a cup of coffee and join me in my office? I'd like to clear the air about yesterday."

In a few minutes, Elena was looking across the desk at Cathy. Were they going to butt heads over something as insignificant as the person with whom Elena had had lunch? If that was the case, better to find out now instead of later.

Cathy leaned across the desk. "I'm afraid I came off a bit strong yesterday. First, let me repeat that I appreciate the way you handled Mr. Nix's case. This morning I spoke with Dr. Rosenberg, and he transferred care back to me. I plan to send Nix home tomorrow. Dr. Rosenberg agrees with me that you did a nice job."

"Thank you."

"I know you're miffed because I showed my disapproval of your having lunch with Frank Perrin. Let me make it clear. You're free to see anyone you want, so long as it doesn't keep you from your responsibilities to the patients in this practice."

Elena gripped her coffee mug tighter. "Then what was it? Because even though you didn't say it in so many words, you disapprove of Frank Perrin. Why?"

"What you've heard so far is only based on rumors, and that's unfair to you and to Frank." Cathy tented her fingers beneath her chin. "I guess it's time to give you more information."

"I finally got Will to admit that the consensus around town was that 'nice women don't go out with Frank Perrin.' Would you care to elaborate?"

Cathy drew in a deep breath and exhaled through pursed lips. "Okay. Part of this is covered by doctor-patient confidentiality, but since you're now my associate I suppose you're entitled to the information as well, since it concerns this practice."

Elena struggled to keep her tone neutral. "Thank you."

"Since I've been here, I've had two pregnant women come to me wanting abortions. I managed to convince one of them to carry the baby to term, but the other was adamant. I later learned that she drove to Dallas for the procedure."

"What does that have to do with Frank?"

Elena said.

"I'm coming to that. Both women were divorced, had been for a couple of years. Neither would name the person responsible for the pregnancy. One followed my recommendation to have the baby. Milton Gaines did the prenatal care and delivery. I later learned from him that Frank Perrin paid that bill."

Elena pondered this. "So Frank was a nice person helping out a woman who made a mistake. I'd think that would be a mark in his favor."

"The clinic in Dallas that terminated the pregnancy of the other woman called our office for information. It seems the receptionist accidentally transposed some numbers and their bill to the responsible party was returned." Cathy's lips tightened. "They wondered if we had the correct address for Frank Perrin."

Elena turned this over in her mind. "That's not exactly firm evidence that he was the father."

"Perhaps, but there are other rumors, ones I can't substantiate, so I won't repeat them. I guess I'd just encourage you to be careful."

"I think I've learned how to assess men," Elena said. *Of course, I thought I'd done a good job when I chose Mark, but look how that turned out. No, she had to put that aside and move on.* "But I appreciate your concern. So far, Frank has been the perfect gentleman. If I see any evidence that's about to change, I'll back away. Fair enough?"

"Fine," Cathy said. She picked up her mug, took a swallow, and grimaced. "I'm not especially fond of herbal tea, and I hate it when it's cold. I need to nuke this."

Elena rose and followed Cathy out of the office. So this attractive man, one who seemed to be interested in her, might be trouble? Well, she was used to trouble — dealt with it on a regular basis in the ER. She was sure she could handle it. And if it got too bad, she'd take the advice of a former president: "Just say no."

"Dr. Gardner, thank you for coming in." Nathan Godwin gestured Elena to a chair on the other side of his desk.

It struck Elena that what she'd observed before held true here: the smaller the man, the larger the desk. Maybe Godwin was compensating for his stature with a desk that appeared to be large enough to require its own ZIP code. Then again, perhaps he had a lot to do and needed room to work. She put that idea aside when she observed that the vast expanse of mahogany was unencumbered by papers. It held a phone with a handful of pushbuttons, a handsome pen and pencil desk set, and a single photo, the frame angled so she couldn't see it.

Godwin fiddled with the cufflinks on a spotless white dress shirt. "We have in hand your application for privileges at Summers County General Hospital, and they will be acted upon in the usual fashion. But right now we need to address an irregularity."

There was a discreet tap at the door. "Nathan, sorry I'm a bit late. I know how you hate to be kept waiting."

The speaker, a middle-aged man, was tall and muscular, a marked contrast to Godwin. Beneath his white lab coat, he wore an Izod golf shirt and khaki slacks. His wavy brown hair receded ever so slightly in a widow's peak. Rimless glasses did little to hide brown eyes that smiled, despite his neutral expression.

Godwin remained seated while he gestured the newcomer to the chair beside Elena. "Come in, Marcus. Dr. Elena Gardner, this is Dr. Marcus Bell. He's a general surgeon who also functions as our hospital chief of staff."

Bell offered his hand. "Pleasure to meet you, Dr. Gardner. I'm glad Cathy is getting some help. I was afraid she planned to work right up to the time of her delivery."

Before Elena could reply, Godwin cleared his throat and said, "Now that Dr. Bell is here, let's get down to business." He produced a thin folder from his desk drawer, centered it carefully on his desk, and tapped it with a manicured forefinger. "This is your application for privileges. It seems to be in order, but there's one problem."

Elena felt a vein in her temple begin to throb and wondered idly if either of the two men could see it. Had what she'd hoped to leave behind in Dallas reached out to grab her already?

Bell hitched himself forward in his chair and picked up the folder. "What Nathan is trying to say is that you saved Milton Nix's life yesterday before you jumped through all the hoops to be formally granted hospital privileges to do so. I've told him that the awarding of those privileges — already scheduled for the next Credentials Committee meeting — is a slam-dunk."

Godwin drew himself up to his full height, a difficult feat when sitting, and doubly difficult when you're only five six. "Dr. Bell, surely you recognize that privileges are granted to each physician based upon their training and qualifications. We've only had

Dr. Gardner's application for a short time. I have not yet seen all her references."

Dr. Bell didn't move, yet gave the impression of a lion crouched to spring on a helpless small animal. "Nathan, I liked it a lot better when our old administrator administered and left oversight of the medical staff to me. But, since you want to make this a contest of wills, I've talked with Dr. Amy Gross, the chair of the Family Practice Department where Dr. Gardner trained. She assures me that when her letter reaches me, along with those of others at that medical center, there will be no question of granting the requested privileges."

"But —"

Bell held up his hand like a traffic cop. "No 'buts,' Nathan. Just before coming here, I spoke by phone with each member of the Credentials Committee." He turned to Elena. "Dr. Gardner, it's my pleasure to advise you that, in a special called vote, all your requested privileges have been granted, retroactive to the moment you walked into the Emergency Room yesterday and took over Milton Nix's care." He beamed, perhaps as much at his triumph over Godwin as in welcome to Elena, and extended his hand. "Welcome aboard."

Elena felt the atmosphere in Godwin's office chill as though an unseen hand had run the thermostat to its lowest level. She tuned out as Godwin and Bell exchanged words that were far from pleasant.

Bell rose. "Well, Nathan, take this to the Board if you want to, but I'm sure you know that your margin there is razor-thin. I'd pick my battles if I were you." He touched Elena lightly on the arm. "Doctor Gardner, let's get out of here."

Godwin was still talking, although with less assurance, as the door closed behind them. Bell steered Elena past the elevators and said, "Let's get some coffee. I'd like to give you a better welcome to the staff than our esteemed administrator has."

They settled in at a table in the back of the cafeteria, each with a cup of coffee. Elena sipped hers and decided that it would never win any competitions for taste.

Bell apparently saw her grimace. "I know. Hospital coffee. And this was probably made for lunch, which was . . ." He consulted his watch. "Which was at least three or four hours ago."

"That's okay. I've had worse," Elena said. "Thanks for defending me to Mr. Godwin."

"My pleasure. As Chief of Staff, I count the day lost when I can't do battle with our Little Napoleon. But don't let him hear you call him Mr. Godwin. Our esteemed administrator is a physician, or so the diploma on his wall from St. George's University certifies."

"I don't believe I've heard of that one. Where is it?"

There was a twinkle in Marcus's eyes that his glasses couldn't fully hide. "Grenada."

"So he doesn't —"

"I think he may have a license to practice in some state, probably the one with the most lenient board exam, but apparently Dr. Godwin decided early in his career he was more cut out to be an administrator than a practicing doctor." Marcus pushed away his cup, still almost full. "Speaking of medical education, one of the responsibilities I'm saddled with is staff education. How about teaching the next CPR class? The groups are usually pretty small — mainly nurses who need to get certified or renew their certification in basic cardiopulmonary resuscitation."

"I guess I could do that."

"Deal. I'll have my secretary call your office with the details. And since we discussed hospital business, now I can turn in a voucher to get reimbursed for the two dollars I spent for your coffee." Marcus laughed. "I wish I could see Nathan's face

217

when that comes across his desk."

Elena pushed back her chair and reached for her purse. "I guess I'd better be running along. It was nice meeting you. And thanks for the coffee."

Marcus gestured for her to stay seated. "I've enjoyed it too, although I don't think either of us had much of an opportunity to get acquainted with the other. Why don't we rectify that by having dinner together sometime?"

Elena wondered how to handle this. She plastered a smile on her face. "Marcus, I'm flattered. But could I have a little time before I take you up on that?"

"Sure. I guess this is sort of a hectic time, getting settled in and all."

Might as well come right out with it. "I don't guess Cathy told anyone. I'm newly widowed. My husband died six months ago."

Marcus's expression didn't change — score one for him. He reached out and covered her hand with his own. "I'm so sorry. You have no way to know this, either, but I'm a widower, although my wound isn't as fresh as yours. If you'd like to get together sometime for a meal and to talk, please call me. But we won't call it a date. We'll call it therapy."

■ ■ ■ ■

"You hardly touched your dinner," Mrs. Kennedy said.

Elena forced a smile. "I'm sorry. Your cooking is wonderful, but I'm just not hungry. It's been a long day."

Matthew Kennedy blotted his lips and folded his napkin. "Would you like to talk about it?"

"No, I think I'd like to get some rest. Would you excuse me?"

In her room, Elena made a stab at rearranging her things, but she had no heart for activity of any kind. She kicked off her shoes and sprawled on the bed. Her eyes were closed, but she still saw the drama that was her life as it unfolded like the scenes of a particularly bad soap opera.

The ring of her cell phone brought her back to reality. She dug it out of her bag and answered the call.

"Elena, this is David. Are you free to talk?"

She almost cried. She'd come close to breaking down and dumping her problems on Pastor Kennedy, but something — some innate caution about letting anyone into her world — kept her from doing it. But David knew her innermost secrets. Well, almost all. And he'd be sympathetic.

"I'm free to talk as long as you want, or at least as long as my battery holds out." She added a second pillow under her head. "I never thought I'd say this, but I already miss the medical center."

"I figured you'd be glad to have your residency behind you. No more early morning rounds. No more poring over textbooks and journals to be able to answer the questions of your staff doctor. No more —"

"I still get up early, but it's to make rounds on my own patients. And if I have a question, there's no calling the staff doctor. I'm my own staff doctor. I have to look up the answers, chase down the weird symptoms."

"In other words, now you're a grownup."

Elena realized that what she felt wasn't a longing for the life she'd left behind. What she really missed was the feeling of security that fled with Mark's death. And she had no idea when — or if — that would come again.

"Enough about me," she said. "How about you? What's new? When will you be coming here? Can I do anything to help you get settled in?"

They talked on and on. That was one of the things she missed about having David near. They never seemed to run out of things to talk about.

"And have you heard that Dean Dunston is retiring?" David asked.

"Oh, I have some insider news on that front," she said. "It seems —"

She heard a click on the line and saw there was another call ringing through. The Caller ID read Sum Gen Hosp. "David, the hospital's calling. I'm covering the ER for Cathy, so I need to take it. I'll call you tomorrow."

She pushed the button to answer the new call. "Dr. Gardner."

A familiar voice responded. "Doctor, this is Glenna in the ER. The EMTs just brought in an elderly man found unconscious by his wife. They don't have a family doctor. Could you come in?"

"I'll be there in five minutes. Meanwhile, please —"

"We'll get an IV going, start him on oxygen, draw blood for a stat CBC and chemistries, put radiology on standby for an MRI of the head. Anything else?"

"Glenna, you're a wonder. I'm on my way."

Thirty minutes later, Elena turned to Glenna and said, "I think he's had a stroke. And with his obesity and his uncontrolled hypertension, it's probably a hemorrhagic

221

one. Let's get that stat MRI of the head, and I need to contact a neurosurgeon. Do we have one in town?"

"The closest one is Dr. Shelmire in Denton. Shall I try to get him on the phone?"

"Please ask the ward clerk to do that. Then I need some Labetalol. I'll give 20 milligrams slow IV push to see if we can drop his pressure some."

Glenna had the vial in her hand almost before Elena finished speaking.

Twenty minutes later, Elena cradled the phone against her shoulder as she reached for her cup of ultra-strong coffee from the ER break room. "I've got the MRI right here," she told Dr. Shelmire. She scanned the images. The story they told wasn't good. "It's definitely an intracerebral hemorrhage. I'm guessing a ruptured aneurysm or AVM."

"Okay, I'm leaving now," Shelmire said. "Talk with the family and tell them he's probably going to need an emergency craniotomy. And you might prepare them for the worst-case scenario."

Elena ended the call and headed for the waiting room where the patient's wife and two adult children waited. Although what Shelmire undoubtedly considered a worst-case scenario was death, she knew of an even worse outcome.

Elena swallowed hard to choke back the bitter taste of bad coffee and bile. She knew what she had to do. Talking with the family would be hard, but she'd done it before. Dealing with the consequences of the stroke and the surgery could be even harder, for them and for her.

Elena hovered behind Dr. Shelmire and admired the way he knelt to be on eye level with his patient's family. "Mr. Lambert is in the recovery room," he said. "A vessel in his brain burst, and the accumulation of blood pressed on some vital structures. Even though we got him to surgery within a couple of hours of the injury, some irreversible damage may have occurred."

The thin, elderly woman sat frozen as Shelmire delivered this news. A middle-aged man and woman flanked her, leaning in as though to keep her from falling. "How much damage?" she asked.

"We won't know until he begins to wake up . . . if he does. I don't look for him to regain consciousness for at least twenty-four hours. If he doesn't, we simply have to wait. Sometimes these patients surprise us."

And sometimes, they don't. Elena turned away and stared into the semidarkness of the waiting room. A television set mounted high in the corner, its sound muted, pelted the area around it with flickering strobes of color. Life moved on in the outside world. But here, for this family, life had come to a dead stop. Now all they could do was wait. Elena wondered if they'd pray, as she had. And if there was no apparent answer to those prayers, would these people ask her or Dr. Shelmire to end their loved one's misery?

Shelmire was patient with the family's questions, the answer to most of them being a simple "We have to wait and see."

He gave Elena a meaningful look, and she returned an almost imperceptible nod. He rose and nodded toward her. "Dr. Gardner practices here, and she'll be looking in on your husband. I'm in Denton, but I'll make it a point to come by every day. We'll consult freely by phone, and if I'm needed I'll come right over."

Elena spoke for the first time. "I haven't had time to have cards printed, but I'm entering the practice of Dr. Cathy Sewell. I'll write down my name and number for you. Feel free to call me anytime." She looked at her watch. A little past 1:00 a.m. "I'd suggest you go home, get a little sleep. This isn't a sprint. It's a marathon. We'll call you if something changes."

An hour later, Elena rubbed her eyes and yawned. Mr. Lambert's condition was stable. What seemed to be an excellent ICU nursing staff was monitoring his status. Maybe she could drive home for a quick nap — at least a shower and a change of clothes — before morning.

"If you need me in the next few hours, here's my cell phone number." Elena handed a card with the information to the charge nurse.

"Thanks, Dr. Gardner. We'll call you if there's any change. But we both know that's pretty unlikely."

Elena wove her way through the dark corridors of the hospital toward the parking lot where she'd left her car. As she stepped through the door, her cell phone chirped. Someone must have called while she was in the hospital and out of cell phone range. She leaned against the doorpost, luxuriating in the feel of the night air against her skin, and pressed the button to retrieve a voice mail message.

"You have one new call," the electronic voice proclaimed. "Wednesday, 12:01 a.m."

Elena wondered who could have called this late when she heard a whiskey alto voice that made her shiver despite the late June heat. "Don't think you can escape. I know what you've done, and you'll pay."

12

"Since you don't have any scheduled patients, you should have slept in a bit," Cathy said. "No need to get to the office this early after a late night."

Elena gripped her coffee cup like it was the last life preserver on the *Titanic*. "No, I've pulled all-nighters before. If I skip out every time I get a late-night call, I won't be much good to you, will I?"

Cathy tried to reassure her new associate. "Listen, you're not on trial here every minute of every day. Relax. Loosen up. You're doing fine."

"Apparently not in my choice of friends," Elena murmured into her cup.

"We've discussed that, and as far as I'm concerned, the matter's closed. Just be careful."

Elena touched the bottom of her cup to the bit of coffee she'd spilled on the break room table and began to form interlocking rings. "There . . . there may be some other problems too."

"Before I forget about it, this came for you. It must have arrived at the medical school after you cleared the campus, so they forwarded it here."

The return address on the legal-size envelope grabbed Elena's attention: Texas State Board of Medical Examiners. "This reminds me, I need to give them a change of address."

"Tell Jane. She'll take care of it for you," Cathy said.

Elena pulled out the single page, scanned it, and felt a hollowness in the pit of her stomach she hadn't experienced since her first roller coaster ride. "This must be some kind of terrible administrative foul-up."

"What?" Cathy asked.

Elena worked to stop the trembling of her hands so she could read. "We have received your request to voluntarily surrender your license to practice medicine. Please reply to this letter, advising in detail your reasons for this request. We must warn you that we are obligated to report any possible criminal activity associated with your actions."

"I take it you didn't make that request."

Elena swept her arms wide in a gesture of innocence, sending her coffee cup to the floor, where it shattered. "This is just one more bit of harassment. I thought that when I moved here it might stop."

Cathy decided that, as usual, her husband had been right. "Want to talk about it?"

"Not really. But I think I need to. You know about the phone calls I got after Mark's death?"

"I remember. From your mother-in-law."

Elena nodded. "That's what I thought. But before I left Dallas I got a letter from a lawyer. Lillian's dead. And she's been dead since shortly after Mark's death. Unless her obituary was some kind of sick hoax, there's no way the calls could have come from her."

Cathy took a moment to think that over. "So we don't know who was making the calls. Still, they should stop now that you've moved away from Dallas and changed your phone number. You did change it, didn't you?"

"I had my home phone disconnected. I gave this office as my forwarding address, and limited even that. As for my cell phone, I didn't think it was necessary to change it. Probably . . ." She ticked off numbers on her fingers. "Probably half a dozen people have the number, and I trust them all."

"So you're through with the calls."

Elena pushed her cup away and put her

fingertips to her temples. "Apparently not. I got another one at midnight last night — the same voice. It said, 'Don't think you can escape. I know what you've done, and you'll pay.' "

"But you've done nothing wrong."

"Evidently my caller doesn't hold that opinion."

"Let me talk with Will," Cathy said. "Maybe the investigator he uses can find out who's harassing you."

Elena moved her hands to the back of her neck and began to knead the muscles there. "There's more to it than that. I don't think I've done anything wrong. But there's a very real chance that I might in the future. I guess it's time for me to get some help."

Will made sure everyone was settled comfortably in his office. Elena and he had diet soft drinks, Cathy sipped from a bottle of cold water. He took a seat behind his desk, centered a fresh legal pad on the blotter, and uncapped a fountain pen. "Cathy has filled me in on what you all shared this morning, Elena. Suppose you tell us what it is that makes you afraid you'll do something wrong."

"I've told you about Mark's death. But I glossed over exactly how he came off life support. I stepped away from his ICU room for a bit. When I came back, they were removing his IV, EKG leads, everything. He was dead. I presumed he'd died in the short time I was gone. But later Mark's doctor, who was the chairman of Neurosurgery, called me on the carpet. I'd waffled about withdrawing life support, and when I finally made up my mind to allow it I wrote the DNR order myself."

"DNR?" Will asked.

"Do not resuscitate," Cathy explained. "And Elena's writing that order instead of conveying her wishes to the attending physician was a significant breach of protocol."

Elena nodded her assent. "The doctor — his name's Matney — the doctor also told me that he hadn't turned off Mark's respirator or authorized withdrawal of life support. He asked me if I'd done it."

Will opened his mouth, but Elena anticipated his question.

"Yes, if I'd done that myself, it would be another no-no. The thing is . . . I don't know if I did or not. I have no memory of the hour before Mark died."

Will looked up from his notes. "Can't you explain that on the basis of . . . what do you call it? Did you block out an unpleasant memory? Sort of a selective amnesia?"

231

"I'd like to accept that, but the story doesn't end there," Elena said.

Will glanced at the notes he'd made. *What more could there be to this story?* He soon found out, as Elena laid out the story of Chester Pulliam's death. "I'll admit it. When I couldn't convince his wife to authorize removing life support, I wanted to take matters into my own hands. I was alone in that room. I even went through the ways I could end his life so no one would ever know. But I didn't. Or at least I don't remember doing it."

"What about the DNR order in someone else's handwriting?" Cathy asked.

"I've thought about that a lot. I knew the signature on the chart wasn't my usual handwriting. That's why I gave Dr. Matney a sample of my signature and used that to bolster my argument that I had nothing to do with Pulliam's death."

"So what's wrong with that argument?" Will asked.

"What if I was functioning in a dream state? Our knowledge on the subject is still evolving. My handwriting might not be the same under those circumstances."

Will frowned. "What do you mean by 'functioning in a dream state?' "

Elena leaned forward as though to explain,

but Cathy waved her back. "No, let me tell him. Because I see where you're going, and why you might be worried about caring for patients in a situation similar to Mark's." She took a long pull from her water bottle. "Elena is afraid she was in a fugue state."

Will said, "Fugue?"

Cathy smiled, obviously enjoying the opportunity to teach her husband something. "I know you think a fugue is some kind of a musical composition that you don't like, but this is different. It's a neuropsychiatric condition. A person in a fugue state can carry out actions with no conscious volition or subsequent memory of their actions."

"Wouldn't that be self-limited? And couldn't it still be due to the stress of Mark's death?"

"Not necessarily," Cathy said. "We used to think fugue states were part of the psychiatric spectrum, but there's a lot of new evidence that they may be related to seizure disorders. And if you've had one, you could have more."

Will made a few more notes. "I guess you'd know more than I do about confirming that diagnosis." He capped his pen. "So now we have the whole story."

"Not quite," Elena said. She turned to Cathy. "Did Dr. Matney contact you and say anything about my being on probation here?"

Cathy's bewildered look answered the question before she confirmed it. "No, not at all. Why should you be?"

"So that was a bluff," Elena said.

"What's Dr. Matney's stake in all this, anyway?"

"He's in the running for Dean Dunston's job, and he's anxious to avoid negative publicity for his department. That's why he wanted to rush me off the campus."

"You mean he just wanted the whole thing to go away," Cathy said.

"Right," Elena said. "I was worried about Matney and my reputation, but something bigger is at stake now. It's possible I might have taken two patients off life support and not even realized it. Now I'm participating in the care of another patient who might be in the same situation. What if I do it again?"

This time Will didn't reach for his pen. Instead, his mind churned with the legal ramifications of the case. Was ending the life of a patient kept alive only by artificial means subject to prosecution for murder? Or manslaughter? Could a fugue state be the basis for a defense based on diminished capacity? Or was someone manipulating these circumstances to cast suspicion on

Elena, bent on wrecking her professional career?

While Elena and Cathy were tossing around phrases like "neurotransmitters" and "subconscious wish fulfillment" and "dissociative reaction," Will tilted his chair back, closed his eyes, and uttered a silent prayer. He certainly hoped God would help out here, because he didn't have the foggiest notion how to proceed.

Elena paused outside the examining room door and scanned the information on the page in her hand. Maria Gomez was not only her first patient of the morning; she was her first patient in private practice. Well, her first office patient, at least.

Mr. Lambert was still in the ICU, still dependent on the respirator, still in a coma with no signs of regaining consciousness. Elena was grateful that Cathy had taken over daily rounds on him. She didn't want to be worried about what she might do if another episode came upon her. If there truly were episodes. The jury was still out on that.

Enough. Time to go to work. Elena tapped on the door and opened it. According to the chart, the woman perched on the edge of the examining table was seventeen years old, but she looked twice that age. Her thin arms and legs were in marked contrast to her distended belly. The record sheet listed a chief complaint of "pregnant." Elena figured she could have made that diagnosis at a distance of fifty feet. The challenge now was what to do about it.

"Good morning, I'm Dr. Gardner." Elena moved a step closer. "How can I help you?"

"She does not speak English." Elena's eyes moved to the young man perched on a chair in the corner. His clothes were clean but very worn: faded jeans, a T-shirt, tennis shoes. *"¿Habla usted español?"*

"Solo un poco. Just a little."

The man's look of disappointment confirmed to Elena that, once more, her lineage had betrayed her. She could imagine his joy at seeing a doctor so obviously Hispanic fade when he discovered her Spanish was limited.

"Your English is fine," Elena said. "If you don't know a word, give it to me in Spanish. I speak some, just not a lot."

"Okay." He swallowed. "Maria is . . . *embarazada.*"

"Yes, I can see she's pregnant. What brings you here?" His puzzled expression told her to stop relying on idioms. Try again. "What can I do to help?"

"Her time is coming near. She has the . . ."
Again, a hesitation as he searched. "She has
dolor de cabeza severo. And sometimes the
things she sees, they are . . . how you say,
not clear."

Elena nodded. Red flags went up immediately. A pregnant woman with severe
headaches and fuzzy vision. "Has she been
eating?"

Embarrassment colored his face. "Sometimes there is no food. I get work where I
can, but . . ." He spread his hands.

So add poor nutrition to the mix. Elena
recognized that getting the entire history
would be a slow process. She already had a
good idea of the problem, and she was itch-
ing to get the pieces of the puzzle that would
tell her how severe it was. "I need to do an
examination. The nurse will prepare her,
and I'll be right back. Do you want to wait
outside?"

"Please, no. I am her *esposo* . . . her
husband." He beamed at finding the word.
"And I must tell her in Spanish what is
needed."

Twenty minutes later, Elena stood outside
the door of the exam room and considered
her findings. Blood pressure sky high. Visual
symptoms. Headache. Elena could make
this diagnosis in her sleep: toxemia of

pregnancy. No convulsions — yet — so it was still preeclampsia. But both mother and child were at grave risk without immediate treatment.

Cathy emerged from the next room, and Elena beckoned her over. "Let me ask you about this one," Elena said. "Young woman, probably eight months pregnant, preeclamptic."

"Let's see what you've got." Cathy studied the sheet, now covered with Elena's notes. She raised her eyebrows, and Elena figured she'd seen the blood pressure readings.

Cathy handed the chart back. "No OB, I guess."

"Nope. I haven't asked, but I'm pretty sure they're both illegals. She doesn't speak English, but her husband does okay with it."

Cathy nibbled at her thumbnail. "Summers County General is the designated regional medical center. Have Jane call the nurse coordinator there. She'll arrange for care by one of our OB's."

"So we can do this locally? No need to send her to Dallas?"

"Not for this. Sure, if there's something so unusual we can't handle it, we send patients to Parkland. But we have good doctors here. There's some kind of administrative payment deal in place so we're re-imbursed for handling indigent care. I don't worry too much about that. That's one way Nathan Godwin earns his pay."

"Good to find that out." Elena scribbled a quick note on the margin of the chart. "You know, I thought I was totally ready to go out into practice. I figured there wasn't anything a patient could throw at me that I didn't have an answer for. But one thing they didn't prepare me for was cutting through administrative red tape to get care for patients. I'd mastered the system at the medical center, but it never occurred to me that I'd have to learn a whole new one here."

Cathy smiled. "Don't worry. You'll find your way through the jungle pretty quickly. Meanwhile, just keep on taking care of the patients."

Elena was about to re-enter the exam room when Cathy called to her. "Oh, and Will wants us to get together again this evening. He has a suggestion about shedding some light on your mysterious caller and the circumstances of Chester Pulliam's death."

Elena froze. She wished she could ignore the whole problem, let it go away. But in her heart, she knew she had to face it. And she was afraid of what she might find.

Elena wasn't really hungry, but the dictum of "eat when you can, sleep when you can" was deeply ingrained. It probably wouldn't hurt her to grab a bite of lunch in the hospital cafeteria. She might even have the opportunity to meet more of the staff.

She saw a familiar face alone at a table for two in the corner. Elena wove through the cafeteria balancing a tray with a ham sandwich and a glass of iced tea. When she arrived at the table, its occupant looked up, smiled, and said, "Dr. Gardner. Would you like to join me?"

"I'd love to." As Elena unloaded her tray, she sneaked a peek at the nametag pinned onto the woman's scrub top. In the ER, Elena hadn't picked up the nurse's last name. The tag gave her that information: Glenna Dunn, RN.

"So are you settled in?" Glenna asked.

"Pretty well," Elena said. "And I want to thank you again for telling me we have an interventional radiologist here. There are so many things to learn when you come to a new hospital — especially when you're thrown in suddenly."

Glenna waved it off. "No problem. And I

hear Mr. Nix is doing well."

"How long have you been working in the ER?"

"About five years now. I planned to quit work and be a stay-at-home mother after Bill and I had children, but —" She bit her lip and stared down at the remains of her salad.

"But you can't have children? Is that it?"

"You might say that," Glenna said. "Bill and I were married less than a year ago. He thought our little apartment was too small, especially if a baby came along. He was driving a truck on weekends to make enough money for the down payment on a house. And then . . . then, about six weeks ago, he was in an accident. Head-on crash. It was terrible." Tears welled up and spilled onto the table.

Elena pulled a tissue from her purse and handed it to Glenna. "I know how you must feel. My husband died recently too."

Glenna looked up with an expression of pure anguish. "Bill didn't die. He had a severe head injury with a massive amount of intracranial bleeding. The neurosurgeon operated, but there was too much damage. Bill's been in a coma ever since. He was in ICU for a week. When he was finally able to come off life support they put him on a regular ward. Now he's in the south wing, the old part of the hospital. They call it 'extended care,' but it's not like he gets a lot of care. The doctor says he won't ever wake up, but he could live for years like this. I don't know what I'll do when the insurance benefits run out. I can't even think about it right now. No, Bill didn't die. But every day I find myself wishing he had."

Elena felt a lump the size of Kansas in her throat. She swallowed hard. "I'm so sorry. I didn't know."

Glenna dried her eyes, excused herself, and hurried off.

Elena was still at the table, her sandwich forgotten, when she felt a gentle touch on her shoulder. She turned and saw Marcus Bell behind her. "I saw Glenna rush out. Did she tell you about her husband?"

Elena gestured for Marcus to sit. "Yes, I'm afraid I put my foot in my mouth. Poor lady dissolved in tears." She sipped her tea, then shoved it aside. She suspected her lunch would remain uneaten today.

"It's a sad story. And every patient who comes into the ER with a head injury seems to freshen the wound. I've asked Glenna if she wanted to transfer to another unit. Her answer's always the same. 'If I can keep another family from facing what I have to live with every day, my work will be worthwhile.' "

Elena wondered if she might have discontinued Mark's life support while in a fugue state to avoid the living death now experienced by Glenna's husband. Had she been fulfilling a subconscious wish? And could she have done the same thing with Chester Pulliam?

"Penny for your thoughts," Marcus said.

"Sorry. Glenna's story just brought back memories of my own husband's death."

"You know, I'd like to offer you that non-date I mentioned earlier. Why don't I buy you dinner on Saturday night? You can talk, we can commiserate, and I assure you I'll be a perfect gentleman."

Elena felt herself tugged in two directions. She'd love some companionship, especially that of someone who'd also lost a spouse. But she got the definite impression that Marcus wanted a relationship that could move beyond the "non-date" phase. Was she ready for that? And if so, was Marcus the one? No, she couldn't make that decision. Not yet. She looked him full in the face. "Marcus, I appreciate the offer, and someday I may be able to take you up on it. But not right now. I hope you'll understand."

The three people gathered in Will's office showed signs of a hard day. Will slouched in his office chair, his collar unbuttoned and his tie askew. Cathy had her feet propped on an extra chair and kept poking at her ankles, apparently trying to decide if the swelling was significant. Elena did her best to look cool, but she couldn't get away from the phone call that had come before she left the office.

"Elena, it's Frank Perrin."

The sound of his voice had made her feel like a schoolgirl again, thrilled that the captain of the football team had called her and a little nervous that she might say the wrong thing. "Frank, it's good of you to call. I'm sorry we had to cut our lunch short the other day. And I really appreciate your using your lights and siren to get me to the hospital quickly. That made a big difference to the patient."

" 'Protect and serve,' that's us," Frank said lightly. "I was wondering if we could make up for that shortened lunch by having dinner together this evening."

Elena almost laughed. Two dinner invitations in one afternoon. Her social life was picking up, and she was nowhere near ready for it. She was exhausted, both physically and emotionally. And she still had the meeting with Will and Cathy.

"If you have to think about it that long, maybe I shouldn't have called." Frank's voice was even, but she sensed an unpleasant undercurrent there.

"No, I was just going over my schedule. Actually, I have a meeting tonight. After that, all I want to do is go home and crash." *Keep it simple. Let him down easy.* "Can I get a rain check?"

"Sure. We'll try again later. Have a good evening."

"Hey, are you with us?" Cathy's voice brought Elena back to the present. "You looked like you were a million miles away."

"Sorry. I can't get my mind off that pregnant girl I saw this morning. Think the OB assigned to her case would mind if I dropped by to check on her?"

"Not at all," Cathy said. "In the morning, call and see which doctor it is. If you go about the time he usually makes rounds, you can introduce yourself."

"If you two doctors are through talking shop, I'd like to get going. We've all had a hard day. Elena, I need your permission to have an investigator look into both the deaths of your husband and Mr. Pulliam. I'll employ him, and if you engage me as your counsel, anything he finds will be privileged and protected."

"You mean that if he discovers I actually did discontinue life support in both cases, that won't necessarily make me end up in court," Elena said. "Is that it?"

"Yes. The guy I want to use — Ramon Campos — is based out of Dallas. He's discreet, very trustworthy, and does a great job of staying under the radar. I can pretty much guarantee that no one will ever know he's investigating these matters."

Elena bit her lip. She hated to open what could be a Pandora's box. "What about the midnight phone calls?"

"That's part of the package. I want him to find out who's been calling you and why."

"How much would this cost?" Elena asked. "I haven't drawn a paycheck yet, and my financial situation isn't very good right now. Between my student loans and the expenses of Mark's death, I'm pretty far in the hole."

Will waved that away. "I'm going to take this on *pro bono,* and I'll handle the expenses of the investigation. You can pay me back after you're on your feet."

Elena felt like she was poised on the edge of the high board. She could jump or back down the ladder. The only sound in the room was a faint click followed by a low whoosh that signaled the air conditioner starting to combat the evening heat.

"Your choice," Cathy said. "But I think you're going to regret it if you don't confront this issue."

"I'm willing — no, I'm anxious to find out who's been calling me. But I don't know how your investigator can talk with the ICU nurses and staff and discover anything about the deaths of those two patients without making a lot of people suspicious. And if Dr. Matney gets wind of this, I can guarantee he'll reach out and do something to get back at me for stirring the pot again."

"So we put that on the back burner. But you will let Ramon check out the calls?" Will asked.

"Okay," Elena said. She reached for her purse. "Do I pay you a dollar or something?"

Will smiled. "No, that's not necessary. There's a Texas case or two upholding the concept that the attorney-client relationship can be implied without the payment of a fee. I can show you the reference if you're

247

worried. I think it's *Perez v. —*"

"I think she gets it, Will." Cathy turned to Elena. "If you won't let the investigator try to discover what happened in the ICU when Mark and Mr. Pulliam were taken off life support, there's another way to get information without Matney finding out."

What else? All Elena wanted to do was go home. Well, not home, but the room in the back of the Kennedy home that was her temporary quarters.

"Remember at our first interview I mentioned a therapist who'd helped me?"

Elena wasn't sure where this was headed. She nodded but kept silent.

"How would you feel about letting him hypnotize you?" Cathy asked. "He might be able to regress you to the times when the respirators were turned off. We could find out if you were the one who did it."

Elena's stomach started churning. "I don't want . . . I can't even think about going through the experience of Mark's death again. Why don't we let the investigator do his work first? I guess I'd try the hypnosis if it's a last resort, but it still won't answer the questions about the phone calls. And if I'm in any danger, I think it must be from the woman who's making those calls."

Will leaned across the desk, his fingertips

steepled. "Have you considered that the two situations might be unrelated? The phone calls and the patient deaths?"

"I don't know. I just don't know." Elena pushed back her chair and rose. "Listen, I appreciate everything you're doing, both of you. But I've had all I can take for one day. Will, thanks for your help. I assume you'll let me know what the investigator finds out. And if there's any information he needs from me, give him my cell phone number."

The night air was warm, but Elena shivered as she hurried to her car. Halfway to the Kennedy home, she remembered she hadn't eaten. The Dairy Queen was only a few blocks out of her way, but she'd have to make a quick right turn. She braked hard and almost skidded around the corner. She was blinded a few seconds later by a set of headlights in her rearview mirror. The car dropped back, and the glare disappeared.

She pulled to the drive-up window and ordered a hamburger and a Diet Coke. A few minutes later she was on her way home, sipping on the drink and wondering how and when her troubles would ever end.

As she climbed out of her car, Elena decided she felt too dirty to eat. First, she'd luxuriate in a hot tub. After that, she could think about eating. She'd eaten enough cold burgers in recent years, so one more wouldn't matter.

In her bedroom, Elena dropped her clothes on the closet floor, intending to stuff them in the hamper later, and wrapped herself in a robe. She padded across the room in her bare feet, anxious to feel the hot water relax her taut muscles.

Maybe reading in the tub would help. She'd brought a few books with her. She pulled one from the bookcase, but it slipped through her fingers. As she bent to retrieve it, her head turned toward the window.

Her scream seemed to go on forever.

13

Will yawned and looked around his parents' kitchen table. His mother and father sat across from Elena, two bulwarks of safety and comfort. Cathy was in the chair beside Elena, struggling to find a comfortable position for her gravid bulk, yet obviously unwilling to leave the side of her frightened associate. Will decided he was expected to take charge of the session.

"Exactly what did you see tonight?" Will held his coffee cup in both hands and looked through the steam at Elena.

"I was about to step into the tub when I glanced toward the window and saw a face. I screamed and ran out of the room."

"Did you recognize him?" Will asked.

Elena shook her head. "I only got the impression of a face, almost like it was floating there at the level of the window. No details."

Cathy patted Elena's arm. "Weren't the

blinds closed?"

Elena ducked her head. "This morning while I was putting on my makeup I raised the blinds in the guest room for more light. Tonight, I was so tired I didn't bother to lower them. I mean, there are gauze curtains across the window, and there are thick bushes outside screening it. I guess this is my fault."

"It's no one's fault," Will said. "Did you call the police?"

Elena huddled deep into her robe. "Your parents insisted."

"And?"

"A patrolman showed up about half an hour later."

Will decided he'd had uncooperative witnesses who were more forthcoming than this. Then again, the witnesses hadn't recently been scared half out of their wits. *Gently.* "What did the patrolman find?"

Elena remained silent. Will looked at his father. "Dad?"

"Norm Thompson came by. Nice young lad. You probably know him."

"I do." *Patience, patience.* "What did he say?"

"Norm found some footprints in the flower bed outside the guest bathroom window. He called them 'partials.' Said there wasn't enough there to identify the prowler even if they caught him. He asked the dispatcher to have a car swing by here every hour or so for the rest of the night. Said they'd keep an eye out for strangers in the neighborhood."

Will was pretty sure the matter would die right there unless there was a repeat performance.

Cathy apparently had the same thoughts. The look she gave him carried a simple message: do something.

"Elena, do you have any idea who might have done this?" No sooner were the words out of his mouth than Will realized how foolish the question was. "Never mind. You're stressed. Why don't you get some rest? We can talk about this tomorrow."

"No!" Elena snapped. "There's no chance that I'll sleep tonight. Can we talk about who it might be? And, more important, what we can do to put an end to it?"

Will wished he had a legal pad. He always thought better when he could make notes. "Okay. We have to start with the possibility this was a random thing. Peeping Toms aren't unheard of, although frankly I haven't heard reports of any in the city lately. That doesn't mean one couldn't have wandered here tonight, though."

"Calling it random doesn't make me feel any more comfortable," Elena said. "He might have . . . might have liked what he saw. He could come back again."

"In that case, let's see if we have any suspects. Are there men you've met since you've been in town who might have done this?" Cathy asked.

"I've been in town for, what, less than a week? And no one I've met has acted creepy. Except maybe that EMT. He seemed antagonistic toward me from the moment we met. And when we ran into each other later, he was pretty surly."

"That would be Eric Burson," Cathy said. "I know what you mean about acting surly. But I don't think you should take that personally. Eric's wife died several years ago of ovarian cancer. They lived in another town then, and the doctor who first saw her missed the diagnosis. After she died, Eric moved here, mainly to get away from his memories, I think. He told people he decided to train as an EMT 'so he could help others.' Really, I think it was so he would come in contact with doctors frequently enough to criticize them."

"Would he do something like this?" Elena asked.

Will shook his head. "Hard to say. But we

can keep him in mind. Who else?"

"Nobody jumps out at me," Elena said. "Other than Eric, the men I've met have been very nice."

"Seeming nice doesn't mean they don't have human frailties." The group turned toward Matthew Kennedy, who spread his hands. "I've known some people who were to all appearances 'nice,' but their sins would make your hair curl. None of us is exempt from the human condition, you know."

Will cringed. *Oh, Dad. Don't start a sermon.* But the elder Kennedy leaned back in his chair, his point made.

"What about Frank?" Will asked.

Elena screwed up her face. "I know everybody tells me to watch out for Frank Perrin. It's been sort of like parents who warn their daughter about who she should and shouldn't date. But so far he's probably been nicer to me than a lot of people. I refuse to consider him a suspect."

"So we've struck out in the suspect department," Will said. "The bottom line is we have no idea who could have spied on you."

Elena seemed to shrink a bit. If the expression in her eyes had been a mystery to Will when they first met, there was no mystery about it now. It was fear.

Will hurried on, trying to reassure her. "For now, be cautious. Keep an eye out for people following you, especially at night."

"I thought someone might have followed me when I left the meeting at your office," Elena said. "But I dismissed that as being paranoid."

"There's something we haven't considered," Cathy said.

"What?"

"We've talked about the stalker being a man, but that's not necessarily true. We haven't mentioned your midnight caller. Could the face at the window have been a woman? Maybe it wasn't the work of a Peeping Tom. Maybe it was one more thing meant to frighten you."

True to her prediction, there was no sleep for Elena that night. She lay in bed, tossing and turning, the light on to dispel the shadows that mocked her as they turned into her stalker. The few times she drifted into a fitful slumber her dreams were of the tribunal, this time sitting in judgment of her for not lowering her blinds.

Cathy had told her not to come to work on Friday morning, but some mixture of pride and stubbornness brought Elena awake at the usual hour. She dressed (with the blinds carefully and tightly closed), armed herself with one of Dora's biscuits and a cup of coffee, and drove to the office.

Elena worked hard to keep her mind on her patients, skipped lunch in favor of reading journals at her desk, and managed to put one foot in front of the other until the work day was over. At last, she heaved a sigh and dropped into the chair behind her desk. *Her desk. Her office.* Nice sound to the words. It was just now soaking in. If things ever settled down, she felt as though she could enjoy it here.

She folded her white coat and laid it on top of her backpack. She'd need to take the coat home and wash it this weekend. Elena hadn't asked her landlady about using their washer, but as nice as the Kennedys had been, there shouldn't be any problem.

"Hey, don't bother taking that coat home." Cathy's voice made Elena jump.

"Sorry. You startled me. What was that?"

"Toss your coat in the hamper in the work room. We have a laundry service. Get a clean one Monday morning. And in a week or so we'll have some with your name embroidered on the pocket. Maybe that will help you feel more at home."

"Sorry," Elena said. "I guess all those

years of laundering my own coat sort of ingrained the practice." She gestured to Cathy to come in and sit down. "Remember all the symbolism of these coats?"

Cathy eased into the visitor's chair across the desk from Elena. "Yeah. Short white coats for the medical students, mid-length ones for the residents, long coats for faculty and attendings."

"My . . . Mark gave me this one. He didn't know it was too long to wear while I was in residency. I kept it in the back of the closet. I could hardly wait for the day when I finished my training, and he could see me wear it. Then . . ." Elena swallowed hard and stared down at the desk.

"Well, he'd be proud of you now," Cathy said. When there was no response, she added, "Want to talk about it? About Mark?"

Mention of Mark made Elena think of the note. The time she'd shared with Mark, no matter how short, seemed so perfect. Now she wondered when he'd begun to drift away from her. Or had he been unfaithful from the start? She'd determined to put it out of her mind, and she strengthened that resolve. "No, I think I'd better move on. But thanks."

Cathy struggled to lift her bulk, making

use of the chair arms to lever herself to her feet. "I'm going to the hospital to make rounds. Would you like to go?"

Elena hesitated.

"C'mon," Cathy said. "I'll sweeten the deal. Come with me, I'll introduce you to some more of the staff, and then Will and I'll take you out for dinner. This is Dr. Brown's weekend on call. Turn it loose for a few hours. You deserve an evening out."

An hour later, Elena stood at Charlie Lambert's bedside in the ICU, looking through his chart while Cathy answered Mrs. Lambert's questions. Now, three days after his craniotomy, he showed a few encouraging signs. There were some spontaneous efforts to breathe, although they were too shallow and slow to allow removal from the ventilator. Currently, the small bag of IV fluid with added Dopamine piggybacked into Lambert's main line was shut off, which told Elena he was maintaining his blood pressure on his own.

Elena eased her hand down to the foot of the bed, where Lambert's right foot protruded from the covers. She squeezed his Achilles tendon and was sure she felt him withdraw his leg a fraction of an inch. Reacting to pain now. Another good sign.

Cathy wound up her conversation with

Mrs. Lambert. "Do you have any questions for me?" she asked.

"Nothing medical, I guess. You and Dr. Shelmire have made it pretty clear. There's progress, but we won't know the final outcome for a while."

"There *may* be progress. It's too early to be sure. And if he does improve, we don't know if he'll recover fully," Cathy warned. "He might have weakness, difficulty speaking, all sorts of problems. And he'll probably need physical therapy."

"I don't care," Mrs. Lambert said. "Just as long as he's alive, I'll devote my life to caring for him." She dabbed at her eyes with the end of a balled-up tissue. "But we have another problem."

"What's that?"

"You see, Charlie lost his job a while back, and our insurance has lapsed. He's not quite old enough for Medicare. I work and bring in a little money — barely enough to keep us going, but too much for us to qualify for Medicaid. And this morning the administrator was arguing with Dr. Shelmire outside the door. Mr. Godwin, I think his name is. He wanted Charlie transferred to another hospital. He said something about 'we're not a charity hospital, and we can't afford this.' "

"I hope Dr. Shelmire —"

"Oh, the doctor stopped that really quick. He said Charlie wasn't going to be moved just to help a . . . I can't say the words he called Mr. Godwin . . . just to help him meet his budget. But it worries me that there's this problem. I don't know how we're going to pay the hospital bill."

Cathy patted the woman's arm. "You let Dr. Shelmire and me take care of this. Your concern is with your husband." She nodded toward Elena. "Either Dr. Gardner or I will be by tomorrow morning. If you need anything before then, ask the nurses to call."

As they waited for the elevator, Elena said, "Sounds like Nathan Godwin is a piece of work. Did I tell you how he and Marcus Bell clashed over my hospital privileges?"

"Nathan wants everyone to kowtow to him. When I first came here, Marcus and I had our differences, but I'll say this for him. He puts the best interests of the patients ahead of anything else. It's too bad they cut back his authority as chief of staff."

"Why was Godwin brought in?"

"This is a municipal hospital with an elected board. Some of the board members thought it was time to take the control out of the hands of the doctors. They called it 'being fiscally responsible.' I call it posturing. But we make do. Most of us have learned to work around Nathan."

"Where to next?" Elena asked.

"I thought we'd go by —" Cathy stopped, bent over, and clutched her abdomen with both hands.

Elena saw beads of sweat form on Cathy's face. "What's wrong?"

"I've been having contractions all day. At first I thought they were just Braxton-Hicks contractions, and they'd stop. But this one was pretty severe. Would you go back to the ICU and get a wheelchair for me? I think I'd better go down to OB and have them call my doctor."

Dr. Milton Gaines leaned against the window ledge in Cathy's room in the OB ward and rolled his head from side to side in an obvious effort to ease tight muscles. "Tough day. I'll be happy when my new associate arrives."

"I know what you mean," Cathy said. She lay in bed, clothed in a hospital gown. There was an IV running at a slow drip into a vein on the back of her hand. A vital signs monitor beeped softly in the background. "It's a good thing Dr. Gardner is here a bit early, since you tell me I'm going to be on enforced bed rest for a while."

"Let's take it a day at a time," Gaines said. "You know the drill for pre-term labor. We'll watch you here overnight. If you don't have more contractions and your exam doesn't change, I'll probably let you go home. But I'd like to let the baby get a little more mature before you go into actual labor, and the best way to do that is to keep you on bed rest for a week or so. After that, we'll see."

Cathy felt as though she was being tugged in opposite directions by a team of horses. Since starting medical school, she'd taken pride in working despite all kinds of hindrances: snowstorms, flooded roads, unbelievable fatigue, and headaches that would fell a bull elephant. But now the health of her baby was at stake. Milton Gaines said she needed to be at bed rest, so bed rest it would be.

Will was by her side, where he'd been since responding to the OB nurse's phone call. He held Cathy's hand and gave it an occasional squeeze. He'd been uncharacteristically silent during Gaines's exam and the discussion afterward. Now he broke that silence. "Cathy, if you don't do just exactly what Milton says, I swear I'll hog-tie you and nail the door to your bedroom shut."

Cathy laughed in spite of herself. This was

about as blunt as she'd ever seen Will. "Don't worry, honey. I'll be a good girl. Elena can fill in, and I'll bet Dr. Brown will help out as well."

She kept the smile plastered on her face, but Cathy was already wondering how her patients would react to the choices presented to them in her absence: a Latina female or an African American male. Well, it was time that the population of Dainger was introduced to a little ethnic diversity.

Elena took one last look at the number on the slip of paper. She raised the phone but paused when she heard the cry of an infant rising above the noise of the OB ward. Life was still going on all around her, and a new one had just been added.

She took a deep breath and punched in the number. "Dr. Brown? This is Elena Gardner. I'm Cathy Sewell's new associate." The word still sounded strange to Elena. Associate. She was part of a practice. And, for who knew how long, she would be the only doctor in that practice. "I'm sorry we haven't had a chance to meet personally. I've been here less than a week, and it's been a whirlwind."

Brown's voice was as soft and smooth as the mocha fudge ice cream that Elena favored, with not a hint of an accent, either regional or ethnic. "Think nothing of it. I've been worried that Cathy didn't have any help lined up. I'm glad you're here, and I can only imagine how busy you've been since you arrived."

Elena gripped the receiver tighter. "I'm afraid I'm going to be busier, and so are you. Cathy was admitted to the OB ward at Summers County General tonight in pre-labor. The contractions have stopped, and the baby's fine, but her OB wants her on bed rest for at least a week. Of course, I'll do as much as I can, but until I get a bit more familiar with practice patterns here in Dainger, you may find yourself seeing more patients as well."

There was no real mirth in Brown's low chuckle. "I'm happy to see as many as necessary, but I think you'll find that there are a number of the fine citizens of our community who balk at treatment by a doctor of color."

Elena's cheeks burned. "If they have reservations in that regard, they may find themselves driving a ways to get medical care. I neglected to tell you. My maiden name is Perez."

If Brown was surprised, his voice didn't show it. "Interesting. Well, I'm glad you're here. Don't hesitate to call me if I can help you. And after you've had a bit of time to catch your breath, you must have dinner with me and my wife. She's Jamaican, and her jerk chicken is wonderful."

Elena hung up, looking forward to meeting Emmett Brown in person and reassured that he'd be a good man to have in her corner if she needed medical backup.

She saw Will come out of Cathy's room. "How's she doing?"

"She's fine. No more contractions after those she had earlier. She's going to take a nap while I get her some magazines."

"Anything I can do?"

"You're doing enough." He took a few more steps away from Cathy's door. "We both think you're going to do fine here. I think the practice is in good hands."

She was in the parking lot, halfway to her car, when her cell phone rang. When she checked the caller ID, she could feel the smile spread across her face. "David. So good to hear from you."

"I've been intending to call all week, but it's been crazy. One of the other residents was sick, and I ended up pulling a couple of thirty-six-hour shifts."

"I thought the new regulations —"

"They do, but babies don't know about

266

Resident Review Commission rules against working long hours. When they're ready to get here, they're ready, and I figured someone should be here to welcome them."

Elena climbed into her car and leaned back in the seat. "I've lost all track of time. How many more days until you arrive?"

"That's another reason I called. The guy I've been covering for is back at work now, and he's going to take my shifts next week. Dr. Cobb said I could leave after today. Tomorrow morning I'm going to head for Dainger. How about dinner tomorrow night?"

"You bet. My treat. Call me after you get into town."

"Sounds great. But what about you? What's new with you?"

"Oh, David. Where do I begin?"

14

Elena pulled her car out of the hospital parking lot, anxious to get home and put this week behind her. Talking with David had made her anxious to see him tomorrow. It would be good to have him here. A phone conversation was a poor substitute for physical presence. And their separation had made her think about what he meant to her. *You shouldn't go there. It's too soon.* Nevertheless, even if David just provided a friendly shoulder to lean on, she'd be happy to see him.

The long summer day was fading to night, and she flicked on her headlights. She'd heard somewhere that the most dangerous time to drive was the hour before full darkness descended. The last thing she needed was an accident.

She'd gone about three blocks when she glanced into the rearview mirror and saw a set of headlights. *Stop worrying. Not every car behind you belongs to a stalker.* Elena wondered if she knew the town well enough to make a few turns. Should she risk getting lost, possibly in a bad neighborhood?

She chanced a left turn. A half-minute later, the headlights appeared behind her. A right turn, then another left put her back on course for home, with the headlights trailing along. There was no doubt in her mind now. The question was what to do about it.

The intersection coming up was a major one, with a four-way stop sign. Elena was pretty sure that a right turn would take her toward the sheriff's office. Without turning on her blinker or hitting the brakes, she decelerated and cranked the wheel hard right. She wrestled the car into submission and stared into the rearview mirror. *Don't be there. Don't be there.* A few seconds later, a set of headlights appeared. The car was far enough back that all Elena saw was two bright white dots in the center of a vague black shape. But that was enough.

Now what? She knew roughly where she was. The sheriff's office was a few blocks ahead. She decided to drive there, pull in, and park as close to the front door as possible. If the car behind her followed suit, she'd lock her doors, dial 911 on her cell phone, and honk her horn until help arrived or her follower left.

There it was, ahead on the right, a squat stone building painted institutional gray on the outside (and, as Elena recalled, inside as well). She swerved into the parking lot at full speed, her left wheels barely touching the pavement. She wove through the vehicles in the lot and skidded to a stop outside the front door in a space marked "Official Vehicles Only." Two floodlights above the doorway spilled a bright pool of light onto the area. She kept the car running, in case she had to make a quick getaway, but eased down until her head was below the level of the seat back. In a moment, headlights appeared in her mirror.

She thumbed the numbers 9-1-1 into her cell phone and had her finger on the "send" button when the vehicle pulled up beside her and parked. When she saw it was a black and white SUV with a light bar on top, she eased up in her seat and cleared the numbers from her phone.

The door of the sheriff's cruiser opened and Frank Perrin stepped out. He leaned against the passenger side of Elena's car and tapped his finger against the window until she rolled it down. He grinned. "Hey, Elena. You know, you ran a stop sign back there. Took a couple of corners awfully fast too. If

I didn't like you so much, I could write you up for about half a dozen violations."

"Frank, I'm sorry. I thought you were following me. There was a Peeping Tom at the house last night, and I'm a nervous wreck."

"I heard about it. When I saw you pull away from the hospital, I figured I'd better follow you and make sure you got home safely." He ran his fingers through his hair, the dark strands falling back into a wave that Elena envied. "Didn't mean to frighten you."

"And I'm sorry I took those turns like a race driver."

"No harm," Frank said. "You know, I'd like to cash that rain check sometime soon. How does dinner at RJ's on Saturday night sound?"

"I'm sorry. I'm really not trying to put you off, but a friend is coming into town tomorrow. I promised to take him out to dinner and catch up. But can we do it some other time?" She summoned up her brightest smile and hoped it took the sting out of her reply. For some reason, she was beginning to feel uneasy with this encounter.

"This friend of yours — is he a 'special' friend?" Frank's voice put the word in quotes.

"He's a doctor I trained with. Now he's

moving here to go into practice with Dr. Gaines."

"I look forward to meeting him. Tell him if he has any trouble he should give me a call. I might be able to help."

"I'll do that. Now I guess I'd better be getting home." She held up her hand. "And I'm pretty sure I can find my way there in the dark, so you don't have to follow me."

"I'll see you around." Frank touched his hand to his forehead in a mock salute, turned on his heel, and disappeared into the building.

As soon as the deputy was through the doors, Elena rolled up her window and took a deep breath. She double-checked to make sure the doors were locked. The first time she met Frank Perrin, she'd been flattered with his attention, but now she felt a little uneasy around him. What had changed? Him? Or her?

Elena worried the thought like a cat with a ball of yarn as she navigated her way to the Kennedys' house. She was sure of one thing. Frank wasn't going to like having David around.

"More coffee?" Dora Kennedy held up the pot like an auctioneer offering a valuable item for sale. "There's plenty, and I can always make more."

Elena shoved her cup across the kitchen table. "Please. It's a lot better than what I'll get at the hospital."

"Do you have to go there this morning? I mean, it's Saturday, and I thought I heard Will and Cathy mention that this was Dr. Brown's weekend on call."

"It is, but Cathy has a patient in the ICU — a man who's recovering from a brain hemorrhage — and I need to check on him. Besides, I want to drop by and see Cathy."

Dora put the last breakfast dish into the dishwasher and wiped her hands on her checked apron. "Tell her we're praying for her. When she gets home, I'll bring meals for her and Will."

Elena savored the coffee. She was so fortunate to be here with the Kennedys. Not just for the coffee and food, either. It had been refreshing to watch them quietly live out their faith. It was almost enough to give her hope that her own could be rekindled some day.

Despite Elena's earlier fears, Matthew Kennedy hadn't gone all evangelistic trying to get her back to church. The only praying she'd experienced here was a simple grace before meals, and not only did Elena appreciate the way Matthew and Dora talked with God, she'd have sat through almost anything to enjoy one of Dora's meals.

Her cell phone rang. She retrieved it from the pocket of her slacks and answered the call.

"Elena, this is David. Did I call too early?"

"You know the answer to that. I'm a doctor. I've had breakfast and was about to leave for the hospital. When will you be in town?"

"I'm here now. I drove in last night after we talked. Just couldn't wait."

"Where are you staying?"

"I'm at the Ramada Inn on Highway 287," David said. "My apartment won't be ready for another week or so."

"Tell you what. Grab some breakfast in the coffee shop there, and I'll pick you up in an hour. I was about to make rounds, but I should be finished by then."

"Sounds great."

Elena ended the call and looked up to see Dora Kennedy smiling at her. "What?" she said.

"Whoever that was, and I suspect it was a young man, you were glad to hear from them."

Elena felt warmth spread across her cheeks. "Am I that transparent?"

"Dear, when you've been a pastor's wife

274

in a small town for so many years, you learn a lot about people." Dora poured herself a cup of coffee and held it to her face, sniffing the aroma. "But don't worry. You also learn how to keep what you discover to yourself." She took a sip from the cup. "Now go do your rounds, then enjoy your time with that gentleman friend. And bring him by here for lunch. I'd like to meet him."

How could Cathy look so good while lying in a hospital bed? In marked contrast to most patients Elena saw in these circumstances, Cathy's hair was combed, her makeup was perfect, even her hospital gown looked fresh and unwrinkled. The glow of pregnancy added the finishing touch.

"I think Milton will let me go home later today if nothing changes," Cathy said.

"Your mother-in-law says they're praying for you. She's promised to bring you meals when you get home."

Cathy smiled. "That's so typical of Dora. And it's not only because I married her son. She and Matthew are that caring about everyone."

"I've noticed. That's why I'm sad that I need to look for an apartment. This arrangement was only supposed to be for as long as it took me to find a place of my own."

"Think about it, Elena. How long have you been in town?"

"A week."

"Have you had a spare hour during those one hundred sixty-eight you've been here?"

Elena shook her head. "Not really."

"I know that Dora and Matthew are glad to have you living with them. Sure, go ahead and look for an apartment, even a house to rent if your budget runs to that. But don't be in a hurry."

As Elena walked through the corridors of the hospital on her way to the ICU, she recognized the truth of what Cathy had said. Given how quickly things happened, Elena could be excused for not having found a permanent home. She'd look at apartments soon, but today she'd relax and enjoy her time with David.

Charlie Lambert was still on the ventilator, but Elena was encouraged that he was now "overbreathing the vent" — breathing spontaneously before the ventilator fired. She squeezed his Achilles tendon between her thumb and fingers and smiled when she felt movement of the foot. Pressure with her knuckle on the patient's sternum resulted in a flinch. He was definitely responding to pain now. Another good sign.

As usual, Mrs. Lambert was sitting at her

husband's bedside, a magazine open on her lap. "What do you think, Doctor?"

"I think he's stable, maybe a little better. We'll see what Dr. Shelmire says, though."

"That nice young man from the ambulance came by this morning."

Elena frowned. "Who was that?"

"I believe his name was Eric. He drove the ambulance that brought Charlie here. He said he was checking to make sure the doctors hadn't fouled up or anything." She bit her lip. "I think he was joking. Don't you?"

"Sure," Elena said. "But if he comes back, remember that now Charlie's under the care of the doctors here. Even though Eric's an EMT, don't let him fiddle with the IV or the respirator. Call for the nurse if that happens."

Mrs. Lambert frowned, but apparently word from a doctor wasn't to be questioned. "Thank you for coming by. Will Dr. Sewell be here tomorrow?"

Elena took a few moments to explain the situation. "So I'll be filling in for her for a while."

"Tell her I'll be praying for her."

So many people were praying for Cathy. Elena wondered why their prayers should be more effective than the ones she offered when her husband lay comatose in the ICU. How could she believe in prayer when her own didn't seem to go further than the ceiling? But obviously other people still had faith. She wished she did.

Elena left the room and made straight for the nurse's station, where she found the nurse assigned to Mr. Lambert. "Did Eric Burson come by here this morning?"

The nurse, an energetic young redhead, said, "Yes. Eric comes by here quite often to check on the patients he's brought to the hospital."

"Does he ever . . ." How could she put this diplomatically? "Does he ever talk about the treatment the patients are getting? Study the charts? Have you ever seen him adjust an IV or change a respirator setting?"

The nurse looked genuinely puzzled. "Sure. But he's an EMT. He's part of the team. Just the other day, he noticed that a patient's IV had almost run out. We were swamped, so he got a bag of D5RL and hung it himself, then charted it. He helps us any time he's here."

"Thanks."

The nurse returned to her charting, and Elena left the ICU wondering whether Eric Burson's motives were totally altruistic.

She'd been told he carried a grudge against doctors. Would he ever take that to the extreme of setting up a medical misadventure of some sort? These patients were, by definition, critically ill. It wouldn't take much. A bit of medication slipped into an IV. A change in a respirator setting to deny the patient needed oxygen. And the logical thought would be doctor error — wrong diagnosis, improper treatment. One more complaint Eric could spread throughout the hospital.

Far-fetched? Elena didn't think so. Because she was pretty sure she'd seen it before, in Dallas. She wasn't sure how the incidents could be connected, but she decided she'd have to be on her guard.

What was the expression? "It's *déjà vu* all over again."

When he saw Elena pull up in the motel's driveway, David wiped his palms on his chinos and took a deep breath. He'd missed her, missed her more than he ever thought he could miss anyone after Carol told him she was tired of playing second fiddle to his medical career. When she left, taking Brittany with her, a bit of David died. It had been two years since that stunning loss. But recently the hope that he could rebuild his

279

life had started to glow like an ember in his heart.

David climbed into the passenger seat and wondered if he should offer Elena a brotherly kiss. She solved his dilemma by shifting into "drive" and pulling away before he could buckle his seat belt. "Hey, it's so good to see you."

"You too, David. Have you had enough coffee?"

"There's always room for more, but I'm fine for now if you have something in mind."

"What I have in mind is to drive around town while we talk. I need to get my bearings, and I suspect you'll find it helpful as well. Will that work for you?"

"Sure. Do you have a city map?"

Elena pointed to the glove compartment. "Cathy and Will gave that to me when I came here for an interview, but I haven't even unfolded it yet. Why don't you navigate? We can learn together."

For an hour, David called out directions and comments while Elena guided them through the streets, both major and minor, of Dainger, Texas. Finally, he folded the map and stowed it again in the glove compartment. "I think that's it. There may be a few places we've missed, but I'm pretty sure

I can find my way around now. How about you?"

Elena didn't take her eyes from the road. "I think so."

"You know, you said we'd drive and talk. To this point, I've done all the talking, and that's been confined to such significant remarks as 'Stratton Street runs into Highway 287 half a mile down that way.' Want to tell me what's bothering you?"

"I don't know where to start. Everything's crazy."

David gestured to a shopping center ahead on the left. "Pull in there. Let's see if we can make sense of it. You always said I understood you better than anyone except Mark."

Elena dabbed at the corner of one eye. Was she crying? Maybe the mention of her dead husband had brought back a painful memory. David could identify with that. For months after his divorce, he'd found himself tearing up at odd times. He needed to assure Elena her reaction was normal. More important, he wanted her to know he was here for her. Not just until the wounds healed and the scars toughened. He was here for the long haul.

Elena dabbed at her eyes, found that the

tissue was sodden, and added it to the pile already building on the floorboard in front of her seat. She pulled another from the box David had retrieved from her glove compartment and blew her nose. "That's it — the totally fouled-up life of Elena Perez Gardner. What do you think?"

"I think you've been handed some tough issues. It's always helped me to break things down so I can deal with them a little at a time. Sort of the way you eat an elephant?"

The out-of-the-blue reference made Elena look up. "What about eating an elephant?"

"It's an old joke. How do you eat an elephant? One bite at a time."

Elena pulled down the sun visor and checked herself in the mirror. Her eye makeup had run, giving her the appearance of a raccoon. "Can you reach into the backseat and hand me my purse? I don't know how you can stand to look at me."

She rummaged in her purse and began to repair the damage. "So tell me about eating this elephant."

"Your midnight phone calls came in on your old home number and, most recently, your cell phone. Given those numbers, Will's investigator should be able to track down the source. If he hasn't found anything by Tuesday midnight, maybe he can make some kind of arrangements to trace the call. I don't know how that stuff works, but he will."

"Okay." The circles under her eyes yielded to cleansing with a Handi-Wipe and she began applying fresh makeup. "How about the suspicion that I'm some kind of mercy killer, starting with my husband?"

"You don't remember taking Mark off the respirator, but you might have. I have an idea how we can get that answer. But you're sure you didn't terminate Pulliam's life. Is that right?"

Could she tell David what she was afraid of? Would he understand?

"Is that right?" David said again.

"Have you ever heard of a fugue state?"

"Sure. A dissociative reaction."

"I'm afraid I had a dissociative reaction that allowed me to discontinue Mark's life support without remembering it. And what if that's how Chester Pulliam died too?"

She watched David's face but saw no evidence of censure or disapproval. Instead, he thought for a few moments, then said, "You need to see a psychiatrist. Maybe he can regress you with hypnosis and put this to rest once and for all."

"That's already been suggested, but I can't. I know it's crazy, but think about it.

Suppose we find out that I did take Mark off the respirator while I was in a fugue state. That's understandable, a one-time thing. But what if I had a similar reaction when I saw Chester Pulliam's situation? Does that mean that every time I'm faced with a patient hanging between life and death there's a chance I'll terminate their existence? It would ruin my career." She clenched her fists. "No, I can't do it."

"Let's talk about this later," David said. "Does that cover everything?"

No, Elena thought. There was Mark's infidelity. But she still couldn't talk about that, not even with David. She'd mentioned it once, that evening when she'd melted into his arms and poured out her heart. Since then, she'd locked the knowledge deep inside her, where it burned like a glowing coal. Maybe if she worked hard enough, she could forget.

She plastered a smile on her newly made-up face and said, "That's enough. Now, what would you like to do?"

"I'm yours for as long as you want," David said. "Why don't we see if we can find you an apartment? Maybe one close to mine."

"Where to?" David put his car in gear but

kept his foot on the brake. "Have you scoped out the good places to eat? I mean, besides eating with the Kennedys. That was a great lunch, by the way."

Elena half-turned in the seat. "So far, besides a couple of burgers, I've eaten at two restaurants, the hospital cafeteria, and in Dora Kennedy's kitchen. I agree that her food gets my vote, but that's not where we're going tonight. After all, it's Saturday night, so I've made some special arrangements." She pulled a sheet of directions from her purse. "Go down this street about a quarter mile to Elm and hang a left."

David shrugged and let the car roll forward. Fifteen minutes later, he pulled to a stop in front of a modest two-story home on the north end of Dainger. "Are you sure this is the place? It doesn't look like a restaurant to me."

"It's not," Elena said. "I haven't eaten the cooking here, but it comes highly recommended. Do you like jerk chicken?"

David wasn't sure what Elena had arranged, but he decided to go with the flow. He helped her out of the car, walked her to the door, and rang the doorbell. Inside, he heard a muted version of the chimes of Big Ben. When the door opened, he saw a tall, strikingly beautiful woman with black hair and skin the color of dark chocolate. She wore a simple white dress, and looked like a million dollars.

"You must be Dr. Gardner," she said to Elena. David thought he detected a slight island lilt to her speech. She turned to him. "And you must be her friend, Dr. Merritt. I'm Dominique Brown. Won't you come in?"

Soon they were settled in a cozy living room. David wasn't much on décor, but he recognized that this one was done with taste.

"Wonderful. Our guests have arrived." A tall black man appeared in the doorway. "I'm so sorry to be late. You know how phone calls for doctors seem to crop up at the most unexpected times." He extended his hand, first to Elena, then to David. "I'm Emmett Brown."

Brown's close-cropped black hair displayed the faintest trace of gray at the temples, although his thin moustache had none. He wore slacks and a sport shirt of the type David associated with the Caribbean.

Elena said, "Thank you for having us here this evening. David's an old friend from residency. He's going into practice with Dr. Gaines, and I thought this would be a good opportunity for him to meet you."

Brown grinned. "David, I hope you like Jamaican food. I didn't when I first met this charming lady, but I found that it came with the package. Since I fell in love with her, I had to learn to eat things like jerk chicken. Now I love it, and I still love her."

"You're kind to have us in your home," David said. "I'm sure the food will be fine."

After Dominique excused herself to put the finishing touches on dinner, Elena asked, "Dr. Brown, how did you two meet?"

"Please," Brown said. "Call me Emmett. And may I call you Elena and David?"

"Of course," they answered in unison.

"I'd finished medical school at Emory and was in New York to start my family practice residency at Montefiore Hospital. Dominique was working as a model in the city. We ended up at the same party, and like the song says, our eyes met 'across a crowded room.' We were married the next year."

"So she gave up modeling in New York to move here with you?" Elena asked.

"I wanted to practice in a town large enough to have good medical facilities, small enough to be family-friendly. Dominique says she gave up nothing and gained everything when we moved here. God hasn't blessed us with children, but we remain hopeful."

"That's a great story," David said. "How do you like practicing here?"

He thought he saw a hint of sadness in Brown's eyes. "There's enough variety to help me keep my clinical skills sharp. The medical facilities and opportunities for specialty consults are quite good for a city this size. Unfortunately . . ." He let the words trail off.

Elena decided there was no reason to tiptoe around the subject. "What Dr. Brown . . . what Emmett is saying is that he's encountered a few patients who won't consider receiving care from a doctor of color." She turned to Brown. "Right?"

"Unfortunately, that's true. And I've sensed a bit of prejudice on the part of one or two colleagues, as well. I hope that doesn't happen to you, Elena."

David frowned. "I visited here a couple of times when I was negotiating with Dr. Gaines, and I didn't see any of that. Would you feel comfortable naming names?"

Brown considered that for a moment. "Most of my colleagues, and that includes Doctors Sewell and Gaines, have been very accepting. I've probably encountered the most resentment from our hospital adminis- trator, Dr. Godwin."

Elena snorted. "Emmett, you're extremely

well-trained — Emory for med school, residency at Montefiore — and you're getting grief from a nonpracticing doctor whose medical education was obtained in Grenada. How's that for the pot calling — ? Sorry. Poor choice of words."

Brown smiled. "That's okay, Elena. I'm not sensitive. Please don't think you have to run everything you say to me through the filter of political correctness. We're all friends and colleagues here. And I look forward to working with both of you."

Dominique appeared in the doorway. "Dinner's ready. I hope you don't mind a bit of spice in your food. In Jamaica, we use Scotch bonnet peppers in our cooking."

David rose. "Dominique, I'm a Texas boy. I'm sure your food isn't any hotter than what I grew up on."

As they moved into the dining room, Emmett whispered in David's ear. "Don't be too sure of that."

Elena sat with her eyes closed, deep in thought as David navigated the car back through the streets of town.

"Earth to Elena."

David's voice shook her from her reverie. "Sorry. What did you say?"

"What was the stuff that Dominique

served? I don't know how long it'll take for my stomach lining to recover."

Elena stifled a chuckle. "Jerk chicken. It's spicy, isn't it?"

"Yeah, but you know, I think I could get to like it. And the other dishes?"

Elena searched her memory. "Rice cooked with red beans and coconut milk. And fried plantain."

She saw David glance in the rearview mirror, an action he'd performed perhaps a dozen times since they'd been in the car. "Is there something wrong?"

"I'm trying to decide why that car has been following us since we pulled away from the Browns' home." He turned right at the next intersection. "You don't happen to have a jealous boyfriend, do you?"

Elena turned to look over her shoulder at the headlights turning the corner and settling in behind them. "I'm not sure what I have. Whoever it is, why don't you see if you can shake them? Then we'll talk."

15

David rolled his car to a stop in the Kennedy driveway. "Good thing I paid attention during our get-acquainted-with-the-city tour today."

"Me too. Between all the turns you made and the way you never touched the brake, I thought I was riding with Mario Andretti tonight," Elena unbuckled her seatbelt and stretched. "I'm glad you finally managed to shake that car. You do agree it was following us?"

"Seemed that way to me."

"That was some pretty awesome driving," Elena said.

David shrugged off the compliment. "I probably watch way too many action movies. The main thing is you're home safely. Now tell me why someone would be following you."

He closed his eyes and leaned back in the seat as Elena shared her story. When she finished, he opened his eyes and turned toward her. "Any idea who could be stalking you, or why?"

"There are a couple of candidates, but I don't have any solid evidence. What would you suggest I do?"

"The usual, I guess. Lock your car. Park in a well-lighted area. Don't —"

"I mean, how do I find out who's following me?"

"Sorry. If you need a baby delivered, I'm your man. But playing Sam Spade, that's not really my strong suit. What do the police say?"

Elena turned toward the window. "I don't really have enough to justify making a complaint. What do I say? We saw headlights behind us? It's a creepy feeling, that's all." She opened her mouth and closed it again.

"What were you about to say?"

"It's like my midnight phone calls. And the notes. I don't have anything substantial. And I don't want to bring in the police until I have a bit more proof. Besides . . ."

"Yes?"

"This is silly. But it's possible the stalker is a deputy sheriff I met my first day in town. And if that's true, going to the police might warn him off. I don't want to do that. I want to catch him so he can be punished."

David took in a deep breath. "I had a patient who was the object of a stalker. They caught the guy red-handed. Do you want to know how that case came out?"

"It sounds like I don't want to know, but tell me."

"In Texas, stalking can be anything from a misdemeanor to a minor felony, depending on the circumstances. This guy got off with a fine and probation."

"What did your patient do?"

"She moved out of state."

"I'm not about to do that."

David turned to face Elena. He put his arm over the backseat and leaned in toward her. "I have to agree with you. The best thing to do is face this head-on. Besides, I can't see you running away from it."

"Will's investigator is trying to track down the phone calls. Maybe he can get a handle on whoever's following me as well."

"Sounds reasonable. In the meantime, don't forget that I'm here for you." *For as long as it takes.*

"I hope you don't mind if I sit down for a few minutes before I fix lunch," Dora Kennedy said.

"Not at all," Elena said. "Just rest for a moment." *If you're cooking fried chicken, I'll*

293

wait as long as I have to.

"I'm sorry you didn't feel up to coming to church with us this morning." Dora carefully put her Bible on the coffee table in the living room, squaring it on top of the magazines there. "Matthew preached quite a good sermon."

Dora eased her ample bulk onto the sofa and patted the seat beside her. Elena joined her, wondering if a sermon, or at least a mini-sermon, was forthcoming. "I had to make rounds, then there was a patient in the emergency room."

"I thought Dr. Brown was on call this weekend," Dora said.

"He is, but I was walking through when the ambulance brought the man in, and . . . I don't know. I guess I hated to see Emmett called away from his Sunday morning when I was right there. As it turned out, it was pretty simple. This woman fainted at church. She'd been put on a new blood pressure medicine, and it dropped her pressure too much. She'll see her internist tomorrow and get the dose adjusted."

"Ever since you came here, Matthew and I have wondered why you've seemed so troubled," Dora said. "I guess you'll tell us about it when you're ready. But something he said this morning might help you."

Elena's guard went up. "Oh?"

Dora reached for the Bible and opened it in the middle. She thumbed through the pages until she found what she wanted. She pointed to a verse she'd highlighted with a yellow marker. "I don't have my glasses. Would you read that?"

Elena took the book, finding it surprisingly heavy. It had been a long time since she'd held a Bible. This one had large print — obviously a concession to Dora's failing eyesight — and ample margins that were filled with scribbled notes. She found the marked passage, cleared her throat, and read. "Where can I go from Your Spirit? Or where can I flee from Your presence?"

"That's from Psalm 139," Dora said. "It's one of my favorites. And what Matthew said was that, like David who wrote that, all of us face problems and trials. Running away does no good. But wherever we are, and whatever we do, God is always there. We don't even have to look very hard for Him. We simply have to open our eyes."

"Thank you," Elena said. "One of these days maybe I'll sit down with you and your husband and tell you all the problems I'm having. But I'm not ready to do that right now."

"You don't have to tell us about them

until you're ready. And God already knows them, you know."

Almost unconsciously, Elena ran her eyes down the remainder of the column. She stopped at the bottom, and the words hit her as though they'd been written especially for her. "Search me, O God, and know my heart; Try me and know my anxious thoughts; And see if there be any hurtful way in me, and lead me in the everlasting way."

"See if there be any hurtful way in me." If she'd acted in a fugue state, she needed to know it — for the safety of her patients. For her own peace of mind. Finding out might mean a major change in the way she practiced medicine. It could even spell an end to her ability to care for some patients. But she needed to do it. She closed the Bible. "Excuse me. I need to call Cathy and get a name and address."

Elena paused in the doorway. "Thank you for sharing that, Dora. And thank Matthew for me too."

Elena's attention was focused on the message slips in her hand and the problems awaiting her on this Monday morning. She tapped absently on the door of Charlie Lambert's ICU room and was about to open the door when a voice inside the room said, "I don't care."

She backed away and listened as the speaker continued. "This hospital can't afford to give free care. I insist you make arrangements for a transfer to a charity facility immediately."

The door opened and Nathan Godwin almost knocked Elena down as he scurried from the room. Through the open door, she could see Mrs. Lambert standing at the foot of her husband's bed, crying. Dr. Shelmire stood beside her, looking daggers at the retreating administrator.

Elena hesitated in the doorway. This really wasn't her fight, and she couldn't add anything right now except maybe a shoulder for Mrs. Lambert to cry on. Then again, maybe that was what would help. She'd been here — sort of — and was more qualified than most to say "I understand."

Dr. Shelmire was the first to see her. "Dr. Gardner, come in. You should hear this too."

Elena eased into the room and took up station beside Mrs. Lambert. On the bed, the endotracheal tube was still in Charlie's throat, but the respirator was turned off, and he was breathing on his own. As Elena watched, Charlie thrashed around a bit and a few nondescript moans escaped around the tube that held his vocal cords apart. "Reacting a bit more, I see."

"Yes," Shelmire said. "He's beginning to react, although he's got a ways to go. I guess you heard what our hospital administrator said. He wants Mr. Lambert transferred to another hospital. Of course I've refused, at least until he's stable and more reactive."

Elena moved a bit so she was in Mrs. Lambert's line of sight. "Dr. Shelmire and I will handle this. Don't let it worry you."

Mrs. Lambert knuckled her eyes, spreading tears across her cheeks. "I slipped out to get some breakfast. When I came back in, that Mr. Godwin was at Charlie's bedside. He started in on me, and then Dr. Shelmire came in." She looked at the neurosurgeon. "Thank you for standing up to that awful man. How can he be making these decisions? He's not even a doctor."

Shelmire and Elena exchanged looks. Elena said, "Actually, he is a —"

"You're right. He's only an administrator," Shelmire said. "Medical decisions are up to us. And rest assured that Charlie is going to get the care he needs."

Mrs. Lambert followed Dr. Shelmire into the hall to talk further while Elena moved to the head of the bed and did a quick exam on Charlie. He was definitely better, but he was a long way from "waking up."

As Elena turned to leave, her hip bumped the partially open drawer of the bedside table. She started to close it but stopped when she saw what it contained, in addition to a washcloth and a Gideon Bible. Nestled in the corner of the drawer was a syringe-needle unit, still in its plastic case. Beside it was a small vial of injectable material. Elena picked it up and read the label: Anectine. Her heart raced and a cold sweat dotted her forehead. Who had put it here? And why would they want to kill Charlie Lambert?

Elena studied the diplomas and certificates on Marcus Bell's office wall. Bachelor's degree from Princeton. Medical school at Columbia. Surgery residency at NYU. Certified by the medical boards of New York and Texas. Fellow in the American College of Surgeons. Master of Business Administration in Health Care Services from SMU.

She could imagine the history behind the displays. His education and training were in the New York/New Jersey area, so he was probably from that region. Marcus had told her he was widowed, and she could identify with a desire for a change of scenery after that event. She wasn't sure why he'd picked this mid-sized Texas town for relocation.

Maybe, as with her, it was the only life raft available in an ocean of trouble.

He'd come here to practice surgery, but somewhere along the line there came an appointment as chief of staff. To be better prepared for that role, he'd done something Elena would never have tackled. He went back to school — probably part-time — to get that MBA. Then, for reasons that apparently had more to do with politics than capabilities, "Dr." Nathan Godwin had taken over most of the administrative duties at Summers County General. That couldn't have sat well with Marcus. Well, if that was the case, he would love what she had to tell him now.

"Sorry to keep you waiting." Marcus sank into the chair behind his desk and handed her one of the two Diet Cokes he carried. "Don't drink it if you don't want it, but I sort of figured that if your day was like mine, you'd either want to rehydrate or use it as an icepack on your head." As if to illustrate, he held the frosty can first against one temple, then the other. He leaned back, put his feet on an open desk drawer. "What's up?"

Elena popped the top on the can and took a long swallow. "I was in Mr. Lambert's room this morning."

Marcus looked blank.

Elena went on to explain. "He's a patient in ICU who had an intracranial bleed six days ago. Mr. Lambert sort of fell through the cracks of the system and has no insurance coverage. He's recovering from surgery. He's off the vent, but he still has a ways to go. Godwin was in there this morning trying to browbeat Dr. Shelmire into sending Lambert to a charity hospital — I guess he meant Parkland."

"Unfortunately, that seems to be Nathan's motto. If it doesn't pay the bills, ship it out. I presume Shelmire stood firm."

"He did, but here's where it gets interesting. The drawer of the bedside table was partly open. On my way out, I started to close it when I saw a syringe and a vial of Anectine inside." She drank deeply from the can, then brushed a stray lock of hair from her eyes. "Someone — and, in my mind, everything points to Godwin — planned to inject Lambert with it."

"Wow!" Marcus chewed on his lower lip. "Clever. Anectine is easy to get in the hospital. Snatch a vial off any anesthesia cart. Inject it IV, just like they do when they put a patient to sleep. But this time, when it paralyzes the muscles, there's no ventilator to take over breathing. And in, what? A couple of minutes? Anyway, in short order, the patient is dead. And the beautiful part is that the drug is metabolized so fast that, by the time of an autopsy, there's no trace. That is, assuming they think to look for it at all."

"That's the way I see it. The question is, what do we do?"

"I don't suppose you brought the vial and syringe with you?"

Elena's mind began to race ahead. She could see where this was headed, and she didn't like it. "No. I was so shocked that I put the vial back in the drawer, slammed it shut, and left. Then I called your office and made this appointment."

Marcus rocked forward, and his feet hit the floor with a resounding splat. "Let's get up to the ICU. I want to see this for myself."

In a few minutes, they stood side-by-side in Lambert's room. Mrs. Lambert hadn't seemed unduly concerned to see two doctors, one of them unfamiliar, show up. By now, she probably wasn't surprised by anything. A week in an ICU would do that, Elena thought.

"Mrs. Lambert, this is Dr. Bell. He's a colleague. I was telling him how well Mr. Lambert is doing." Elena tried to muster her biggest smile. "We're going to be here

302

for a bit. Would you like to slip out and get something to drink, maybe get a sandwich in the cafeteria?"

"That would be lovely. I'll only be a few minutes."

Marcus closed the door behind Mrs. Lambert. He drew the blinds, cutting off the view of the room from the nurses' station. "We don't need anyone else peeking at us right now."

Elena's hand hovered over the drawer pull. She started to use the tail of her white coat to open the drawer, then realized that there were dozens of fingerprints already there. No need to try to protect against adding more to the drawer pull. And what about the vial? Were there fingerprints there too? If so, maybe they could be checked. If the culprit had ever been fingerprinted, that would pin down his identity — or hers. Of course, Elena would have to give her prints for comparison, because they'd be on the vial as well.

"Well, open it." Marcus's voice had an edge. Was he as nervous as she was?

She yanked the drawer open and gasped. It contained the same Gideon Bible and washcloth she'd seen earlier. Nothing else. The syringe and the vial — with her fingerprints — were gone.

■ ■ ■ ■

Restless nights were nothing new to Elena, but this one had them all beat. For hours she watched the numbers on the clock change. The minutes ticked away, the hours rolled over, but still sleep eluded her. Instead, her mind called the roll of the demons pursuing her.

When she finally fell into a troubled sleep, somewhere near dawn, wakefulness gave way to nightmares, always featuring the triumvirate of doctors she'd come to call "the tribunal."

"You were going to kill that patient," the monk-like doctor said.

"We have your fingerprints on the vial," came the pronouncement of the doctor with Coke-bottle glasses.

"Your only hope is to beg us for mercy," said the movie star clone.

"I didn't do it. I didn't do it." Elena tried to say the words, but nothing would come out. They lodged in her throat like a lead weight. She couldn't swallow. She couldn't breathe. She was choking, suffocating.

"This is your punishment." The middle doctor looked over his glasses at her, and his countenance was like an Old Testament

304

prophet proclaiming doom on a city. "Just as your patient was to die, so shall you be starved for life-giving oxygen. Your brain cells will begin to die like waves of soldiers advancing into a cannon's fusillade. Your heart will quiver in fibrillation, no longer able to pump blood. Soon, all your organs will cease to function."

"When?" she choked out.

"Your death will be announced by the ringing of this bell." The handsome doctor held up a small brass bell and began ringing it. "When it stops, you will cease to exist."

Elena tried to reach out her hand to grab the bell and ring it. No matter how far she reached, it always remained just a few feet away. She stretched out her arm, again and again.

Her hand hit something, there was a crash, and Elena snapped awake. The tribunal was gone. She was in a strange bed, in a strange room. The lamp she'd knocked off the bedside table lay on the floor, its shade askew. Slowly it came to her. This was the Kennedy home. She was in their guest room. And the ringing was her cell phone, the ring tone she'd assigned to the hospital.

Elena sat up, pulled the covers around her to combat the chill she felt, even though the room was warm. She picked up the phone from her nightstand.

"Dr. Gardner."

"Doctor, I'm sorry to bother you this early. This is Glenna Dunn. I'm working in the ICU, and your patient, Charles Lambert, has a temp of a hundred and two. What would you like us to do?"

"Give me a second." Elena looked at the clock. Four-twenty-two. She'd been asleep less than two hours. She padded to the bathroom and splashed water on her face. She cupped her hand and drank from the faucet. Better, but only slightly. She struggled to get her mind back in gear. "Glenna, I'm back. When did you notice this?"

"We didn't wake him for vital signs through the night. That was Dr. Shelmire's order."

"That's okay. So, what was his 9:00 p.m. temp?"

"Ninety-nine two. He was a little behind on his fluids, so we speeded up his IV. He seemed okay during the night, but honestly, I didn't keep a really close eye on him. We had a couple of pretty sick patients, and we're working short-handed. That's why they called me in to work up here on my day off from the ER."

"So why did you take his temperature now?"

"When things finally settled down, I had a look at my other patients. He looked flushed, so I used the old manual thermometer — you know, hand to the head — and he felt warm. That's when I checked his temp."

"Get a CBC. Urinalysis and culture from his catheter. I may want some other things, maybe a chest X-ray and blood cultures, but I want to see him first. I'll be there in about an hour. Call me if something else comes up before then."

"Do you want me to give him an aspirin suppository?" Glenna asked.

The mental index cards rippled in Elena's brain. Lambert wasn't taking anything by mouth — didn't even have a feeding tube in place. So oral meds were out. There were no IV drugs proven to effectively lower fever. An aspirin suppository would be the best choice, but aspirin had an effect on bleeding and clotting. It was a long shot, but if the fever was due to seepage of blood from the brain into the spinal fluid, aspirin might aggravate the bleeding. Besides, fever was a sign, not a disease. With a temp no higher than this, it was better to hold off and find the cause.

It took only a couple of seconds for Elena to parse the possibilities and say, "No. Hold off on any meds until I get there. See you soon."

She replaced the lamp on the table and started climbing into the clothes she'd laid out the night before, a habit born of long experience with calls in the middle of the night. As she dressed, she wondered what this latest development in the Lambert chronicle might represent. Was it something simple, like a urinary tract infection? More intracranial bleeding was possible, but quite unlikely. As she dressed, she tried unsuccessfully to ignore the possibility that kept popping into the forefront of her thoughts. Did this represent another attempt to kill Charles Lambert?

All the way to the hospital, she couldn't get away from the idea that perhaps this was more than a simple fever in a post-op patient. But how could someone infect a comatose patient? Material from a contaminated syringe injected in his IV? Bacteria from a lab culture introduced into his lungs via the endotracheal tube? She discarded some of the possibilities as ridiculous, but then again, this whole scenario was ridiculous. Why would someone want to keep an unemployed truck driver from recovering?

Had he been hauling illegal cargo, like drugs or stolen goods? Was this an attempt to keep him from talking?

Or was this another move to discredit her? She was already under a cloud of suspicion for the deaths of two critically ill patients. Would Charlie Lambert's death be the third strike that ended her ability to practice medicine, here or anywhere?

16

The OB doctors' lounge at Summers County General was cool enough this morning, but David was sweating. When he'd been in residency, even though he might have gone to a new service or a new hospital, adjustment was relatively easy because things were done with a surprising amount of uniformity in the medical community in Dallas. And most of the town doctors there, except a few stubborn souls, took their lead from what was taught at the medical school.

Here, he not only had to become familiar with a new hospital with a new cast of characters, but he'd already discovered a couple of things his new partner liked to do that were different from the practices he'd learned. How many more would there be?

"Don't worry," Milton Gaines said. "I don't expect you to copy everything I do. We'll iron out the differences. I imagine you'll teach me a few things, and maybe I've learned some stuff along the way that will help you. The main thing is that our patients get good care, with as much uniformity as we can offer. That way they feel more comfortable no matter which of us they see."

David drew a cup from the industrial-sized urn in the corner, tasted what apparently passed for coffee in the lounge, wrinkled his face, and tossed the Styrofoam cup into the trash.

"I see you've learned a valuable lesson already," Gaines said. "Don't drink the coffee in the OB doctors' lounge unless you have a death wish. I'll buy you a cup in the cafeteria after we finish rounds. It's better than this, which isn't saying much. The best coffee comes from the nurses' break room. Be nice to them, and they'll share."

"Fair enough." David popped a stick of gum into his mouth, but it was no match for the lingering bite of the coffee. "Ready for rounds?"

Gaines eased himself to his feet. "Let's go."

Gaines had two postpartum patients still in the hospital, both doing well after delivering healthy babies, both anxious for discharge. He introduced David to each woman. "This is Dr. Merritt, my new associate. If I'm out or tied up, you'll see him. He's a good man, well-trained and caring. I know you'll like him."

In the hall, Gaines said, "I have one other patient. She's a Hispanic female, nearly at term, admitted recently with preeclampsia. It's a struggle to keep her blood pressure down, and I'd appreciate any help you can give me."

David took the chart Gaines offered and studied it. His senior partner had done all the right things: magnesium sulfate, hydralazine, beta-blockers, oxygen, careful control of fluids. The woman — Maria Gomez — had not yet had a seizure, which was in her favor, but her blood pressure remained high despite treatment.

"I see you estimate that she's at thirty-three to thirty-four weeks gestation," David said. "Are you thinking of inducing her?"

"Definitely. I figured one of us can manage the induction while the other takes care of the office. Want to handle it?"

David closed the chart. "Sure. Why don't we examine her?" *My first OB in private practice and it's a patient with early toxemia of pregnancy. Welcome to the real world.*

David could see that the girl — and that's what she was, just a girl — was frightened.

He could understand why. About to have a baby, lying in a bed in a strange hospital being cared for by people who didn't speak her language; no wonder she was scared.

Gaines warned David that the husband would be his interpreter, but one of the first things he'd learned in medical school was that in any encounter, especially the first one, the patient should be the focus. He stood at Maria's bedside and lightly touched the back of her hand, careful to avoid the IV there. "Maria? *Soy el Dr. Merritt. Cuidaré de usted.*"

She nodded and managed a weak smile. The husband offered his hand. "*Soy* Hector."

"Hector, I've used up most of the Spanish I know to introduce myself to your wife and tell her I'll take care of her. Can we speak English?"

"My English is not so good, but I will try."

David explained that he and Dr. Gaines needed to examine Maria. "We think that it may be best to help the baby get here as soon as possible."

"I understand. Do what is needed, and I will share what you tell me with Maria."

Thirty minutes later, the three men stood at Maria's bedside. In simple English, augmented by the few Spanish words he

313

had picked up during his residency, David explained what was planned. Medication given in Maria's IV would stimulate labor. He would be at the bedside or nearby during the process. The baby was old enough to safely come into the world, and that was necessary to lower Maria's blood pressure and prevent such complications as convulsions. David stumbled on the last word, but Hector assured him it was the same in Spanish.

Maria was nodding even before David finished. *"Sí, comprendo."* Obviously, she understood more English than he or Gaines realized.

"If you're okay to stay here and handle this, I'll get back to the office," Gaines said. "I'll check with you later today. If you need me to relieve you, we can switch."

David took the chart Gaines handed over, feeling like a runner who'd just been handed the baton for the final leg of the race. He prayed he wouldn't stumble.

Elena handed Jane the chart and yawned for what seemed like the fiftieth time that morning. Her jaw popped. "Excuse me."

"Tough night?" Jane asked.

"They called me about four. Mr. Lambert was running a fever."

"Anything serious?"

"Nope. Just a urinary tract infection."

"Glad it wasn't anything worse," Jane said.

Elena thought again about the dictum she'd heard repeatedly since her first physical diagnosis class in med school. When you hear hoofbeats, think horses, not zebras. But last night she'd focused on zebras as soon as the call came.

All the way to the hospital, she'd imagined all the worst possible causes for Charlie Lambert's fever. As it turned out, a third-year medical student could have made the diagnosis and started treatment. Elevated white blood count and pus cells in the urine added up to a urinary tract infection, the most common cause of fever in a patient with an indwelling urinary catheter, and one that was easily treated.

After ordering the appropriate antibiotic, with a mental note to adjust it after the urine culture results were available, Elena carried out a thorough neurological evaluation. Although his endotracheal tube was still in place, Lambert hadn't required ventilator assistance for thirty-six hours. He was moving all four extremities in random fashion, occasionally bucking against the breathing tube in his throat. He uttered a few groans, although the presence of the

315

tube prevented him from talking. *Time to take out the endotracheal tube.* She left a note for Shelmire, letting him make the final decision.

Jane's voice brought Elena back to the present. "That's the last patient until this afternoon." The nurse strode off toward the front office to file the morning's charts.

Elena was barely through the door to her office when her cell phone vibrated. She pulled it from the pocket of her white coat. The Caller ID showed "anonymous caller." What now?

"This is Dr. Gardner."

"Elena, Sam Shelmire."

She closed the door, dropped into her chair, and leaned back. "Are you a mind reader? I was thinking about you."

"No psychic powers. Just responding to your note. I'm on my cell, headed back to Denton."

They spoke for a few minutes, ironing out details of treatment. Shelmire agreed with her suggestion to remove Lambert's breathing tube. Elena said she'd take care of that on rounds this evening.

"How long do you think it will be before he can go to a regular room?"

Shelmire paused, apparently measuring his words. "Don't quote me on this, but the moment Lambert leaves the ICU, your martinet of a hospital administrator is going to be all over me to get him to another hospital. He's still upset that there's no insurance coverage in this case. Frankly, I don't think a long ambulance ride up the road to Parkland is in Lambert's best interest quite yet. Do you?"

"You're the surgeon," Elena said. "But I think you're right. So, what you're saying is that we need to be very slow in moving Lambert out of the ICU."

"We won't make up anything, but I'll bet you can find a reason he needs skilled nursing care, even after he regains consciousness."

"If he regains consciousness," Elena said. "Just because he moves and groans doesn't mean he's going to wake up again."

After she ended the call, Elena sat for a moment and stared at the ceiling. She would love nothing more than to head home and fall into bed, but she had a full schedule of patients this afternoon. Or rather, Cathy had a full afternoon, and now these patients were Elena's.

She was about to slip out and grab a sandwich when Jane tapped on the door and opened it halfway, her expression apologizing for the interruption. "Frank Perrin's on the phone for you. Do you want to take the call?"

Elena noted that when Jane spoke Frank's name, she looked like she'd bitten into a persimmon. "I'll take the call," Elena said. As Jane was withdrawing, something made Elena add, "And I'll be careful."

Elena lifted the receiver and hesitated with her finger over the blinking button. How should she handle this? Chummy? Distant? Formal? She settled for neutral. "Dr. Gardner."

"Hey, Elena. This is Frank Perrin." Chipper, perky, just a friend calling another friend.

Elena adjusted her tone accordingly. "Good to hear from you, Frank. What's up?"

"I was wondering if you could break free for lunch. I know you're snowed under, what with Cathy out of the office for a while."

How did he know that? Was she the only person in town not on that grapevine? She shrugged. "I . . . I guess so. But I'll have to be back here by one. Will that work for you?"

"Grab your purse and walk out the back door. I'm sitting out here waiting for you."

Elena wasn't sure how to react to that news. How long had he been sitting out

318

there? And how many times before that had he sat outside her office or home? *Get a grip. Now you're being paranoid.* Still, despite the bright summer day, she felt a shiver move up her spine as she climbed into Frank's patrol unit.

The vehicle must have been here in the sun for quite a while. The vinyl seat was searing, so Elena hunched forward.

Frank started the SUV and flicked the air conditioner to high before he lifted the microphone off its hook. "This is Frank. I'm out of service for lunch, but I have my radio on." He replaced the microphone and put the SUV in gear.

"I thought you'd say something like 'Base, this is Unit 3. I'm ten-ten.' What happened to those codes?" Elena asked.

Frank shrugged. "You've watched too many police shows. We did away with those a few years ago. This is more direct. If we want to say something without it going out over the air, we have cell phones."

"You're taking all the mystery out of police work," Elena said. "I've always pictured what you guys do as exciting."

Frank half-turned his head and shrugged. "Do you like burgers?"

The abrupt change of subject caught

Elena off guard. It took her a moment to process the question. "Sure."

"Got anything against eating them in a hole-in-the-wall?"

"I've done that before and survived. I'll bet I can do it again."

He flicked his turn signal. "Then prepare for a taste treat."

This time Elena paid close attention to the route Frank took. She was never going to be lost in this town again. The unit rolled to a stop in a gravel parking lot before what could charitably be called a house, although Elena's description leaned toward "shack." The paint had at one time been blue, probably at least three shades of blue, but now the building was a uniform gray. Two windows, one of them covered with plywood, flanked a front porch that leaned at a precarious angle.

Frank followed her up the rickety steps and opened a warped front door with a loud scraping sound. Inside, Elena stepped into a room filled with picnic-style tables and benches. It seemed to her there was hardly room to maneuver around the tables and through the people who stood waiting for a place to sit. Frank's entry parted the stand-ees like the Red Sea before the rod of Moses, and in a moment he and Elena were standing at the counter that ran across the back of the room. A black woman, her gray hair barely contained by a net, stood sweating behind the counter. Behind her, a man of similar age and coloration was flipping patties and assembling hamburgers at a record pace.

"Two, please, Hattie," Frank said. He turned to Elena. "Everything?"

"No onions."

"One no onions. Two iced teas."

Hattie barely nodded. "Two — one, no onions — for Frank."

Frank pointed toward a middle-aged couple leaving one of the tables, and Elena followed him. Two men moved toward the spot, but when they saw Frank, they veered off and headed toward the wall where stools and a chest-high shelf afforded a place for the overflow.

Frank pulled a couple of sheets of paper towel off the roll in the middle of the table. He shoved a squeeze bottle of mustard, another of catsup, and shakers of salt and pepper toward Elena. "Not the Ritz, but I'll bet you've never had a better burger."

"I'm sure it'll be great. But —"

A young black man hustled up to the table and set two plates before them. "The one with the toothpick in it's the one without onions," he said, his eyes never meeting theirs. "I'll bring your tea."

"That's Sam. He's Hattie's grandson. She's raising him."

"Shouldn't he be in school?" Elena asked.

"He dropped out after tenth grade. He wasn't an athlete, so there was no way he'd ever get into college. Hattie figured he might as well go to work."

The young man was back with teas before Elena could speak. Again, he kept his eyes downcast, as though afraid to meet the gaze of the deputy.

They ate in silence, partly because of the din surrounding them and partly because the food was so good that bite followed bite without interruption.

Back in the parking lot, Elena said, "Thanks for lunch, Frank. I'm glad we had an uninterrupted meal this time. And I'll certainly come back here again. That was probably the best hamburger I've ever tasted."

"I hope those return trips will be with me. Next time, though, I'd like to take you out in the evening to a nicer place."

Elena said something noncommittal. She wasn't sure about the vibes she was getting from Frank Perrin. She was noticing little things: the way the help at the cafe looked at him, the two men who almost fell over themselves getting out of his way, the fact that he hadn't even offered to pay for his meal. No, the more she learned about Frank, the more she understood the warnings she'd received. She needed to be careful around him.

"Time for a break, Dr. Gardner." Jane motioned to Elena's office, where a cold Diet Coke and a package of mini-Oreos were centered on her desk blotter. "I think this is what you like."

"Jane, you're an angel. How did you know?"

"I pay attention. You've got half an hour before your next patient. Now sit down and relax. You've done a great job today, but I don't want you to wear yourself out." Jane grinned. "I'm pretty sure Dr. Sewell's going to want you around for a good while."

"I hope so." Elena eased into her chair and motioned Jane to the one opposite.

Jane remained standing in the doorway. "Thanks, but I've got things to do." She started to close the door.

"One thing," Elena said. "The office is closed tomorrow afternoon . . . right?"

"Right." Jane eased the door closed.

Elena extracted a wrinkled post-it note

from her desk drawer. If she did this, there was no turning back, and the results might change her life. On the other hand, she couldn't go on this way. She pulled the phone toward her and tapped out ten digits.

A man's voice answered on the second ring. "This is the office of Dr. Josh Samuels. I'm probably with a patient, but if you'll leave your name, number, and a brief message, I'll call you back, usually within an hour. In the meantime, relax. Together, we can get through this."

Elena smiled. She could see what Cathy meant. This wasn't your ordinary psychologist.

"This is Dr. Elena Gardner. I'm a new associate of your former patient, Dr. Cathy Sewell. I need to see you tomorrow if at all possible about an urgent matter." She added the numbers of the unlisted office line and her cell phone, and hung up. She hoped she was doing the right thing.

She'd eaten one cookie and drunk half her Diet Coke when the back line rang. She snatched up the receiver. "Dr. Gardner."

"Elena, this is Will. I was hoping I'd catch you between patients. Do you have a moment?"

She tried not to let her disappointment show. "Sure. What's up? Is Cathy okay?"

"She's fine. She's at home and champing at the bit to get out, but Milton Gaines wants her on bed rest for a bit longer. We can talk more about that when I see you. Can you come by our house this evening about six?"

Elena did some rapid calculations. Finish with office patients, make rounds and pull Mr. Lambert's endotracheal tube, pick up her dry cleaning. "Sure. Can I bring anything?"

"No, we're fine. I'm going to get some Chinese takeout. Will you eat with us?"

"Sounds good." Tex-Mex, Chinese, American. The cuisine in Dainger was a veritable United Nations. "I'll see you at six."

She'd just hung up the phone when it rang again. The blinking light told her the call was on the private line. Dr. Samuels? She felt a mixture of hope and fear wash over her as she lifted the receiver and answered.

"Dr. Gardner, this is Josh Samuels. How may I help you?"

How could anyone help her? Elena did her best to give Samuels a concise summary of her situation.

He listened without interruption. When she wound down, he said, "Two questions. First, why tomorrow? And second, what do you hope to get from the session, assuming

I can hypnotize you and regress you to the times in question?"

"The first is easy. I've taken over the practice while Dr. Sewell is confined to bed, and tomorrow afternoon is the only time I can get away. Besides, I'm afraid that if I delay this, I won't go through with it."

"Fair enough. I can see you after my scheduled patients. Be here at five. Do you need directions to my office?"

"I'll see Cathy tonight. I can get them from her. And thank you for seeing me."

"I asked two questions. What's your answer to the second one?"

What did she hope to gain? To find that she'd caused the death of two patients, one of them her husband, while in a fugue state? To learn that she was a danger to those she was sworn to help? She turned it over in her mind for another thirty seconds while Samuels waited patiently on the other end of the line. Finally, she said, "I guess I've decided that knowing, even knowing something bad about myself, is better than wondering for the rest of my life."

"Good answer. Once we know what's wrong, we'll work on fixing it."

After she hung up, Elena sat with her eyes closed, searching for encouragement to go through with what she'd set in motion. A phrase began to percolate to the top of her mind like the first bubble of coffee in an old-fashioned pot. She made her way to Cathy's office and looked in the bookshelf behind the desk. Yes, there it was, right where she remembered seeing it.

Elena took down the book, opened it, and thumbed through the pages until she found the one she wanted. There it was, Psalm 139. She slumped into Cathy's chair and let the words soak in. This was a modern translation, unfamiliar to her, but that only seemed to make the words more powerful.

> "Investigate my life, O God, find out everything about me;
> Cross-examine and test me, get a clear picture of what I'm about;
> See for yourself whether I've done any-thing wrong — then guide me on the road to eternal life."

That was it. She'd let Josh Samuels inves-tigate her life, look in the hidden corners, peek into the dark closets. Then she and Samuels would have a clear picture of what she was about. After that, the two of them — and, yes, God, if He was still interested — could set about fixing what was wrong in her life.

Elena looked at her watch and quickened her steps. Her last patient had taken more time than anticipated, but the end result certainly justified her efforts. The woman beamed when Elena assured her that an adjustment of her medication would almost certainly provide relief from the headaches that plagued her. *Sometimes you do something that makes it all worthwhile.*

In the ICU, it was the work of a moment to remove the breathing tube from Mr. Lambert's throat. Although he was improving daily, Elena warned his wife there was no guarantee he wouldn't awaken with a neurologic deficit that could range from mild to severe. "He's not out of the woods, by any means. And you should prepare yourself for the possibility that he might need institutional care for the rest of his life."

"I entered this marriage for better or for worse, and I'm not about to back out now," the woman said.

As Elena hurried down the hall toward the hospital exit, she thought back to the time when she prepared herself to take care of Mark, no matter how severe his impairment. Would she have been so eager if she'd known about his unfaithfulness? Was it even possible that she had some inkling of it before his stroke? And could that have affected her taking him off life support? Perhaps it was a case of *I was prepared to take care of you forever, no matter the cost to my own life — but no more. Better for both of us to end your life right now.* Was that how it went down?

She shrugged without slowing her steps. Tomorrow afternoon she'd know more about what she'd actually done. Until then, no need to worry about it.

Her car was in the ER parking lot. She was halfway there when tones from her cell phone told her she had a voice mail message. Maybe there was something she could do — maybe get a different phone or change carriers — to allow calls to reach her inside the hospital. Meanwhile, it was a real inconvenience.

She stabbed at the button to retrieve the message and beeped her car unlocked as she waited. When she recognized the voice of her caller, she rolled her eyes and looked skyward. How much more did she have to suffer at the hands of this megalomaniac?

"Doctor Gardner, this is Doctor Godwin. Please come by my office as soon as you get this message. I'll be here until six this evening."

That was it. No explanation. Not a request. A command.

Elena scrolled down the numbers on her phone and put in a call to Will's cell. Maybe she could catch him and not disturb Cathy. She counted five rings, and was about to end the call when he answered.

"This is Will."

"Elena here. I was on my way to your house when our administrator issued a summons to his office. Sorry, but it looks like I'll be a little late."

"No problem," Will assured her. "We'll save you some food. I'd offer to delay eating until you get here, but Cathy's in that 'I'm pregnant and if you don't feed me I can't be responsible for the consequences' mood."

Elena managed a brief smile. "I'll call you when I'm on my way."

Five minutes later, she tapped on the door of Godwin's office.

"Come." In that one-word response, Godwin managed to convey the image of a man wrestling with the problems of the world, resigned to interrupting his important work to deal with a supplicant.

She advanced and stood before his desk. He looked up and motioned her to sit.

"What's so important?" Elena heard the irritation in her voice. Then again, that's how she felt.

"I've been advised today that during your residency training you were suspected of irregularities in the death of two critically ill patients. Is that correct?"

Wham! Where did this come from? Who could have done it? She started to go down a mental checklist, but Godwin interrupted her.

"I asked you a question, Doctor."

"Your information appears to be flawed," she replied in a cool voice. "My husband was in a coma from which there was no hope of recovery. I was involved in the decision to remove him from life support."

"And the other instance?"

"A patient in a similar circumstance was taken off life support. I was assisting in that patient's care. I left my residency without any blot on my record. My chair released me two weeks early because Dr. Sewell needed me." She paused a beat. "And, since she's now on bed rest and I've taken over her practice entirely, that was probably a good thing."

Godwin sat silent for a moment. "I'll be looking into the circumstances of those deaths. Meanwhile, to prevent any such incidents at this hospital, I'm going to suggest that the chief of staff temporarily suspend your privileges in the ICU." He picked up his pen and pulled a stack of papers toward him. "That's all."

17

Will did what he'd learned to do best. He listened, filed away information, and waited for the speaker — in this case, Elena — to run down.

"More shrimp fried rice?" Cathy asked.

Elena shook her head. She chewed, swallowed, and said, "No, that's plenty." She turned to Will. "What can Godwin do? Can he suspend my ICU privileges?"

"With the usual lawyer's disclaimer that I don't have all the facts, it seems that Godwin's within his rights to investigate a complaint against a physician. He should, and probably will, consult Marcus Bell. I don't know how those lines of authority are drawn now." He saw Elena's mouth open and stopped her with an upraised palm. "But I'm betting that he can't curtail your ICU privileges. First, I'm pretty sure the Credentials Committee would have to be involved, and any action would require a hearing. If I were representing you — and I'd be happy to do that if you like — I could make a pretty compelling case that Godwin is interfering with your right to practice."

Elena shoved her plate aside and folded her napkin. "So, what should I do?"

"I'd call Marcus Bell and give him a heads-up. It's better that he hear your side before Godwin gets hold of him." Will leaned back in his chair. "And I'd call him now. Don't embellish. Don't do too much explaining. Simply tell him what you told Godwin."

Cathy pushed her chair back from the dining room table. "I agree with Will. You can call from our bedroom. Meanwhile, we're going to move to the living room, where it's more comfortable."

Will helped get his wife settled into an armchair. "Shouldn't you go back to bed?"

"Milton said I could be out of bed. I just can't exert myself." She wiggled in the chair. "Don't make me more of an invalid than I am." Another wiggle. She looked down at her bulging belly. "But I'm sure ready for our offspring to make an appearance. It's like carrying around a medicine ball inside me — a medicine ball that kicks."

In a couple of minutes, Elena joined them. "You were right, Will. Marcus said not to worry. He thinks Godwin's flexing his administrative muscles."

Will retrieved a legal pad from the end table beside him. "Why don't we get down to the business I wanted to discuss?"

"I'm sorry," Elena said. "I got so involved in my problems I forgot that you asked me here."

Will waved that away. "Five days ago, I engaged an investigator to look into your Tuesday night phone calls." He held up the legal pad. "He called me today and gave me a verbal report."

"He actually traced those calls?"

"Yes. He's identified your caller." Will consulted his notes. "The calls came from —"

"Wait." A flush painted Elena's face crimson. "Slow down. I'm not sure I'm ready for this. How did he get this information?"

"I asked my investigator not to be too specific when he reported. After all, I'm an officer of the court."

"You mean he may have done something illegal?"

"More likely he got someone to bend the rules a bit." Will waited to be sure there were no more questions. "I gave him your former home number in Dallas and your cell phone number. What I suspect he did was search the call logs of your carriers until he found the calls to those numbers at midnight on the dates in question. If they all came from the same number — and apparently they did — he had his answer."

"The number, but what about who made the call?" Elena asked.

"Once he had the number, it would be simple to identify who owned the phone. The only problem would be if the call were made from a so-called disposable cell phone. Fortunately, your caller wasn't that devious."

"But every time my Caller ID showed the number as 'private,' or 'anonymous,' or something like that."

Will smiled. "That means you, as the party on the other end, can't see it. But nothing is hidden from the phone companies."

"The first calls were to my home phone. That's an unlisted number. Then, after I arrived here, she called my cell phone. How did she get those numbers?"

"There are several ways, but I suggest you ask her that the next time she calls." He noticed that Elena's high color had faded a bit. "Are you ready to know the identity of your midnight caller?"

Elena wondered why she was so hesitant to

hear Will say the name. Maybe it was because to this point the midnight caller was only a disembodied voice, popping up once a week to torture Elena. But once Will gave the name, the voice would become a real person, someone she had to deal with. She wasn't sure she was ready for that. She knew it wasn't logical — but what was logical about the merry-go-round her life had become?

The ring of her cell phone brought her up short. She looked at the display and started to ignore the call. *Not now, David.* But she pushed the button. "Hello, David."

"Elena, I need your help. This is an emergency."

She sat up straighter and pressed the phone to her ear so hard it hurt. "What?"

"I'm doing an induction on Mrs. Gomez. She's the lady you referred, the one with preeclampsia."

"I remember. What's the emergency?"

"We started the Pitocin drip this afternoon. Things were slow at first, then she started making some progress. But now she's bleeding and having constant contractions. Fetal heart tones are rapid and getting fainter."

Elena quickly connected the dots. *Abruptio placenta.* A premature separation of the placenta, the organ that nourishes the fetus, from the wall of the uterus. More common with preeclamptics. "Abruption?"

"Grade three. I don't think we can deliver her fast enough to save her or the baby. I'm taking her for a stat C-section."

"What do you need from me?"

"I need an assistant. My partner's delivering breech twins, and has another woman in labor after that. The other OB in the area, Tom Denson, is tied up in Bridgeport."

"I just talked with Marcus Bell. Call him."

"I did. While I was on the phone with him, he got a second call — a patient with a perforated peptic ulcer. He's probably on his way to the OR by now."

Elena was already on her feet. "Guess it's me, then. I'll be there in fifteen minutes."

She saw the puzzled looks from Will and Cathy. Elena rattled off a brief explanation as she snatched up her purse and headed for the door.

"Here," Will ripped the page off his pad and stuffed it into her purse. "You can read this later."

The tension in the operating room was like an over-tight violin string.

"How's the baby?" David worked to keep his voice steady.

The pediatrician didn't look up from the fetal monitor. "Fetal heart tones weaker and slowing. We need to get that baby out of there."

The anesthesiologist's voice was strained. "Her pressure's dropping, pulse up to one twenty. I'm running a unit of blood in each arm, full open."

David held out his hand, and the nurse slapped a scalpel into his palm. He looked across the operating table. "Ready, Elena?"

She nodded. He knew she was nervous. But he also knew she was well prepared. This wasn't her first C-section, nor was it his. But still, his pulse was racing, and he suspected the same held true for Elena.

"Fast as you can, David," the pediatrician said. "This baby's in trouble."

David did what he'd always done in emergency situations. He put his mind on automatic pilot and let muscle memory and hours upon hours of study translate to actions. Elena kept up with him, step-by-step, her hands working in unison with his.

"Opening the uterus," David said. A gush of blood spilled out into the operative field.

The anesthesiologist said, "I can't get the blood and fluids in fast enough to keep up."

David willed himself to work steadily. In a moment, he held up the baby, clamped and cut the cord, and passed the infant into waiting arms. "Okay, let's get this bleeding under control."

David removed the placenta, but the bleeding continued unabated. "Are those coagulations studies back?"

The reply came from the anesthesiologist. "Yep. No abnormalities. And I'm having a hard time keeping her stable. BP's at shock levels."

"Emergency hysterectomy?" Elena asked.

"Not if I can help it. This is a young woman. Maybe she and her husband want a brother or sister for this baby." He pointed with a hemostat. "Find the aorta and compress it."

Elena reached gingerly into the abdominal cavity.

David tapped the back of her hand with the instrument. "Don't be tentative. Find it by feeling for the pulsations, then use gentle pressure to shut off blood flow. Just be careful. We don't need a ruptured aorta to deal with."

Seconds passed like hours until Elena said, "Got it."

In a moment the bleeding slowed. David quickly identified and tied off first one uterine artery, then the other. Smaller vessels would nourish the organ, but ligating these arteries should stem the tide. "You can release your pressure now." He held his breath.

Elena withdrew bloody, gloved hands from the wound and let them rest, clasped together, at her waist.

Blood still oozed into the operative field, but it was nothing like the flood of five minutes before. David exhaled, then refilled his lungs. "That's better. Now let's clean up all the other bleeders and get this wound closed."

Elena showered in the nurses' locker room and changed into street clothes. She borrowed a white coat from a hook on the wall and headed for the ICU. David was at the bedside of Maria Gomez. The breathing tube was still in her throat, and a ventilator puffed oxygen into it at a steady sixteen breaths per minute.

"What do you think?" David asked.

The anesthesiologist shook his head. "Her pressure got pretty low. I tried to keep her well-oxygenated, but with the blood loss and poor perfusion, there's no way to know how much brain damage there might be."

"I'll keep the blood going until we get her back to more normal levels. Will you be around if I need you again tonight?"

The anesthesiologist yawned. "Sure. You've got my cell phone number." He extended his hand to Elena. "I'm Charlie Tandy."

"Nice to meet you. I didn't know I was signing on for this when I came to Summers County General."

"We're large enough to have every specialty you might need, but small enough that the docs sometimes have to pitch in when it's crunch time." He grinned. "You did fine."

Elena dropped into a chair at the doctor's charting station. In a moment, David joined her. He nodded toward the door leading to the waiting room. "Now I've got to go out there and tell Maria's husband that his baby girl is fine, but there's a chance his wife won't wake up from the operation."

"You did everything you could," Elena said. "All you can do is play the cards you're dealt. And we don't know yet what the outcome will be." She ran her fingers through her still-wet hair. "You'll keep her here in the ICU, won't you?"

"Yeah. One nice thing about this hospital — we have lots of ICU beds." He managed a wry grin. "Of course, this is going to drive Nathan Godwin up the wall. The payment we get for an uninsured OB isn't much, and there's no way it's going to cover time in the ICU."

"So, what are you going to do?"

"What's best for the patient, of course. Our esteemed administrator can go fly a kite." David flashed a grin. "But there's no need for you to worry. It's me he'll come after."

"He's already after me," Elena said. She told him about her visit in the administrator's office earlier. "I've talked with Marcus Bell. He told me not to worry, but that's hard to do." She picked up a pencil from the desk and started tapping out a nervous rhythm on a metal chart cover. "Why is Nathan so uptight about insurance and payments?"

"I can answer that," David said. "My associate told me the whole story when I first interviewed here. Marcus was doing a good job as chief of staff, but he wasn't riding herd on payments. You and I both know that most doctors aren't wired that way. So the hospital board hired Nathan. His contract specifies that Summers County General has to show a profit within two years, or he's gone. And the contract only has a few more months to run."

"So the more nonpaying patients he can move out of here, the better his chances of keeping his job. Right?"

David touched his nose. "Bingo. You got it."

Elena finally told David goodnight, promising to call him tomorrow. She was driving out of the parking lot when her cell phone rang. Without taking time to see who was calling, she answered.

"Elena, this is Marcus. Did I catch you at a bad time?"

She wheeled into an empty parking space and killed the engine. "Not at all. Just tired. Are you through with your case?"

"Uh-huh. Perforated peptic ulcer. Did it laparoscopically. Isn't modern technology wonderful?"

"I don't think laparoscopic surgery would have worked for what we did. David did a stat C-section for a placental abruption."

"Yeah, that's one reason I called. I wanted to thank you for stepping in. That's something the doctors here at Summers County General have to do — help out in a pinch."

Elena pushed the lever to lean back in her seat. "Glad I could do it." She unfastened her seat belt. "You said one reason. Was there another?"

"Um, yes. I didn't bring this up when we spoke earlier. It didn't seem like the right time. Would you like to have dinner with

344

me some night this week?"

"Marcus —"

He hurried on. "As a friend. Remember, I know you're widowed, and as a widower I've been down that road. I just want to offer a listening ear. About anything."

Now Elena knew what it felt like to be caught between the proverbial rock and hard place. Maybe it would be good to have someone else besides David to talk with about the struggles she'd had since Mark's death. On the other hand, Marcus might be called on soon to deal with a request to suspend some of her clinical privileges. Would a social relationship between them jeopardize their professional one?

"I've had a really hard day, and it's hard for me to think," she said. "Can we talk about this later?"

"Sure. Would you like me to call you, or shall I wait for you to call?"

Elena yawned. "Call me tomorrow night. Is that okay?"

She reached across to the passenger seat and dropped the phone into her purse. *Oh, please let me make it home and into bed without any more interruptions.* She navigated flawlessly through the dark streets, proud of how familiar she'd become with Dainger. *Oh, don't mind the name. It's just named for some early settler.* That might be true, she decided, but there was plenty of danger here as well. The threat to her career had followed her here. Someone was stalking her. And apparently her midnight caller hadn't given up after Elena relocated.

She'd forgotten about her midnight caller. And this was Tuesday. She looked at the clock on the car's display. Two minutes to midnight.

Elena saw a strip shopping center ahead. It was deserted at this hour, but the parking lot was well lit. It would be a good place to pull in. She wanted to focus her full attention on her caller tonight.

She turned off the engine, checked to make sure her doors were locked, and reached into her purse. First she removed her cell phone and placed in on the dash in front of her. Then she rummaged until she found the slip of paper Will had given her. She unfolded it carefully, as though the information written on it might escape if mishandled. The light under which she was parked was bright. The words were clear, but the first time she read them Elena couldn't really process them. Surely not. There was no way.

The phone rang. She looked once more at the name on the paper. Then she pushed

346

the button to answer the call. Elena struggled to make her voice steady, her words neutral. "Hello, Karri. Why do you keep calling me?"

There was a sharp gasp, then a click and silence.

18

Elena leaned across the table to be heard over the din of the hospital cafeteria. "I'm glad we could get together for lunch."

David took a sip of iced tea. "Sorry we had to eat here, but I have a lady in labor upstairs, so I need to be in the hospital."

"How's Maria?"

"Still in ICU. Showing a few signs of waking up. Breathing on her own now, so I've unhooked the respirator. Maria's still got a ways to go, but I think she's going to make it."

Elena swallowed another bite of her BLT sandwich. "And the baby?"

David beamed. "Beautiful baby girl. Everyone in the nursery's crazy about her."

"Doctor Gardner. Who's your friend?"

Elena's sandwich turned into a lump of lead in her stomach. "Hello, Eric."

David stood and extended his hand. "David Merritt. I'm a new OB in town."

"Eric Burson." Elena noticed Eric's hesitation before he returned the handshake. "I'm an EMT."

"Nice to meet you. I look forward to seeing you around. Just not professionally."

Eric scowled. "What's that supposed to mean? That you don't want me taking care of any of your patients?"

David made a patting motion with his open palms. "Maybe I didn't say that well. I hope none of my patients have an emergency. But I do look forward to seeing you around the hospital. It's nice to meet you."

The last words were said to Burson's retreating back.

"Don't mind him," Elena said. "That's the way he's behaved since the first time I saw him." She went on to relate what she'd been told about Burson's wife and the effect her death had had on his view of doctors.

"Whew. I wonder why he became an EMT. I'd think that being around doctors all the time would only keep him stirred up."

"I guess we all wonder that. But everyone agrees he's good at what he does, so they put up with his attitude."

"You don't suppose . . ."

"What?" Elena asked.

"If Burson's got something against doctors . . . Well, there's an old saying. 'Keep your friends close and your enemies closer.' You don't suppose he wants to be around doctors to look for a chance to get some sort of revenge, do you?"

It sounded crazy when I first thought of it. Now I don't know. Elena looked at her watch. "I've got to get up to the ICU and see a patient."

"I'll go with you," David said. He shoved the remaining potato chip remnants on his plate into his mouth, chewed and swallowed, and said, "Let's go."

In the ICU, they split up. Elena took Mr. Lambert's chart from the rack and went into his room. The patient was still breathing on his own, and his vital signs remained stable. She called his name. No response. She pressed her knuckle into his sternum, and he seemed to pull away from her. Maybe his level of coma was lighter. Or maybe that was wishful thinking.

"Do you think he'll ever wake up?" Mrs. Lambert asked. "What's going to happen?"

Elena was totally conflicted in how she wished this scenario would play out. She settled for, "No one knows. We have to be patient."

"I guess I'll just keep on praying."

"You do that. And we'll keep taking the best possible care of your husband."

Elena stopped at the nurse's station and made a couple of adjustments in Lambert's IV fluid orders. She wondered if Shelmire had considered a feeding tube or a gastrostomy. It was apparent that the man was likely to survive the bleeding into his brain, but Elena was afraid that Charlie Lambert might remain in a vegetative state for a long time. Maybe years.

Elena paused at the door of Maria Gomez's room. David was standing silently at the bedside, his eyes closed. She wasn't sure how long he stood there — maybe a minute, maybe five. She waited in uncomfortable silence until David turned toward her.

"Oh, Elena. I was praying."

"I wish I thought it did any good." She covered her mouth as though she could stop the words. "I'm sorry, David. I know you have deep faith. But I'm not sure I do anymore."

David motioned her outside, and they found a quiet spot in the back hall. "I know you prayed after Mark's stroke. Did the fact that God didn't restore him to health mean that God didn't hear your prayers?"

Elena knew the answer David wanted, but she answered with her heart, not her head.

351

"Yes! That's exactly what it felt like. Doesn't it say somewhere in the Bible that whatever we ask, we'll get?" She swallowed hard. "Now that seems like a lie."

"You're right about the passage. That's hard to understand when we ask for something and don't see the result we want. But there are other places that assure us God knows not just what we want, but what we need."

"So why bother to pray, anyway?"

David shrugged, as though the concept was beyond words. "I guess it's a way of staying connected. For me, part of praying is listening. It's a two-way conversation."

"Right now, I'm not sure I feel like talking to God."

"No problem. Just listen."

Code Blue ICU! Code Blue ICU!
Elena hurried down the hall and pushed through the double doors into the ICU. Her heart dropped when she saw the activity in Charlie Lambert's room. She edged nearer and saw an anesthesiologist at the head of Lambert's bed. He'd reinserted a breathing tube and was squeezing an Ambu bag to force air into Lambert's lungs. Another doctor — it looked like Marcus Bell — pumped on Lambert's chest at a pace of one hundred

beats per minute. Just a couple of days ago she'd told her CPR class they could achieve the proper rhythm by humming the Bee-Gees song, "Stayin' Alive." The class thought that was comical. Now it was a serious matter.

The drama dragged on, but eventually Marcus looked at the anesthesiologist. Both shook their heads and straightened, flexing their backs to ease tired muscles. Elena turned away and saw Mrs. Lambert huddled at the nurse's station, shivering despite the blanket someone had thrown over her shoulders.

Elena eased over and stood beside the woman. "What happened?"

"I slipped out to make a phone call. I was only gone for five or ten minutes. When I came back, Charlie wasn't breathing. His lips were blue. I screamed. A nurse came running in. They brought me out here, so that's all I know." She looked at the room, where the blinds were now drawn. "Is he . . . ?"

"I wasn't in the room. I'm sure someone will be here soon to tell you."

Mrs. Lambert ignored Elena's carefully neutral answer. She seemed to shrink in on herself and started sobbing. A woman in a plain blue dress covered by a short white coat eased into the chair beside her. "Mrs. Lambert, I'm Chaplain Fulmer."

Elena moved aside, her mind already locked in a comparison of this episode to the death of Chester Pulliam. Although she had no idea who could have done such a thing, she had a very good idea who might be blamed for it. She felt a tingling between her shoulder blades. Just as surely as if she had a target pinned to her back, she knew what was coming.

Elena wished she'd sneaked a peek at the thermostat as she entered Nathan Godwin's office. Surely he had the air conditioning cranked up full tilt. She shivered inside her white coat. Then again, maybe the fault lay not with the thermostat but with her situation.

"Doctor Gardner, I appreciate your coming by." Godwin's voice showed none of the appreciation his words supposedly conveyed. "Please have a seat."

Elena took one of the two visitor's chairs. She hitched it forward so that only an expanse of uncluttered mahogany separated her from the administrator. *Don't show your fear. Don't get angry. Let it play out.* "Under the circumstances, I expected the call." She looked at her watch. Still plenty of time to get through this before she left for Fort Worth.

"I perceive you're in a hurry," Godwin's smile carried more triumph than mirth. "Very well. I'll get right to it. As you know, I'm already aware of your involvement in the suspicious deaths of two patients during your residency training."

Elena bristled. She leaned forward until she was halfway across Godwin's desk. "For the last time, these deaths were the result of withdrawal of life support from two patients with no hope of recovery. And one of those patients happened to be my . . ." Her throat caught. She couldn't say the word.

"Your husband," Godwin said. "Yes, I know. Nevertheless, you left your residency under something of a cloud, with your ability to deal with brain-dead patients in question." Not only was the administrator capable of using the dreaded phrase, he seemed to delight in it.

"What's your point?"

"You were in the ICU at noon, shortly before your patient, Mr. Lambert, was found unresponsive, with no respirations and only a faint heartbeat. Efforts to resuscitate him were not successful."

"I don't deny that. I saw him, talked with his wife, and then met a colleague to discuss one of his patients. After that I went to medical records to sign some charts. I was on my way back to the ICU when I heard the emergency page."

Godwin opened his desk drawer and pulled out a plastic bag containing a small vial and a syringe. "This was found in Mr. Lambert's bedside table. It's succinylcholine, commonly known by its trade name of Anectine. I believe someone injected Lambert with this drug. Since he no longer had the respiratory support of a ventilator, when the Anectine paralyzed him he stopped breathing."

Elena clamped her jaws shut. *Don't say anything. See where he's going.*

"I intend to turn this evidence over to the police. At that time, I'll make them aware of your history and suggest they investigate Mr. Lambert's death as a homicide." He turned the bag, letting the light catch the vial. "It appears to me that there's a clear set of fingerprints on the vial. If they're found to be yours, I have no doubt that you'll be charged with murder. At that time, I intend to summarily suspend your hospital privileges."

"You can't do that. This is America. I'm innocent until proven guilty."

Godwin pointed to a thick binder on his

desk. "I've carefully researched the hospital bylaws. If there is reasonable suspicion that a staff member's continued practice in this hospital constitutes a threat to the well-being of its patients, the hospital administrator may suspend that doctor's privileges pending a full investigation. I don't need the approval of the Credentials Committee or your precious Dr. Bell. It is within my power, and that's exactly what I intend to do at the first opportunity."

He dropped the bag back into his desk drawer. "Good day, Doctor."

As Elena left the city limits of Dainger, she wished she could leave her troubles behind as well. All the way to Fort Worth, thoughts circled in her head like a cloud of vultures over carrion. She felt certain this vial of Anectine was the same one she'd found in his bedside table earlier — the one she'd so innocently picked up and examined — which meant that her fingerprints would be on the vial. Someone was trying to frame her. But who? And why?

Was Nathan Godwin the culprit? He had no reason to hate her. But she'd aligned herself, no matter how innocently, with Marcus Bell, and the enmity between Bell and the administrator was obvious. Could

Godwin have gone so far as to kill a man in order to cast suspicion on her as a way to demonstrate his power? It was far-fetched, but so was everything else that had gone on in her life recently.

Then there was Eric Burson. He made it a frequent practice to be in the ICU. He'd been there right before the first episode that almost took Lambert's life. As an EMT, Burson had access to Anectine and was familiar with its action. He hated doctors. That was no secret. And he'd apparently directed some of that hate toward Elena from the moment they'd met. Was this the endgame of some arcane plot to harm her? Elena found it hard to believe that someone whose profession involved the daily saving of lives could sacrifice one in order to get revenge on a member of the medical community.

Marcus Bell? He'd been in the ICU at the time of Lambert's death, but she couldn't think of any motive he might have to do such a thing. She'd tried to turn away his advances graciously, pleading her recent widowhood. Surely he understood that, since he'd gone through the same experience. No, Elena couldn't bring herself to consider him a suspect.

She thought of her midnight caller, the

mysterious Karri. When she'd first seen the name on Will's note, Elena couldn't place Karri Lawson, but soon the picture came clear. Karri, the attractive brunette nurse who'd cared for Mark during his terminal stay in the ICU. Karri, who was so attentive. Karri, who always seemed to be around Mark. Could they have been having an affair before Mark was stricken? Was Karri the reason for Mark's note? Was it jealousy that drove Karri to torment Elena with the cards and midnight calls? But did it go even further? Had Karri somehow managed to arrange for Charlie Lambert to die under circumstances that would cast suspicion on Elena?

What about Mark's sister, Natalie? Elena had no idea the woman even existed until the name appeared in Lillian's obituary. Had Natalie come out of the shadows to carry on the vendetta against Elena that her mother had started? Could she have had a hand in Lambert's death? Was it possible that she was in Dainger even now? Perhaps under an assumed name?

A loud honk from behind her brought Elena's attention back to the road. A glance at her speedometer told her she'd slowed to forty miles an hour. Ahead of her a solid double line divided the highway as far as she could see, while behind her was a string of cars almost a half mile long. She waved an apology and pulled onto the shoulder. She sat there, her emergency flashers going, while car after car passed. As the slipstream from each passing car rocked her little Ford, Elena fought back the tears.

The last car passed, but she didn't pull out. Instead, she did something she hadn't done in months. She'd read somewhere that the two most fervent prayers anyone could utter were "Please, please, please" and "Thank you, thank you, thank you." Before Elena turned the wheel and pulled back onto the road, her lips formed the words: "Please. Please. Please."

Every step from the parking garage to the elevator to Josh Samuels's office was like moving through a field of tar. To dredge up the events of five months ago was more than Elena could contemplate. Yet she trudged on.

Once she stopped in her tracks, frozen, until words began playing in her head like an endless loop: "Investigate my life, O God . . . See for yourself whether I've done anything wrong." Surely God already knew whether she'd done anything wrong. Now it was time for it all to be brought into the light. It would either help . . . or hurt. But it was time.

The waiting room was small, neat, and empty of patients. Elena took a seat in the farthest corner and picked up a magazine, hiding behind it as though it could shield her from unseen eyes.

"Elena?"

She hadn't heard the inner door open. Now Josh Samuels filled it, a look of genuine welcome on his face. Knowing gray eyes stared out from a craggy face with a distinct five o'clock shadow. Ridges marked his shaved head like a relief map. Samuels wore a starched white dress shirt, open at the collar, the cuffs laid back two neat turns. Creased Dockers and white Reeboks completed his outfit. Not exactly what she expected a psychologist to wear. But, according to Cathy, Samuels wasn't a typical psychologist.

She followed him into an office that was just as small and cozy as the waiting room. A desk sat butted against the far wall, facing a landscape Elena thought was by Monet.

Samuels led Elena to the corner of the room where a group of three armchairs formed a semicircle around a coffee table. He motioned her to take one of the chairs.

A number of certificates and plaques hung on the wall nearby, and she tried to sneak a look as she was seated.

"Perfectly normal to be curious about the credentials of someone to whom you're about to pour out your secrets," Samuels said. "Let me save you the trouble of straining your eyes." He pointed to two certificates in the center of the grouping. "Undergraduate work at USC. Graduate degree from Stanford. Stayed on the faculty for a couple of years. Married a Texas girl and moved here." He crossed his legs, revealing white crew socks. "Now, how can I help you?"

Once Elena started, the words tumbled out one after the other with hardly a pause for breath. Samuels didn't move, didn't ask a question, didn't take a note. He spoke only when it was obvious she had finished.

"You want me to see if I can regress you to those times in the ICU when your husband and Mr. Pulliam died. Is that right?"

It seemed to Elena that she had no more words, might never speak again. She nodded.

"You realize that I have no legal privilege. If I find that you committed a crime, I have to report it."

"Both Mark and Chester Pulliam were essentially . . ." She swallowed hard and forced out the hated word. "They were brain-dead. I'd already given permission to withdraw Mark's life support. Mrs. Pulliam was reaching the same conclusion. My attorney tells me that the worst thing I could be guilty of was going outside ethical boundaries. If something else comes up, and you think there's a crime involved, I'd ask that you discuss it with an attorney before proceeding."

Samuels was silent for several minutes, his gaze fixed on the painting across the room. Finally, he nodded. "Fair enough. I'll hypnotize you, and we'll see where it takes us."

Elena looked around. "Do you want me to lie down on a couch or something?"

A ghost of a grin flitted across Samuels's face. "You're fine right where you are. Are you comfortable?"

Elena nodded.

"There's a lot of misinformation about hypnosis. Some psychiatrists use a drug like amytal to induce a hypnotic state. I'm not an MD, so that's not an option. However, I've found that it's easy to hypnotize a cooperative subject. If we had time, I could teach you self-hypnosis. I've helped people lose weight and stop smoking that way."

"I just want you to get that information. Please."

"I'll do my best. Now lean back. Close your eyes. Concentrate on the sound of my voice."

Elena recalled having her tonsils removed in childhood. As she came out of the anesthetic, she heard the voice of her mother as though it were issuing from a tunnel, echoing and hollow but still recognizable. She remembered the pleasant feeling as though she were emerging from a deep and restful sleep into a day full of promise. Of course, then the pleasant feeling gave way to a terrible burning in her throat and things went downhill from there.

This time she was experiencing the pleasure without the pain. The voice that echoed through the tunnel of her mind wasn't that of her mother. Nevertheless, it was associated with a feeling of comfort, of security. "Elena, wake up. You're coming awake now. Can you open your eyes?"

She did, and saw Josh Samuels sitting in his chair opposite her. "Did . . . did you get what we wanted?"

"Yes. I took you back to the day of Mark's death. Then we went forward to Mr. Pulliam's death. You were a very easy subject."

364

"Did . . . did I do anything bad?"

Samuels pointed to a small tape recorder on the table. "I took the liberty of recording the session. You can listen if you wish. If not, I'll let you erase the recording."

Elena was already shaking her head. "No, I can't relive those times. Will you just tell me what you learned?"

"Very well. Would you like some water? A soft drink?"

Her throat was parched as the Sahara, but she couldn't wait even another minute. "After we finish. Tell me, please."

"Let's start with Pulliam. You spoke with Mrs. Pulliam. When she left the room, you spent five minutes considering all the ways you could put an end to his life — your words were 'give him a death with dignity' — but you didn't act on those impulses."

Elena felt tears forming in her eyes. "Thank God."

"That's another interesting thing. Before you walked out of the room, you paused at his bedside, took his hand, and prayed. For him, and for you."

"Are you sure? That would be so out of character," Elena said. "I stopped praying when Mark died."

Samuels's hand moved toward the recorder. "Want to hear it?"

"No, I believe you." There it was. She hadn't removed Pulliam's life support while in a fugue state. She wasn't really a danger to terminally ill patients. Elena couldn't process all the implications yet, but she would eventually. "What about Mark?"

"Before we go there, you mentioned one more thing that might be important. As you left the ICU, you felt for your pager at your waist but didn't find it. You turned back toward Pulliam's room, thinking it might have slipped off in there. Just as you found it in the pocket of your white coat, you saw a nurse going into that room. Your words, as I recall, were 'I wonder what Karri is doing in there?' "

19

Even after the puzzle piece marked "Karri" dropped into place, Elena still had more questions than answers. But she could think about that later. Right now, all she felt was a sense of relief.

Samuels leaned toward her. "Are you all right?"

"I'll take that water now, if you don't mind."

The therapist disappeared through a side door and returned in a moment with two frosty bottles of water. Elena drained hers fast enough to make her temples hurt. Samuels uncapped his bottle and sipped, his eyes never leaving her.

"Do you want to go on?" he asked.

"Yes. Obviously, it's a relief to hear that I wasn't responsible for Chester Pulliam's death, but I need to know for sure about Mark."

He put his almost-full bottle on the table.

"By your recollection, you sat with Mark as you had done for two weeks, holding his hand and talking to him, hoping he could hear you. You'd decided there was no hope of recovery for him, so you told him what was coming. You kissed him and said, 'May God give you peace. May God give both of us peace.' "

"Is that when I turned off the ventilator?"

"No, that's when you went to the family room to cry. That's where they found you to tell you Mark was dead."

Elena couldn't hold back the tears.

"Does this help?" Samuels asked.

"More than you can ever know," Elena said. "I didn't act in a fugue state. I'm not a threat to patients. The only thing I did wrong was write Mark's DNR order when I couldn't find Dr. Matney to tell him I'd finally reached that decision. Oh, yes. It helps."

Samuels remained silent, apparently waiting for her to say more. What more was there to say? She felt as though a huge weight had been lifted from her shoulders.

He sipped once more from his water. "Don't you wonder who actually was responsible for these deaths? And why?"

And with those words, she felt her shoulders sag once more.

Summer days were long in Texas, and daylight savings time added yet another hour of sunlight. When Elena pulled out of the parking garage, the setting sun was low on the horizon, almost blinding her. She looked at the dashboard clock and did some fast calculation before she pulled into the parking lot of a steak house near Samuels's professional building. If she took her time over dinner, the sun wouldn't interfere with her drive home.

An hour later, Elena climbed into her car, started the engine, and cranked up the air conditioner to high. There was no reason to hurry home, and this was probably as good a time as any to try the call. She pulled her phone from her bag and checked the display: three-fourths charged.

The yellow slip was still in her purse. Elena's fingers hovered over the phone keys like a scared diver peering over the edge of the high board. She took a deep breath and punched in the number.

One ring. Two. Three. Four. Then a soft voice answered. "Hello?"

Even if Elena hadn't been aware of the number she'd dialed, she would have recognized that husky alto from the single word. She'd never thought much about the expression "her blood boiled," but it was as though she could feel it roiling through her veins at this moment.

Again, "Hello?"

"Karri, this is Elena." She rushed on, anxious to get the words out. "Don't hang up. I'll just keep calling. We have to talk."

"Why?"

"Why? Because I know you've called every week to torment me. I suspect the letters came from you too. And now I know that you took Chester Pulliam off life support. Tell me why."

There was the click of a lighter, the sound of a deep inhalation, a satisfied exhalation. Elena pictured Karri drawing on the cigarette, blowing smoke into the phone. Her next words dripped with venom. "You poor sap. You never knew, did you?"

"Knew that you and Mark were having an affair? No, I didn't know until after his death. That's when I found the note he'd written, the one telling me it was over between us."

Karri's cackle was right out of the story of Hansel and Gretel, the wicked witch enjoying the confusion of her victim. "Like I said, you never knew. I met Mark when he was working on some computer issues at the hospital. We seemed to click. For a while I thought something might come of it. Then I asked him to leave you."

Elena struggled to keep control of her voice. "What happened?"

"He told me he loved you. He planned to beg your forgiveness. It was over between us. That note you found was meant for me."

"So Mark —"

"Mark was unfaithful to you a couple of times. Big deal. When it came down to it, he wanted you, not me. Then he had that stroke and died." Another puff of the cigarette. Elena could almost smell the smoke. "When I couldn't take my anger out on him, I decided to vent it against you. That's the reason for the calls and the notes. I wanted you to worry that you'd ended his life without knowing it. I wanted to wreck your life, the way Mark wrecked mine when he got my hopes up and then dashed them."

"And Chester Pulliam?"

"Same thing. I thought it would really mess up your head if you were accused of that one as well. I even transferred from Zale to St. Paul to get the opportunity." Elena heard another puff.

Elena remembered the dark-haired nurse who ducked into a room in the ICU to avoid her. "How could you know I wasn't the one who took Mark off life support?"

"Because I did! I waited until you left. Then I sneaked into his room, shot him full of some morphine I'd been saving out of patient shots, and turned off his respirator. As much as he hurt me, I couldn't stand to see him go on the way he was. He was going to die anyway. And I figured I might as well use it to hurt you."

A car pulled up beside Elena. A couple got out, favored her with a curious glance, then walked side-by-side into the restaurant.

"One more question," Elena said. "How did you manage to get into the ICU here at Summers County General? How could you arrange the patient death here?"

Karri seemed genuinely puzzled by the question. "I don't know what you mean. I don't even know where Summers County is. All I know is you must not have changed your cell phone, because I used the number we had in the ICU at the hospital."

Karri was still talking when Elena broke the connection. She'd solved one mystery, but another one remained. Who killed Charlie Lambert? And why did they want to blame it on her?

The insistent tapping roused Elena. She

372

raised her head from its resting place on the steering wheel of her car and turned to look at the couple she'd seen enter the restaurant earlier. The man tapped once more, and Elena lowered the window.

"Are you all right?"

"I'm all right. I've just had some disturbing news."

The woman leaned over her husband's shoulder. "Is there anything we can do? Are you okay to drive?"

"I'm fine. Thank you."

Elena watched them climb into their car and pull away. She'd have to stop using parking lots for her private pity parties. Having strangers stop to offer assistance was embarrassing.

It was almost dark now. Time to head back. She glanced at the reverse directions she'd printed, making sure she knew how to get out of Fort Worth and onto the road to Dainger. There it was again. Even though the experience had been emotionally draining, she'd felt safe in Josh Samuels's office. Now she was driving back into danger.

As soon as she cleared the Fort Worth city limits, she engaged the car's cruise control and tried to do the same with her mind. She determined that she wouldn't worry for the next half hour. After all, she should feel relieved. It was unlikely that Karri would call again. Elena would have to talk with someone, perhaps Will, to see how to convey this new information to Dr. Matney.

What did she have to substantiate what Karri told her? The recording Samuels had made during her regression therapy would back her up, but she could imagine a lawyer tearing it to shreds. Could she have recorded her conversation with Karri? Maybe, if she'd thought of it. But she hadn't. No, Karri had told her what she needed to know. That was more important than any legal confession.

As her car moved through the gathering darkness, Elena saw two bright pinpoints in her rearview mirror. How long had that car been back there? She was going the exact speed limit, and in her experience that was an invitation for every car on the road to pass her. But this one hung back. Either they were extremely law-abiding, or they were following her.

You're being paranoid again. No, the person looking into her bedroom window hadn't been a figment of her imagination. And she was a woman driving alone at night. Reason enough to be a bit jumpy. She checked to make sure that her doors were locked. Her eyes scanned the gauges. Plenty of fuel, temperature fine, no red warning lights showing.

She added ten miles per hour to her speed. The lights in her rearview mirror maintained their position. She slowed, and so did the car behind her, trailing as though at the end of an invisible cable. Elena saw the lights of home on the horizon. She sped up, determined to lead her pursuer to a safe, well-lit place as quickly as possible.

She decided to head for RJ's. She took the appropriate exit and the car behind her did the same. Two short blocks brought her to the restaurant. She pulled into the parking lot, encouraged to see that it was almost full of cars, with people coming and going almost constantly.

She kept her eyes glued to her rearview mirror. In a moment, a car slowed as though about to turn in, then accelerated away. There was plenty of light in the parking lot, but that just made the street leading to it seem darker, and it was impossible for Elena to make out details of the car. No matter. At least she'd managed to scare away her stalker.

Elena restarted her car and had her hand on the gearshift when another car came down the same street she'd used. She recognized this one as soon as it entered the parking lot. She watched the black and white SUV rock to a stop in a no parking zone in front of the restaurant. Frank Perrin climbed out and gave her a casual wave.

Elena rolled down her window but kept the engine going.

Frank leaned against the driver's side door. "Aren't you even going to ask?"

"Ask what? Why you followed me all the way from Fort Worth?"

Frank showed a perfect poker face. "Actually, I didn't. I had a call to a fender-bender out near the Tarrant-Summers county line. I was about to head back when I thought I saw your car go by, with a black Chevy right behind it. It looked like he was following you, so I just made myself a caboose to your little train."

Elena had a momentary pang over her decision to seek a safe place. Why couldn't she have simply driven home, so Frank could identify the man following her? Then again, who was to say that Frank wasn't the real stalker, and the car she'd seen was one he'd let get between his and hers to avoid identification?

"Do you want me to follow you home?" Frank asked.

Elena did her best to sound calm and casual. "No, but I appreciate your looking out for me like that."

"All part of the service." He tipped his hat back and smiled. "Now that's two dates you owe me."

"Thanks for bringing lunch." Cathy spooned up the last bit of soup and chased it with Diet Sprite. "I hope you didn't mind coming here. Milton still wants me to take things easy."

"No problem," Elena said. "I wanted to talk with you, and this is a great way to do it. I just wish we had more time to get together."

The two women were seated in the dining room of Cathy and Will's home. Elena looked around her and decided that one day she'd have a cozy house like this — neat but functional, attractive without being frilly. But that was a dream for another day.

"What's on your mind?" Cathy asked.

The front door opened and Will called, "Anybody home?"

Cathy answered. "We're in the dining room. Elena brought soup and sandwiches. They're in the kitchen. Help yourself and then come join us." She looked at Elena. "Does Will being here affect the talk you wanted to have?"

"No, actually I think some of this may require a lawyer's perspective."

In a few minutes, Will was settled at the table, across from the two women. "Hope you don't mind if I dig in. I only have a half hour for lunch today."

"Eat and listen," Cathy said. "Elena has some things to tell us."

Elena took them through the story of her session with Josh and the conversation with Karri Lawson that followed. "It's good to know that I wasn't directly responsible for either death. Will, here's my question for you. Since neither Mark nor Mr. Pulliam had any chance of surviving, was Karri's action in discontinuing life support murder? Homicide? Manslaughter?"

"Realize that this is pure conjecture on my part, but I can't imagine a district attorney taking a case like that to a Grand Jury. So the answer is probably 'None of the above.' "

Elena nodded. "That's what I thought. Which brings me to my second question. What should I do about her confession? Should I contact Dr. Matney and tell him about it?"

Cathy put down her glass. "Let me take that one. You and I both know how things work in a medical center. By now, Dr. Matney is knee-deep in the politics of trying to get that appointment as dean. Situations like this one fall into the category of 'out of sight, out of mind.' Why bring it up again? You don't need his recommendation. You've completed your training. You have a job. Your employer knows the truth and is satisfied. I'd leave it at that."

Will held up his finger while he chewed and swallowed the last bite of his sandwich. "I think you should sit down tonight and write out a complete account of your conversation with Karri. Make it as close to verbatim as you can. Tomorrow, call Josh Samuels and ask him to lock up his notes of your session, including the recording he made."

Elena thought about that for a minute. "Is that really necessary?"

"It may never come up again," Will said. "But, if it does, it'll help that you put the story down while it was fresh. And Samuels's corroboration of what you said under hypnosis would be important."

"I can see that, I guess," Elena said. "But it worries me that Karri is still working in the ICU. What if she decides that disconnecting people from life support gives her a thrill? Maybe she'll start to think she should be the one to decide who lives and who dies."

"Don't you think that's a bit far-fetched?"

Cathy asked.

"After what she's done, I'd believe anything," Elena replied.

They were silent for a couple of minutes. Then a smile brightened Will's face. "How about this? Karri doesn't know my investigator, Ramon. Nicest guy you'll ever meet, but he can act pretty tough if the situation warrants it. He could 'run into' Karri in the hospital cafeteria, draw her aside, and say something like, 'We know what you did. And if you so much as think of doing it again, we'll see that your license is lifted and you face the stiffest criminal penalties possible.' "

Cathy chimed in. "What if she asks, 'Who's this we?' "

Will grinned. "I suspect he'd give her a knowing look. 'You know. And don't forget it.' How's that?"

Elena pondered that for a moment. "We could try it. I'd like to think this was a one-time thing, a way of hurting me because Mark dumped her to stay with me."

Cathy tilted her glass and crunched a piece of ice. "That's settled. Now what about the person who murdered Charlie Lambert? We're not talking about withdrawing life support from a patient who's dependent on it. This was a man on the road to recovery. He might not be the same person as before his stroke, but he'd be alive."

"I've been waiting for the police to come knocking on my door," Elena said. "If Nathan Godwin gives them that bottle of Anectine with my fingerprints on it, I don't see how I can avoid being arrested."

"Either he hasn't called the police yet, or they're taking their time with their preliminary investigation. In either case, we still have some time. We'll try to come up with a solution before they get to you." Will pushed back his chair. "Right now, I'm due back at the office. We'll talk about this later."

"Jane, this is Dr. Gardner." Elena snugged her cell phone against her ear with her shoulder and used both hands to wheel her car into the hospital parking lot. "I have one more stop to make before I come back to the office. Anything going on?"

"Nothing that can't wait until you get here. Your first patient of the afternoon cancelled, so you've got a little time."

"I'm at the hospital. Given the cell phone reception here, you'd better have the operator page me if you need me."

Elena wasn't sure where the office she wanted was located, so she took a moment to consult the directory in the main lobby.

She envied David the opportunity to get to know the place he'd practice, instead of being thrown into the middle of it with almost no warning. But she was proud she'd been able to adapt so well to her role in Cathy's practice. If only everything else was going smoothly.

She found the office number, determined its location using the map alongside the directory, and set out in that direction. As she walked, Elena rehearsed her speech. The Jefferson family had come to the office that morning with their mother. A review of Cathy's previous notes confirmed Elena's impression that this was a woman slipping further into the heartbreaking world of senile dementia. Mrs. Jefferson was totally out of touch with reality now, and there was no way her family could care for her at home. Elena hoped that the hospital's social worker might be able to help find an answer.

Here it was, room 1003. She read the name on the door: N. Cook, Social Worker. Elena tapped on the door, and a pleasant female voice replied, "Come in."

File cabinets occupied the space along every wall except for the door through which Elena entered. A scarred metal desk sat in the center of the room, and the woman behind it was almost hidden by a stack of papers. She motioned Elena to one of the two mismatched client chairs across from her and beamed a thousand-watt smile at her visitor. "Have a seat. I'm Natalie Cook. How can I help you?"

Elena offered her hand. "I'm Dr. Elena Gardner. I —"

The social worker's expression was one of pure shock. "How in the world did you ever find me?"

"I beg your pardon?"

"You're Mark's wife, aren't you?"

"Do I know you?"

"No, my mother made sure of that long ago." She leaned across the desk and Elena saw the resemblance before the next words confirmed it. "I'm Natalie, Mark's sister."

20

Elena felt as though she were inside a huge snow globe that some giant hand had given a shake. Her world had just turned upside down. "Natalie? But your name is Cook, not Gardner."

"Cook is my married name. After my mother threw me out of her house, calling me a hippie who'd never make anything of her life, I migrated to Santa Fe. I was scratching out a living selling trinkets in the town square when I met Clark. He was the youth pastor at a church there. We started dating and were married six months later."

"Your mother never mentioned you."

"No, when I didn't live up to the image she had in mind for her daughter, it was as though she'd taken white-out and erased my name from the family Bible. She wouldn't take my calls, returned my letters unopened. The only reason I know that you and my little brother were married is that one of my high school friends had my address and sent me the clipping from the paper."

Elena tried to assimilate what she was hearing. "How do you go from selling jewelry on the square in Santa Fe to practicing social work in Texas?"

"Clark was called to be associate pastor of the First Methodist Church here in town, and we found out the hospital was looking to add a social worker. I didn't have any training, just a couple of years of college, but I bluffed my way through the interview and got the position. I've been learning on the job ever since."

"Do you and Clark have any children?"

Natalie bit her lip. "Last year, Clark decided he wasn't cut out for ministry — or for marriage. I'm alone now."

Elena hitched her chair closer. "Natalie, you're not alone anymore. I'm glad I found you. But I have some news about your family."

"Sorry I'm late." Elena tossed her purse into her desk drawer. She snatched her white coat from the hook behind the door and shrugged into it, then scanned the hall. The plastic bins outside every exam room door held a chart. She was starting behind, and to catch up she had to put aside the events of the past hour. There'd be time enough to think about them this evening when she had dinner with David.

Elena tapped on the door of the first exam room and entered to find an elderly woman fidgeting on the edge of the exam table. Her right shoe lay on the floor, and she was flexing the toes of that foot.

"Mrs. Musgrove, I'm Dr. Gardner. I'm terribly sorry to keep you waiting. I was held up at the hospital." Elena perched on the rolling stool and studied the chart. This was the woman's first visit to the practice. She listed a chief complaint of foot trouble. "Tell me about the problem with your feet."

The woman kept her eyes fixed on her foot, as though her gaze alone might make it well again. "I've got this place on it that won't heal."

"How long has it been there?"

"Maybe six months, might be a bit longer."

"Does it hurt?"

"No. But I told my daughter about it. She took one look at it and made this appointment. I don't think it's much, do you?"

Elena had no trouble finding the ulcer on the bottom of the woman's foot. It was about an inch in diameter, fairly shallow, with a clean central crater. She placed her fingertips lightly on the top of the foot. The pulse was weak, and the skin was cool. Elena pulled a hatpin from the lapel of her white coat and lightly jabbed the woman's foot. "Feel that?"

"Not really. But I don't have much feeling in my feet, anyway."

Elena thought she knew what the woman's problem was, but she wanted to be certain. "How's your weight?"

"I don't see what that has to do with my feet, but now that you mention it, I've been losing weight, even though I eat quite a bit."

Elena went through several more questions. She made a couple of notes on the chart, then set it aside. "Mrs. Musgrove, I think you have diabetes. I'm not sure how long you've had it, but it's affected the nerves and the circulation in your feet. I'm going to have my nurse set up an appointment for some lab work to confirm that diagnosis. Meanwhile, here's what you need to do to keep that ulcer from getting worse."

She gave the woman comprehensive directions, all the while trying to ignore the clock in her head that was saying, "You're behind. Hurry up." This patient deserved her best, and if it took a bit of time, so be it.

The afternoon went by quickly. Some

patients presented with problems that were simple, some with problems that were challenging. When she finished with the last patient on her list, it was almost six o'clock. She looked into the waiting room, expecting it to be empty. Instead, she saw a middle-aged Hispanic man in the far corner thumbing through a magazine. He wore a dark blue uniform of some kind. Maybe this was a mechanic, here to see her about an injury.

Jane was still checking out the last patient, so Elena approached the man and said, "I'm Dr. Gardner. Are you here to see me?"

The man put down his magazine and stood up. Elena got a closer look at his uniform, and his solemn expression confirmed her fear. "I'm Jesus Hernandez, Dainger Police Department. I wonder if I might have a few minutes of your time, Doctor?"

He retrieved a worn leather briefcase from near his feet and followed Elena into her office. She eased into the chair behind her desk and waved him to a seat opposite her. It took everything she could muster not to show the panic she felt. "How can I help you, Officer?"

"Doctor, we're working a case that involves a patient of yours, Charles Lambert.

To assist us in our efforts, I'd like you to allow me to take your fingerprints."

So that was it. No questions. No Miranda warning. Just a request for fingerprints. Elena had never been printed before. No military service. No fingerprinting when she began her residency. The police couldn't say the prints on the Anectine bottle were hers unless she gave them this sample.

Should she call Will? Surely they had to have some sort of warrant to do this. Wasn't there something in the Constitution about unreasonable search and seizure? She might be able to delay the process for days, maybe even weeks. But what would that gain her?

She pushed back the sleeves of her coat and held out her hands. "Certainly."

As the man went through the process, Elena had a thought. "Tell me, did the police chief send you to do this because you're Hispanic? Did he think that would make me more cooperative?"

A ghost of a smile flittered across Officer Hernandez's face. "No, ma'am. I'm a second-generation Texan. I can't do much more in Spanish than order in a Mexican restaurant." He handed her a moist towelette to clean her fingers. "The chief sent me because I'm the best one on the force at taking fingerprints."

Will stopped his client in mid-sentence with an upraised index finger and reached to punch the flashing button on his private line. Only a few people had this number, and he didn't want to miss a call from any of them. "Yes?"

"Will, it's Elena. Can you talk?"

"Let me call you back in five minutes."

It was actually ten minutes before Will shook hands with his client and showed him out of the office. The incorporation of a small business for the man was a simple matter. Will had a hunch that Elena's call didn't signal anything simple. Five minutes later, he knew he'd been right.

"The police came for your fingerprints? Did they read you your rights?"

"No," Elena said. "No questions. Not even any pressure to cooperate. He just said, 'I'd like you to allow me to take your fingerprints.' I started to tell him I'd need to call my lawyer, but then I decided there was really no benefit to refusing."

"You could have made them come back with a warrant, but you're right. This way, you paint yourself as a cooperative citizen with nothing to hide."

"How long do I have before they show up with handcuffs, though? If Godwin gave them the Anectine bottle, they're bound to identify my fingerprints on it."

Will pulled a legal pad toward him and scribbled a few words. "First they'll take a statement from you and ask you a bunch of questions. How do you explain the fingerprints on the bottle? Can you account for your whereabouts during the time of Lambert's death? By the way, where were you then?"

"I was in medical records, signing charts. And, before you ask, there was no one else around. The place was empty."

"Not good," Will said.

"But I have a little time. Right?"

"Some. Let me call my source at the police department and see what he knows." Will scribbled a note on his pad. "Can you come by this evening to talk about this?"

"Ummm . . . I'm supposed to have dinner with David tonight. There are some things we need to discuss. Can this wait until tomorrow?"

Will wondered what could be more important than avoiding an arrest for murder. "I suppose so. Meet me in my office at noon tomorrow. If you hear from the police before then, call me immediately."

"It seems to me that the only way I can be cleared is —"

The silence stretched on. "Elena, are you still there?"

"Let me think about this."

Will heard a click, and realized he was holding a dead phone. He wasn't sure what Elena had in mind, but he was willing to bet it involved thinking outside the box. Way outside.

David paused with a bite of enchilada halfway to his mouth. He'd hoped this would be a quiet dinner, one when he could convey to Elena how he felt about her. But she'd led with startling news, and that had been the topic of their conversation since. "She didn't know about Mark?" All around them, the little Tex-Mex restaurant buzzed with conversations, but David kept his attention riveted on Elena. "What an amazing story."

Elena dipped a chip into the salsa. "Her mother had effectively disinherited her, cut off all communication. She knew we were married because a high school friend tracked down Natalie's address and sent her a copy of the story. She recognized me from the picture. We're still not sure how her name ended up in the list of survivors in

Lillian's obituary. Probably one of Lillian's acquaintances mentioned her."

David chewed and swallowed. "Wow. Sort of like the line from *Casablanca*. 'Of all the hospitals in all the states, you had to come to the one where she works.' "

"I don't think that's what Bogart said, but I get the picture. And I'm glad I found her. I think there's a connection there that will be good for both of us. I really need a friend right now."

"Excuse me, but what am I?" David's words were light, his tone serious.

"I'm sorry. Of course you're a friend. A good one, too."

David forced a smile. *Tell her now. She knows it, but she just won't let herself admit it.* "Elena, let's not ignore it. You know how I feel about you. Mark's been gone for more than half a year. Isn't it time you began thinking about the rest of your life?"

He saw her open her mouth, then close it again. Maybe his words had hit home this time. Finally, she shook her head. "There's just too much uncertainty in my life right now. Maybe, when I get out from under this cloud —"

David nodded. At least it wasn't a "no." Just a "maybe later." He could live with that.

Elena bit into a chip, then licked a bit of

salsa off her fingertips. "Tell me, how's Mrs. Gomez?"

"Good news there. Today she roused when her husband called her name. She's still in and out of consciousness, but she's breathing on her own. I think she's going to make it."

"Still in ICU?"

"Yeah. I figure I've got at least another day's grace before Godwin really pushes me to transfer her to a postpartum room."

As David watched, Elena seemed to retreat deep inside herself. "Penny for your thoughts."

She shook her head and pushed away her plate. "Would you mind if we cut this short?" Elena dipped into her purse and dropped some bills on the check. "I hate to hurry off, but I was thinking about something I have to do, and it looks like I don't have much time."

Darkness was descending on the city, but still Elena sat in her office, her fingertips pressed to her temples. The lamp on her desk provided the only illumination of the yellow legal pad before her. Random thoughts flew through her head, while she did her best to capture them and arrange them to make some sort of sense. Who would want to kill Charlie Lambert? And why?

She ran down her list of suspects once more. Nathan Godwin. Marcus Bell. Eric Burson. Frank Perrin. Natalie Gardner Cook. She could imagine motives for each of them. What about access?

Godwin could go anywhere in the hospital without question. Eric was a frequent visitor to the ICU. So was Marcus. Frank made calls to the hospital to take statements from accident victims — could some of those take him to the ICU? Natalie worked in the hospital.

Elena dropped her head to the desk. *God, I don't know what to do.*

There was no divine voice from the clouds, no lightning flash or burning bush. Instead, the answer came to her the way algebra had finally begun to make sense to her in high school. One minute it was a crazy, senseless exercise. The next, everything fell into place.

Now she knew who the killer was. Even better, she knew who the next victim would be, and when the attempt would take place.

She picked up the phone, found the number she wanted, and dialed it. "Hi, this is Elena Gardner. Listen, I need a big favor from you."

■ ■ ■ ■

Elena stood in the closet and listened to the hospital sounds around her. The overhead paging system was silent at 2:00 a.m. The squeak of rubber soles and the occasional murmured conversation marked the passage of nurses on their rounds, accompanied at times by the clacking wheels of a medication cart.

Elena had taken the head nurse aside and asked her to avoid this room as much as possible. The nurse seemed puzzled, but at last she agreed.

This had to be the room. This had to be the patient. And, most important, if rumors spread throughout the hospital as rapidly as Elena thought, this had to be the night. It would happen on the 11:00 p.m. to 7:00 a.m. shift — the time when life was at its lowest ebb, for medical staff and patients alike.

Elena stretched, and listened to her bones creak. She'd stood here for three hours. How much longer could she —

The door opened. A dark form slipped into the room and pushed the door closed. The soft "whoosh" of the pneumatic closer ended with a sharp "click." The intruder crept further into the room. The beam of a pencil flash, softened by a finger over the lens, swept over the bed and picked out a form hidden under the covers.

The intruder pulled a cylindrical object from a pocket and flicked a plastic cover off the tip.

Elena stepped from the closet. "That's enough. Stop right there." Her hand found the light switch, and light flooded the room.

Glenna Dunn shielded her eyes with her hand, still holding the pencil flash. She put the syringe behind her like a child caught with a forbidden cookie. "Dr. Gardner, you surprised me. I came by to check on my husband."

"At 2:00 a.m?"

"I'm working a double shift in the ER tonight. I thought I'd slip up here on my break."

Elena closed the distance between them. "Great alibi, Glenna. Your husband stops breathing, and any number of people would say you were in the ER the whole time. Nobody pays any attention to the time you're gone on break, especially if things are busy down there."

"I don't know what you mean."

"By the way, you can put down that syringe of Anectine. Your husband was

moved to another room earlier today. This
—" She whisked back the covers. "This is
Resusci-Annie, the mannequin I use for
CPR classes. Makes a pretty realistic patient
in the dark, doesn't she?"

Glenna lunged forward, the syringe held
like a knife, the deadly needle poised to
plunge into vulnerable tissue. Elena dodged
back like a matador avoiding the horns of a
charging bull.

This wasn't the way Elena pictured the
scene. She'd confront Glenna, the nurse
would break down crying, and Elena would
call the police to take her. But apparently,
Glenna had no intention of going quietly. If
she could jab that needle into one of Elena's
muscles and empty the contents of the
syringe, paralysis would occur within a
minute, giving Glenna plenty of time to get
away. Since Elena wouldn't be able to
breathe for five minutes or more, she'd die.

Elena locked Glenna's right wrist in both
hands, fighting with all her might to keep
that deadly point away. Glenna tried to
scratch Elena's eyes with her free left hand.
Elena dodged just in time.

Back and forth the battle raged. At last,
Elena focused every ounce of strength she
could muster, and began to bend Glenna's
hand backward. Elena gave one final heave,

and the needle jabbed into the base of Glenna's neck. Glenna strained to pull the syringe away, but only succeeded in pushing down on the plunger.

Elena pulled back in horror. Glenna stood for a moment, the syringe dangling from the needle still sunk into her neck.

Elena ripped the syringe away. "Glenna, breathe," she yelled. "Take some deep breaths while you can."

Glenna fell to the floor. It seemed that all her muscles contracted at once. Then she went limp as a rag doll.

Elena knelt at the woman's head, positioned her head to open her airway, and put her lips around Glenna's mouth. Elena gave three quick breaths. She didn't think she could do that for five or six more minutes. There had to be a better way.

Her eyes swept the room. There was a ventilator in the corner, left there when Glenna's husband was moved earlier in the day. But how to put it to use?

Elena bent and gave Glenna another four breaths. As she straightened, she saw the case she'd shoved under the bed when she put Resusci-Annie in place. It contained the laryngoscope and endotracheal tubes she'd used to teach advanced resuscitation techniques.

Elena pulled the case toward her and opened it, then turned away to breathe for Glenna once more. She had to hurry. Elena made a quick guess about the size tube needed. She pulled it from the case and snapped the laryngoscope open. The light didn't go on.

Breathe for Glenna again. Look back in the case and see the batteries lying free in one corner. Insert the batteries, open the laryngoscope, mutter a quick "thank-you" when the light came on.

Four more quick breaths. Elena inserted the laryngoscope, pulled upward to visualize the larynx. Hard to see the vocal cords. Try anyway. She shoved the tube into Glenna's throat. Two quick breaths into the tube with one hand on Glenna's chest. No movement. Move her hand downward, another couple of breaths. The stomach rose. Glenna produced a massive belch. The tube was in the esophagus — the swallowing tube — not the airway.

Elena removed the tube, gave Glenna three mouth-to-mouth breaths. One more try with the laryngoscope. This time she got a good view of the vocal cords, and slid the tube between them. Two quick breaths. The chest rose. She was in.

Elena scrambled to roll the ventilator close

enough for the tubing to reach Glenna's endotracheal tube. She flipped the switch, adjusted the dial, and relaxed as the rhythmic "chuff, chuff" filled Glenna's lungs.

Elena sat back on her heels for a moment. Then she rose and reached across the bed to ring the call button.

"Yes?"

"This is Dr. Gardner. Please get hospital security up here stat. Then put in a call to the police. We're going to need them."

21

Elena stretched and yawned. She decided the police station in Dainger was nicer, both outside and in, than the sheriff's office. On the other hand, the personnel were definitely less inclined to be friendly. Elena and Will sat in chairs apparently chosen with an eye toward cost rather than comfort. All things considered, she would have preferred bright lights and a rubber hose to four hours in these chairs.

Officer Hernandez, whom she now knew was actually Sergeant Hernandez, consulted his notes. "Doctor, you took a big chance trying to catch the perpetrator yourself. If you'd simply shared your suspicions with us, we could have investigated Mrs. Dunn and saved everyone some excitement."

Will leaned forward. "We've been through this twice now. My client appreciates the civics lesson, but we both know she's innocent. If Mrs. Dunn's actions didn't indicate her guilt, her voluntary confession afterward certainly buttons things up. What more do you want?"

"I want Dr. Gardner to go over her story one more time."

"Why?"

Hernandez rose in response to a tap on the door. He returned accompanied by a middle-aged woman dressed in a navy business suit. Her red hair was perfectly styled, her makeup was understated but flawless, and her manner said, "I'm in charge, and don't you forget it."

Hernandez pulled out a chair for the newcomer. Elena noticed it was padded, in contrast to the ones on which she and Will sat. "Mr. Kennedy, I believe you know Mrs. McMurray?"

Will and the woman shook hands, not necessarily like old friends but at least long-time acquaintances. "Diane, what brings you out at this hour?"

"Two reasons, Will — getting the story firsthand before taking on this case, and the fact that I'm up for reelection next year."

"Score one point for honesty." Will turned to Elena. "Dr. Elena Gardner, Diane McMurray, Summers County District Attorney."

Mrs. McMurray nodded once. "Doctor,

I'm glad you came out of this unharmed."

Elena started to respond to the "un-harmed" description, but decided it wasn't worth it. "Are you going to charge Glenna with murder in the death of Charlie Lambert?"

"Honestly, I'm not sure. Manslaughter might be more appropriate. Then again, a grand jury might be sympathetic to a woman whose husband was in a permanent coma."

Like mine was, but I didn't try to kill him. On the other hand, I was willing to withdraw life support and let him die. She'd leave the moral distinction to lawyers and theologians. Diane McMurray would do what she had to do. It was out of Elena's hands now.

McMurray crossed her legs and leaned back in her chair. "Would you please go over your story once more?"

Elena wanted to scream. "If I have to."

Hernandez punched the key on a battered tape recorder in the center of the table. He recited the day and hour, named those present, and said, "Doctor, you make this statement voluntarily?"

Elena nodded. Will nudged her and she realized her mistake. "Yes."

She gave a brief account of the deaths of her husband and Chester Pulliam, explained

404

what she'd since learned through hypnotic regression by Josh Samuels and from her phone conversation with Karri Lawson. "That led me to the conclusion that the death of Charlie Lambert was unrelated to the events that took place in Dallas. But I wasn't sure who was behind it, or what their motive was."

"Tell us about that," McMurray said. Elena noticed that she hadn't taken any notes. Either the tape would be sufficient, or McMurray had a phenomenal memory.

"Realize that Charlie Lambert had suffered a severe stroke," Elena said. "The likelihood that he'd recover was slim. So whoever ended his life might have thought they were doing a favor for him and his wife. But several people had other reasons as well."

"Go on."

Elena went through her list of suspects and the reason each of them might have wanted to kill a patient and put the blame on her.

McMurray leaned forward as though this was the most interesting story in the world. "So how did you come up with Glenna Dunn?"

"Glenna's husband was in an auto accident that left him in a vegetative state.

She was worried about what she'd do when her insurance benefits were exhausted. Marcus said she told him she kept working so she could save others from going through what she experienced. I thought she meant she wanted to help keep patients alive. Then I realized maybe she meant using her position in the ER and ICU to put an end to the lives of patients in a vegetative state."

"What made her think she could get away with that?"

"With me around, who'd ever think about suspecting anyone else? It was a perfect setup for her."

McMurray nodded. "Why did you think she'd strike last night?"

Elena emptied the water bottle that sat in front of her. "Gossip travels like wildfire in any hospital, and this one is no exception. Glenna's position in the ER gave her a direct line to both hospital news and tidbits from law officers. She knew I was under suspicion for Charlie Lambert's death, just as she'd planned." She indicated Hernandez, who sat poker-faced across from her. "The sergeant here fingerprinted me yesterday. The odds were that I'd be arrested soon. She had to end her husband's life while I was still in circulation so I could be blamed for it."

"That's a pretty slim reason," McMurray said.

"There's more. Last night, I called the hospital's business manager at home. I asked her a question, and she knew the answer immediately because she'd worked on it all day. Bill Dunn's insurance coverage runs out today."

After leaving the police station, Elena wanted to go home and sleep for a week. Unfortunately, that wasn't an option. Cathy was out of the office until after the baby came. So Elena sucked it up and, with the help of more cups of coffee than she could count, made it through the day.

It was almost six o'clock when Jane took the last chart from her. "Dr. Gardner, I hope you can rest this weekend. Did Dr. Brown agree to cover for you?"

"Yes, bless his heart. He's a good man and a good doctor."

"That he is," Jane said. "You know, when you came here I was afraid Dr. Sewell's patients might be a bit hesitant to see a doctor . . . I mean —"

"You mean they'd be influenced by skin color," Elena said. "Emmet is almost charcoal; my complexion is sort of like café au lait. Cathy's so fair she'd disappear against new snow. But in the short time I've been here, I've noticed people paying less attention to the color of their doctor's skin and more to the person inside. That makes me happy."

In her car, Elena set a course for home. Well, the Kennedys' home. She'd lived with them half a month, and already it was home to her. Next week she'd look for a place of her own — maybe that apartment near David.

Dora Kennedy met Elena at the door and gave her a hug that threatened to crack a couple of ribs. "You come in here and sit down. I saved you some supper. There's meat loaf, mashed potatoes, sliced tomatoes, corn, peas, and biscuits. And if you're still hungry, I think there's some chocolate cake left."

Elena tried to remember when she'd last eaten. "That sounds marvelous. Thanks so much."

As they entered the kitchen, David rose from the kitchen table, almost knocking a cup of coffee onto the floor.

"I took the liberty of inviting Dr. Merritt to eat with us," Dora said. "I figured a bachelor couldn't turn down some home cooking. Now you two just visit a minute, while I finish reheating everything."

Elena covered the distance to David in three swift strides. He enfolded her, and she buried her head on his chest.

"How could you put yourself at risk like that?" David asked.

"I had to. It seemed the only way to trap Glenna."

"You could have asked me to be there with you."

"I . . . I guess I wanted to do it myself."

David smoothed her hair and held her a bit tighter. "It's time you realized that you don't have to do things by yourself for the rest of your life."

"I hate to interrupt you two young people," Dora said, "but my food tastes better when it's hot." Soon, the three of them were seated at the kitchen table, Elena and David with heaping plates, Dora with a cup of coffee.

Two weeks with Matthew and Dora had conditioned Elena. She didn't pick up her fork. Instead she took her hostess's hand and bowed her head. David reached out and completed the circle.

"You do it, dear," Dora said.

Elena almost panicked. She swallowed twice. "Dear Lord, thank you for so many blessings. Not just the food, not just this home that's been opened to me, but for your protection and presence — even when I didn't recognize it. Thank you for David, who's always been there for me. I promise not to take him for granted anymore. I know I haven't been in touch with you for quite a while, except when I really needed something. But now I ask you to speak to me. Now I'm listening. Amen."

After supper, David and Elena said goodnight on the front porch. "I'll call you tomorrow," he said. "Get some rest."

"I'll look forward to your call. Right now, I just want a hot bath and a soft bed."

Elena went to the closet and exchanged her slacks, blouse, and low-heel dress shoes for a robe and slippers. She was headed for the bathroom for a long, hot soak when she had a brief perception of movement outside the window. *Is someone out there?* She opened the bathroom door, stepped inside, and turned on the water in the tub. Then, as though she'd forgotten something, she turned back into the bedroom.

Out of the corner of her eye, she saw something move in the bushes outside her window. Once more, she'd forgotten to draw the blinds. Well, too late now. Was she certain there was a face at the window? She reran the film in her mind. Yes, someone was there.

What now? Call the police? Even as she debated what to do, Elena sidled toward the easy chair that sat hard against the wall, out of the window's line of sight. She reached behind the chair and retrieved the object she'd placed there after the first Peeping Tom incident.

Stop it. Call the police. No, by the time the police get here, the prowler will be gone. Then she'd be sentenced to weeks more of dodging shadows, wondering when her stalker would turn up next.

Elena eased into the hall and hurried to the outside door. She slid through it with no sound and moved gingerly around the side of the house, keeping to shadows. He was standing in the bushes, his head a few inches from the window. Apparently, he thought the possibility that she might return and shed her robe made the wait worthwhile.

Every step took an eternity. Don't make a noise. Her whole plan was predicated on surprise. What if it didn't work? What if the surprise she had in store for the perverted peeper didn't immobilize him? What would she do if he turned on her? Fight? Run?

Elena crouched to stay under the prowler's line of sight and duck-walked the last six feet. She stopped an arm's length away, straightened, and shoved her weapon forward until it touched the intruder's back.

Next came what Elena had been told was the most chilling sound in the world — *chik-chuk* — as she racked the slide of the shotgun she held pressed against his spinal column.

The man's hands shot up as though jet-propelled. "Don't shoot! Don't shoot! Don't shoot!"

"Get on the ground, hands behind your head. Now!" Elena reached into the pocket of her robe and pulled out the cell phone she'd dropped in as she left the house. As she punched in 9-1-1, Dr. Nathan Godwin sank to his knees, laced his fingers together behind his head, and eased to the ground like a candle melting in the sun.

Saturday night was always busy at RJ's, and Elena had to remind him of her relationship with Will and Cathy before the restaurant owner agreed to set up the party in a private room. These five people had helped her through some tough times, and she thought a celebratory dinner with them was fitting. Cathy and Will were seated across from her. David occupied the chair to her left, Natalie was on her right. Marcus Bell sat across the table from Natalie.

412

Elena waited until the water glasses were filled, then raised hers. "I'd like to propose a toast to friendships, old and new."

Glasses touched, murmurs of "hear, hear." Then the conversational buzz began.

Elena leaned across the table toward Cathy. "I'm glad your OB let you come tonight."

"I'm doing well, so he decided to turn me loose for an evening. Thank you for inviting us."

To Will, she said, "I'm grateful for all your legal help, but more important, I appreciate your support. I can never repay you for all you've done."

"Consider the bill paid. You've been a great addition to Cathy's practice. Well, I guess it's yours too, now."

"Thank you for inviting me," Natalie said to Elena. "I don't have many friends in town, and even though I work in the hospital, I don't come in contact with the doctors very much."

"Maybe Marcus can help you with that," Elena said.

"I'll do my best," Marcus said. "I have to admit that the social worker's office isn't somewhere doctors like to hang out, but maybe I can buy you coffee in the cafeteria and introduce you around."

Natalie turned toward her sister-in-law and mouthed, "Thanks." And was she blushing just a bit?

Elena decided to ask the question she knew was on everyone's mind. "Will, what do you think will happen to Dr. Godwin?"

Will put down the roll he was buttering. "I heard through the grapevine that he left the police station, went home, emailed his resignation to the members of the hospital board, and started packing."

Cathy looked puzzled. "Won't he have to be here for a trial?"

"He'll be charged with a misdemeanor. I'm pretty sure his lawyer will plead it out and ask for probation. In the meantime, Nathan will probably move on to another town and most likely repeat the pattern."

"I guess repeating the pattern is pretty typical in cases like that," Elena said.

"In his case, very typical." Will replied. "One of my sources in the police department tells me this isn't the first time Nathan has done this. Marcus, is there anything you can do to spread the word about him? Ethically, of course."

Marcus nodded. "I expect the hospital board to ask me to resume the duties they gave to Nathan, so I'd be the one responding to any requests for references. I'll have to be careful what I say, but I think I can get the message across."

"Elena, I still can't believe you confronted Nathan instead of calling the police," Cathy said.

"I'd forgotten that shotgun was still at my folks' house," Will said. "But there was no ammunition for it."

"Nathan didn't know that," Elena said. "And I'll have to admit, that sound even scared me, and I was the one holding the gun."

Elena let her gaze sweep around the table. She felt blessed by the presence of these people in her life. Coming to Dainger had indeed involved danger. But the process had left her better equipped to move on with her life.

Natalie was chatting with Marcus. Cathy and Will had their heads together, whispering as only a married couple could do. Beside her, David pretended to study his menu, but she saw the glances he directed toward her.

Elena knew she had to face her feelings for David soon. Marcus had become a friend, but she was convinced that was all he'd be in her life. Frank Perrin — well, Frank was a "bad boy" who might provide a thrill, like seeing how close to a flame you could get your hand without getting burned. But she was certain the threat of a burn would always be there.

Mark's death had taken away a part of her life that could never be replaced. His infidelity, even if he had planned to end the affair, left her with a sense of distrust, but it was unfair to let that carry over to David. More and more, she felt certain that he was the best candidate to help her rebuild her life, if she'd just give him the chance.

As though he'd been tuned in to her thoughts, David leaned in toward her and whispered, "Would you like to go to church with me in the morning?"

"I'd like that."

"And sometime next week, I want to take you out for dinner and a movie."

"You mean like we used to do back in Dallas. As a friend?" Elena struggled to hide the grin she felt coming.

"Absolutely not. Like a real date."

"Sounds fine." She let the smile break through. "I think we have a lot to talk about."

EPILOGUE

Summer moved to fall, and winter followed. But at last spring came to Dainger. White clouds of blossoms filled Bradford pear trees. Delicate red flowers decorated the redbuds. Along the highway, bluebonnets sprang up in random profusion. The earth was green with the promise of new beginnings.

As was the case every year at Easter, the sanctuary of the First Community Church overflowed. Faithful and occasional worshipers shared pew space as they came to celebrate this holiest of days. Pastor Matthew Kennedy had no need to follow the familiar words in his hymnal, so he let his eyes roam over the congregation as he sang.

Will and Cathy sat in their usual place, halfway forward and on the aisle. Next to them, Dora, the proud grandmother, gently rocked young David Matthew Kennedy in her arms.

Seated in the back of the sanctuary, Marcus Bell and Natalie Cook shared a hymnbook. He'd seen them a few times around town, but this was the first time they'd appeared together in church. He hoped things went well between them. They'd both been dealt disappointment and deserved a new chance for happiness.

At first he almost missed them, but at last he spotted Elena and David. He'd never get used to calling them Dr. Gardner and Dr. Merritt, so it was a good thing they'd granted him first-name license. At first Elena's attendance was spotty, but recently she had been right there beside David for every service. That boded well for the forthcoming marriage that the ring on her finger signified.

The hymn ended and so did his reverie. Time to open God's Word to the people.

"Before we consider the glorious event that we mark today, I'd like to share something that seems quite appropriate. There are many of you in this congregation today who've been in a tomb of your own, a dark and forbidding place from which there seemed to be no exit. But God, in His mercy and power, brought you forth into the light. Yet you fear for the future, because you're not certain He can or will do it again.

"Listen to these words from a very wise man: 'What God has done in the past is both a model and a promise of what He will do in the future; but He's too creative to do the same thing the same way twice.'

"Don't forget what's been done for you in the past. But always remember that there's more to come."

Matthew glanced up from his notes in time to see Elena give David a knowing look and reach for his hand. The pastor imagined he could read the young man's lips, as he leaned in toward his fiancee and whispered, "I can hardly wait to see what comes next."

DISCUSSION QUESTIONS

1. Elena had multiple fears — a lonely house, loss of a place to practice medicine, being thought a mercy killer, perhaps being a menace to her own patients. What do you think was the most significant? What things make you afraid? Which one is the most significant? What have you done to address your fears?
2. Do you think Elena was overly sensitive about her racial background? Was that the only factor that estranged her from her mother-in-law? Was that relationship typical of any families you know? Could it have been repaired?
3. What were Cathy's major concerns about taking Elena into her practice? Did Will have different areas of concern? When taking on someone in a business or similar relationship, what factors do you consider?
4. With what characters did you most closely identify? Why? Were there charac-

ters who "turned you off" from almost the moment they were introduced? Why?

5. What is your assessment of Frank Perrin? Why do you think that? What advice would you have given Cathy about him when you first learned of their relationship?

6. What did you like about Marcus Bell? What did you dislike about Nathan Godwin? In what ways were the two men similar? What differentiated them? Did you see any of your own characteristics in either man?

7. What is your reaction to the final statement from Pastor Matthew Kennedy in the epilogue? How is that applicable to your life?

8. What single thing did you take away from this novel? Is it worth sharing?

ABOUT THE AUTHOR

Richard L. Mabry, MD, is a retired physician and medical school professor who achieved worldwide recognition as a writer, speaker, and teacher before turning his talents to non-medical writing after his retirement. He is the author of one nonfiction book, and his inspirational pieces have appeared in numerous periodicals. He lives in Frisco, Texas.